The
White
King

The
White
King

György Dragomán

Translated from the Hungarian by Paul Olchváry

Houghton Mifflin Company
Boston • New York • 2008

For information about permission to reproduce
selections from this book, write to Permissions,
Houghton Mifflin Company, 215 Park Avenue South,
New York, NY 10003.

www.houghtonmifflinbooks.com

Library of Congress Cataloging-in-Publication Data
Dragomán, György, date.
[Fehér király. English]
The white king / György Dragomán ; translated
from the Hungarian by Paul Olchváry.
    p. cm.
ISBN-13: 978-0-618-94517-7
I. Olchváry, Paul. II. Title.
PH3382.14.R34F4413 2007
894'.51134—dc22   2007036124

Book design by Melissa Lotfy

Printed in the United States of America

MP 10 9 8 7 6 5 4 3 2 1

This work received aid for translation from the Hungarian Book Foundation:
www.hungarianbookfoundation.hu.

Chapter 2, "Jump," appeared in *Paris Review*, no. 178, fall 2006.

FOR MOTHER

The
White
King

1

Tulips

■ ■ ■ ■ ■

THE NIGHT BEFORE, I stuck the alarm clock under
my pillow so only I would hear it ring and Mother
wouldn't wake up, but as it turned out I was awake
even before it went off, that's how wound up I was for the
surprise. After taking my extra-special nickel-plated Chinese
flashlight off the table, I pulled the clock from under the pillow and lit it up, it was quarter to five. I pressed the button so
it wouldn't go off, and then I took the clothes I had put on the
back of my chair the night before and dressed in a hurry, careful not to make a sound. While pulling on my pants I accidentally kicked the chair, which luckily didn't topple over but
only thumped against the table beside it. Carefully I opened
the door to my room, but I knew it wouldn't creak because
the day before I'd rubbed the hinges with grease. I went over
to the cupboard and slowly pulled out the middle drawer and
removed the big tailor's shears Mother always used to cut
my hair, and then I opened the lock on our apartment door
and slipped out, quiet as could be, not even hurrying until

I reached the first turn in the stairwell, where I broke into a run. By the time I reached the bottom of the stairs and stepped outside our apartment block, I was warm all over, and that's how I went toward the little park, whose flower bed, next to the iron spout where people went for spring water, had the most beautiful tulips in town.

By then we'd been without Father for more than half a year, though he was supposed to go away for only a week to a research station by the sea on some urgent business, and when he said goodbye to me he told me how sorry he was that he couldn't take me with him because at that time of year, in late autumn, the sea is a truly unforgettable sight, a lot fiercer than in summer, stirring up huge yellow waves and white foam as far as the eye can see. "But no matter," he said, and he promised that once he got home he'd take me too, so I could have a look for myself, why, he just couldn't understand how it could be that I was already past ten years old and still had never seen the sea. "But that's okay," he said, we'd make up for this along with everything else we'd make up for, no sense in rushing things, there would be plenty of time and more for everything because we had a whole life ahead of us, yes, this was one of Father's favorite sayings, and I never did quite get it, but then when he didn't come home after all, I thought about it a lot, and that farewell came to my mind a lot too, when I saw Father for the last time, when his colleagues came to get him with a gray van. I'd just come home from school when they were about to head off, if our last class of the day, earth science, hadn't been canceled I wouldn't even have met them, they were just getting into the van when I got there, they were in a real hurry, Father's colleagues didn't even want to let him talk to me, but then Father told them not to do this, they had kids too, he said, they knew what this was like, five minutes really wouldn't make a bit of difference, and then one of his colleagues, a tall silver-haired man in a gray suit, shrugged and said he didn't mind, five minutes really wouldn't make a bit of difference here. So Father then came over and stopped right in front of me, but he gave me neither a pat nor a hug, no, he just kept clutching his sport coat all the while in front of him with both hands, and that's when he told me about how he was needed urgently in that research institute, he'd be there for a week, and if it turned out the situation was really serious, then he'd be there a little while longer until he put things right, and then he got to talking about the sea, but suddenly that tall silver-haired colleague of his came over to him and put a hand on his shoulder. "Come on, doc," he said, the five minutes were up, now it was really time to go or else they'd miss the plane, and Father then bent down and kissed my forehead, but he didn't hug me, he just told me to take good care of Mom and to be a good boy, because now I would be the man of the house, time to raise that chin up high. And I said, "Okay, I'll be good," and told him he should take care of himself, and then his colleague looked at me and said, "Don'tcha worry, little guy, we'll take care of the doctor all right," and he gave a wink, and then he opened the side door of the van for Father and helped him get in, and meanwhile the chauffeur started the engine, and no sooner did the door slam shut on my father than the car headed off, and I picked up my school knapsack and turned around and went toward the stairwell because I got a new forward, one more button for my miniature soccer team, all its players were buttons, and I wanted to test the forward on the oilcloth to see if it slid as well on that as it did on the cardboard, so anyway, I didn't stay there and I didn't even wave, and I didn't keep watching that van, and I didn't wait for it to disappear at the end of the road. I remember Father's face clearly, he was scruffy, he smelled of cigarette smoke, and he seemed really, really tired, even his smile was a bit crooked. Anyway, I thought about this a lot later on, but I don't think he suspected beforehand that he wouldn't be able to come home.

A week later we got just one letter from him, and in it he wrote that the situation was much more serious than they'd figured, not that he could give details, seeing how this was top secret, but he'd have to stay on there for a while yet, and if everything went well maybe he'd get one or two days' leave in a couple of weeks, but for the time being he was needed there every moment. Since then he sent a few other letters too, every three or four weeks, and in every one he wrote that he'd come home soon. But then he couldn't come for Christmas either, and we waited and waited for him even on New Year's Eve, and before we knew it April had arrived, and no more letters were coming either. Which is when I got to thinking that Father had in fact fled abroad like the father of one of my classmates, Egon, whose dad swam across the Danube and went to Yugoslavia and from there to the West, but they hadn't heard a thing from him since then, they didn't even know if he was alive.

Anyway, that morning on my way to the park I slunk along behind the apartment blocks because I didn't want to meet up with anyone, no, I didn't want anyone at all asking where I was off to so early. Luckily no one was at the waterspout, so I was able to climb over the chain and right into the flower bed where the tulips were, and I took out the shears and started cutting the flowers, snipping their stems way down by the ground because my grandmother once told me that the lower down you cut tulip stems, the longer the flowers will last, that it's best if you just cut the whole thing, leaves and all. Anyway, at first I wanted to cut only twenty-five stems, but then somewhere around fifteen I lost count so I just kept cutting one after another, meanwhile my jacket was getting all covered with dew, and my pants too, but I didn't bother about it, no, instead I thought of Father, of how he too must have done something like this every year, he too must have cut the tulips like this each spring. Mother told the story lots of times of how he gave her tulips when he proposed, how he courted her with bouquets of tulips, and how he gave her tulips every year on their anniversary, every April 17 he surprised her with a huge bouquet. Yes, by the time she woke up, the flowers were there waiting for her on the kitchen table, and I knew that this anniversary was going to be their fifteenth, and I wanted Mother to get a bouquet bigger than any she ever got before.

I cut so many tulips that it was all I could do to hold them right, and since the bouquet only slid apart in my hands when I tried hugging it tight, I laid it down on the ground beside me, shook the dew off the shears, and went on cutting one stem after another, and meanwhile I thought of Father, how he must have used these very same shears, and I looked at my hands and tried imagining Father's hands, but it did no good because all I saw were my own thin, pale hands, my fingers in the shears' worn metal rings, and then all of a sudden this old man shouted at me, "Get over here at once, what do you think you're doing, cutting those flowers? I'll have you know I'll call the police and you'll wind up in reform school, which is where you belong," but I looked up and luckily didn't recognize him, so I shouted right back, "Shut your trap, stealing flowers isn't a crime," and I pocketed the shears and gathered up the tulips with both hands. A couple of stems fell away, but by then I'd already jumped out of the flower bed, and I heard the man shouting after me that I should be ashamed of myself for talking that way, but no matter, he'd jotted down the ID number on my arm, but I didn't even look back because I knew he couldn't have done that, since I had come on purpose in the jacket without my school ID number sewn onto its arm, and so I ran right on home holding the flowers in both hands, carefully, so they wouldn't break, the flowers

5

were smacking against each other and sometimes touching my face, the broad leaves were swishing and swooshing and flapping about, and the smell was like freshly cut grass, only much stronger.

When I got to the fifth floor I stopped in the hallway in front of our apartment, crouched down, and put the flowers carefully on the doormat, and then I stood up, slowly opened the door, and stepped over the flowers and just paused there in the dark hall, and listened. Luckily Mother wasn't yet awake, so I carried the tulips right into the kitchen and put them all on the table, and next I went into the pantry, got the biggest empty pickle jar out from under the shelf, and took it over to the faucet, where I wiped it clean with water and set it down on the middle of the kitchen table and went right to work stuffing the tulips into it. But there were so many tulips that they didn't all fit in the jar, about ten stems just wouldn't slide in, so I put those in the sink, and then I went back to the kitchen table and tried my best to set the bouquet right, but it didn't work too well. What with all those leaves, the tulips were really tangled up, some stems were too short and others were too long, I knew I'd have to cut the stems the same length if I wanted the bouquet to look decent, but then I thought that if I got the big washtub from the pantry, all the flowers would fit in that, and maybe I wouldn't even have to cut their stems, so I went back to the pantry door, opened it, bent down, and pulled the tub out from under the shelf, which is when I heard the kitchen door open and I heard Mother's voice. "Who's there?" she said. "Is there someone in here?" She didn't see me yet, on account of the pantry door being in the way, but through the crack in the door I could see her standing in her long white nightgown, she was barefoot, and her face turned pale when she noticed the tulips, and she leaned with one arm against the doorjamb and her mouth opened. I thought she was about to smile, but instead her face looked more like she wanted to cry out or shout, as if she was really angry or something was really hurting her, she bared her teeth all the way and she scrunched up her eyes, and I heard her taking really deep breaths, and then her eyes began scanning the kitchen, and when she noticed the open pantry door her hand came off the doorjamb and swept the hair away from her face, and she let out a big sigh and asked, "Son, is it you, dear?" But I didn't say a thing just yet, no, I first came out from behind the pantry door and stopped beside the table, and only then did I say that I wanted it to be a surprise, and I begged her not to be angry. "I didn't want to do anything bad," I said, "I did it only because Father asked me to be the man of the house while he was away." Mother was straining to smile, but from her eyes it was obvious that she was still really sad, and now she said in a deep, raspy voice that she wasn't angry, no, she wasn't angry, she repeated, "Thank you very much, dear," and as she said that, she stepped over and gave me a hug, not her usual sort of hug but a whole lot tighter, she held me really tight the way she did when I was sick one time, and I hugged her back and held her tight too, and through my clothes and through her nightgown I could feel her heart beating, and I thought of the tulips, of how I'd knelt there in the earth in the park, cutting one tulip after another, and I felt Mother hug me even tighter, and I hugged her even tighter too, and my nose was still full of the tulips' smell, that thick green scent, and then I felt Mother shudder, and I knew she was about to cry, and I knew I would start crying too, and I didn't want to cry, but I couldn't let her go, I could only hold her tight. I wanted to tell her not to be so sad, that everything was okay, but I couldn't say a thing, I couldn't open my mouth at all, and at that very moment someone pressed the buzzer on our apartment door, and the person sure did press it hard because the buzzer buzzed really loud and long, once, twice, three times, and I could feel Mother letting me go, her whole body seemed to turn cold all of a sudden, and then I also let her go and I told her, "Wait here, I'll go and see who it is."

On my way to the door I thought it had to be the police, yes, that old man in the park had recognized me after all, he'd reported me and now the police were here, they'd come to get me and take me away for vandalizing public property and cutting tulips, and I thought that maybe I'd better not open the door after all, but the buzzer just kept buzzing really loud, and by now there was knocking too. And so I reached out a hand all the same, turned the lock, and opened the door.

It wasn't the police standing there in front of the door but Father's colleagues, the ones I saw him leave with on that day a while back, and I was so surprised I couldn't get a word out, which is when the tall silver-haired man looked at me and asked if my mother was home, and I nodded, thinking Father must have sent a gift with them for his and Mother's wedding anniversary, and I was just about to tell them to come on in, I wanted to say, "My mother will be really glad to see you." But before I could get a word out, the silver-haired man snapped at me, "Didn't you hear me, I asked you something," and I said, "Yes, she is home," and then the other man, the shorter one, snarled at me too. "Well then," he said, "we'll just come on in," and he pushed me away from the doorway and both of them did come right in, they stopped in the hall and then the shorter one asked which room was my mother's, and I said, "Mother is in the kitchen," but by now I was leading the way, and I called out to Mother that Father's colleagues were here, that they must have brought a letter from him or maybe he'd sent some gift.

And right then Mother was drinking water from the long-eared mug we usually used to fill the coffeemaker, but her hand stopped in midmotion, she looked at me but her eyes then fixed on Father's colleagues, and I saw her turn pale behind the mug, which she then lowered, and I saw her mouth turn to stone like it did whenever she got really angry, and then, in a really loud voice, she asked Father's colleagues, "What are you doing here?" and she slammed the mug on the counter so hard that all the water splashed right out, and she said to them, "Get out of here," but by then both of them had followed me into the kitchen. The tall silver-haired man didn't even say hello, but instead he said to Mother, "What is this, you haven't even told the kid?" And then my mother shook her head and said, "That's none of your business," but the tall silver-haired man said, "Well, that was a mistake because he'll find out sooner or later, anyway, best to get this sort of thing over with from the start, because lies breed only lies," and then Mother gave a laugh and said, "Yes, of course, you two gentlemen are the guardian angels of truth," and then the shorter one told Mother to shut her trap, and Mother really did turn all quiet, and the silver-haired man stepped in front of me and asked, "Hey, son, do you still believe that we're your father's colleagues?" I didn't say a thing, but I felt my body turn cold like in gym class after a timed run when you have to lean forward because there's no other way to catch your breath, and then the silver-haired man said, "Why then, I'll have you know that we're not your father's colleagues, we're from the state security service, and your father's been arrested for conspiring against the state, so it'll be a while until you see him again, a good long while at that, because your father is shoveling away clear across the country at the Danube Canal, which they're digging to shorten the winding Danube. Do you know what that means?" he asked. "It means he's in a labor camp, and as scrawny as he is, he won't be able to take it for long, and he'll never come back from there ever again, maybe he's not even alive anymore, who knows," and as he said this Mother took up the mug from the counter and flung it on the floor so hard that it broke into pieces, and the

9

officer then got all quiet, and for a moment you couldn't hear a thing, but Mother then said, "Enough of this, stop it right now, if you want to take me too, then take me, but leave him alone because he's a child, understand, leave him alone, and tell me what you want, tell me what you're doing here."

The shorter man said they'd just been passing by and as long as they were here anyway, they figured they'd look around a bit, maybe they'd find something interesting in the doctor's room.

Mother asked if they had a search warrant, and the tall silver-haired man smiled at her and said they didn't need a warrant for every little detail, that there was nothing wrong with their looking around a bit, besides, he didn't think we had anything to hide.

Mother now said really loud, "You have no right to do this, get out of here, go. If you don't leave right this instant, why then I'll go to city hall and stage a sit-down strike, yes, I'll publicly demand my husband's release, what is this, keeping him locked up for half a year already without a trial and without a sentence? Be this country what it may," she said, "we have a constitution all the same, we have laws all the same, searches still require a warrant, so you'd better show one or get out of here, now."

The silver-haired man then smiled at Mother and said that this scrappiness really looked good on her, and no doubt my father down there on the Danube Canal must really miss her, for she was truly a beautiful woman, too bad they'd never meet again.

Mother's face turned all red and her whole body tensed up, I thought she'd go right on over there and slap that silver-haired officer, I couldn't remember seeing her that angry ever before, and then Mother really did move, but not toward the officer, no, instead she went straight to the apartment door, opened it, and said, "Enough is enough, out, get out of this building at once, because if you don't," she said, "I'll call my father-in-law." She told them they knew full well that he was a Party secretary, and although he'd been sent into retirement he still had enough friends in high places so he could arrange, on account of what they'd done here, to have the two of them transferred to the traffic division, so if they knew what was best for them, they'd better get out right this instant. Mother said this so firmly I almost believed it, even though I knew full well she would never call my grandfather's home of her own free will because ever since my grandmother said to her face that she was a screwed-up Jewish slut, yes, ever since then Mother wouldn't give her or my grandfather the time of day, but from the way Mother spoke now, you couldn't tell that at all.

The shorter officer now said that if she thought the old man had any clout left, especially now that his son had been taken away, well, she was quite mistaken, my grandfather could thank his lucky stars he himself hadn't been interned, but if my mother wanted to pick up the phone and complain, why then, she could go right ahead, and he stepped over to the counter, took the silverware drawer by the handle, and yanked it right out with such force that although the drawer itself stayed in his hand, the knives, forks, tablespoons, and teaspoons flew all over the kitchen, and the officer then slammed that empty drawer back down onto the counter so hard that its back edge tore right off, and he said, "There you are, now you have something to complain about, but this is just the beginning, that's right, just the beginning," and he bared his teeth, and I knew he was about to knock over the table. But then the silver-haired man put a hand on his shoulder and said, "Take it easy, Gyurka my boy, take it easy, let it be, it seems we misjudged the lady, we thought this was a missus with brains, we did, we thought she knew when and with whom she has to be polite, but it seems she doesn't have the sense to recognize her well-wishers, it seems she's dead set on getting herself all mixed up in trouble too. Fine, then, let it be, just like she wants." The officer called Gyurka now flung the broken drawer to the floor where the silverware was all scattered about and he said, "Fine then, Comrade Major, let's do as you wish, let's go."

The officer called Gyurka now looked at Mother and nodded, and then he turned and looked me square in the eye and said fine then, they'd leave, but only because he saw that we liked flowers, and anyone who liked flowers couldn't be bad, and as he said that, he stepped over to the table, and I thought for sure that he was about to fling that pickle jar to the floor, but all he did was pluck out a single tulip, he held that flower to his nose, gave it a sniff, and said, "The only problem with tulips is that they have no smell, otherwise they are really lovely flowers," and then he left the kitchen. "Let's go, Comrade Major," he said, to which the silver-haired man didn't say a thing but only waved his hand for him to go, and the officer called Gyurka began heading out, and on reaching Mother he stretched that tulip out to her and Mother took it from him without a word, and the officer called Gyurka said, "A flower for a flower," and he turned toward me again and looked me square in the eye and gave a wink, and he went out the door and right down the stairs.

The major then also stepped out into the hall, and Mother was just about to slam the door on him when he suddenly stepped back over the threshold, put his foot in front of the door so Mother couldn't shut it, and said, nice and calm, "You'll come to regret this, lady, because when we return we'll yank the floor right up, we'll scratch the putty right out of the window frames, we'll look under the bathtub too, and into the gas pipes, we'll take apart the whole place bit by bit, and you can be sure we'll find what we're looking for, you can be certain of that," he said before falling silent, turning, and heading down the stairs.

Mother slammed the door, but before it closed all the way I heard the major say, "See ya around," and then Mother turned and fell against the door, she just stood with that red tulip in her hand, looking at the pieces of the broken mug, the silverware thrown all about, the drawer broken in two, and her mouth winced before slowly hardening, she now squeezed her lips tight and looked at me and said, quiet as could be, "Go get the dustpan and the broom, let's pick up the pieces of the mug." And I then looked at the tulips on the table in that pickle jar and I wanted to say to her, "It wasn't true what those officers said about Father, was it, he'll come home, right?" but then I turned toward Mother and saw that she was sniffing at that single tulip, and her eyes were glistening so much that I knew she could hardly hold back her tears, so instead I asked her not a thing.

2

Jump

· · · · ·

SZABI AND I figured out pretty fast that chalk doesn't give you a fever at all, that it's just a legend, because we each ate one and a half pieces of chalk and nothing happened to us, we even tried the colored chalk, Szabi ate a green piece and I ate a red one, but it did us no good waiting under the bridge by the school for an hour and a half, nothing happened to us except we peed in color, my pee was on the reddish side and Szabi's was greenish. And as for the thermometer trick, we didn't dare try that either, because Mother caught me red-handed the other day sticking the end of the thermometer on the cast-iron radiator, and two weeks earlier, before our math exam, Szabi had even worse luck, he held a thermometer up against the bulb of his little lamp and the mercury got so hot so fast that it exploded right out of the end of the thermometer, and his father gave him a whipping with the buckle end of a belt, so the thermometer trick was out of the question, but we had to come up with something all the same.

If we didn't manage to get sick by the next day, we knew that it would be the end of us, the other kids at school would knock our brains out because that's when they would find out that we'd accidentally let those slot machines wolf down all our class money, the cash we were supposed to use to buy materials for a flag and for the placards we had to make to carry in the May Day parade. Yes, it would turn out we'd spent all of that money on those machines in the cellar game room off the side of the Puppet Theater building because Feri lied that every third player wins on those new automatic machines. "That's why they're automatic, after all," he said, and the first time we tried, we really did win, we won a ten, but from there on in we only lost, and in the end we only wanted to win back the money, we broke the third hundred bank note only so we could win back what we'd lost. It almost worked too, but then we couldn't get the proper rhythm, right when we pressed the button, the flash switched from EXTRA SUPER BONUS to nothing, and so we lost all the money, and then it didn't do any good telling the cashier it wasn't our money and that he should give it back, he just laughed. "That's a game of chance for you," he said, and if we went on shooting off our traps, then he'd see to shutting them up for us, and if we didn't want to play anymore, why then we should get the hell out of there because we were only taking space away from paying customers.

Anyway, when we got out to the Street of the Martyrs of the Revolution, Szabi and I looked at each other, and both of us knew we were in for it, and then Szabi said it would be best if we went to the station and stowed away on a freight train and rode it to coal country and became miners, because kids could work there too, so he'd heard, you didn't get asked a thing when you went to sign up for work because the coal mines always need workers. And I said he should go if he wanted, but I was staying put because I wasn't in the mood to die of silicosis. "Let's get sick instead," I said, because if we went about it properly then we could get out from under the May Day mess altogether, and then Szabi said, "All right, eating chalk gives you a fever," and so we tried it right away, but it wasn't worth shit, and even pissing that reddish pee did me no good, it didn't look bloody at all, and even its smell was all wrong, so we knew we had to think up something else. And then Szabi said it would be best if we went to the water-spout and tried to drink as much as we could stand, because if we gulped down that ice-cold spring water fast enough we'd be guaranteed a decent case of pneumonia, and that would mean at least three weeks in the hospital, not to mention that everyone would feel sorry for us, so the money would be the last thing on their minds, that's for sure.

There was hardly anyone at the spout, only four people were standing there, and while they filled up their jugs one after another, Szabi and I took turns climbing the pedestal of the statue that was missing on account of its being stolen, pretending we were the Torchbearer of the Revolution, the main thing was to stretch out your right arm in front of you as far as possible like you were really holding a torch, and you weren't supposed to move at all, while the other person was allowed to throw only one speck of gravel at a time at the one playing the statue, but not at the face, and the statue who could take it longer would win, and I happened to be up there being the statue when the last person in line filled up her jug, and Szabi then scraped up a whole handful of gravel and flung it all at me, and he said, "Let's get going, we still have to go catch ourselves a little pneumonia," and I said okay, but he should go first, seeing how it was his idea and because he cheated at playing statue, and he said he knew I was chicken, all right, but he'd show me how to go about it.

The water flowed out of a thick, horizontal iron pipe set in the wall under a memorial plaque to Jánku Zsjánu, the famous outlaw, protector of the poor, who relieved his thirst at this very spot when fleeing from the posse that was out to hang him, and the plaque also said that this was medicinal water and that pregnant women and nursing mothers were not allowed to drink it, so when Szabi bent over toward the pipe to begin drinking, I said, "Stop, slow down, haven't you read on the plaque that pregnant women aren't allowed to drink this water?" But now Szabi didn't laugh at all, though at other times he always did, he even told me not to kid around because this was dead serious business, first you had to stick your mouth on the spout to keep the water from flowing out, and then you had to start counting until you reached at least one hundred, and when the pressure was so great that you could hardly stand it, you had to suddenly open your mouth, which was when the ice-cold water would shoot down your throat and your gullet really fast, it would fill your gut all at once, and your insides would cool down so much that pneumonia was as good as in the bag, and if you did it right you'd faint straightaway. But the other person shouldn't go slapping the one who drank the water but only splash cold water in his face, because then he'd come to on his own right away, and I said, "Okay, but don't talk so much, get going already, we should take advantage of no one coming by for water just now," because if anyone saw us, sure as hell they wouldn't be happy about our trying to block off the spout with our mouths.

Szabi said I was right and that he would now begin, and he crouched right down in front of the spout and pressed his mouth against its end so not a drop of water could flow out, and I started counting out loud, so he could hear it too, so he would know how long to keep the pressure up, and Szabi's head turned red nice and slow, at first as if he had blushed from all the kidding around, but then his face got redder and redder, I hadn't even reached fifty yet and his face was beet red, then it started slowly turning blue. He shut his eyes and I saw that he was now holding the spout with both hands and his face was completely blue, and I was only at eighty-five when all of a sudden he let go of the pipe, and the water came gushing out so hard that Szabi reeled back, his clothes got sopping wet but he was still trying to drink all the same, his mouth was wide open and he was gulping down the water, but all that pressure must have sent some of the water up his nose because when he wiped his face with the sleeve of his official school shirt, he said this wasn't worth shit, this was a bunch of crap because he didn't feel anything at all in his lungs, which should be hurting by now, so this method wouldn't do the trick, either. But he said that if I wanted, I should go ahead and give it a try, maybe it would work for me, but that I shouldn't let the pressure build up so much in the pipe, it would be enough if I just pinched my nose shut and drank as much water as I could stand, and I said okay.

And so I crouched right down in front of the spout, pinched my nose shut, and used the palm of my other hand to direct the rush of water into my mouth, and I began swallowing the water, it was pretty cold all right, but the less air I had, the warmer the water seemed to get, and by the time I stopped, it seemed burning hot, that's how little air I had left in me, and I too nearly fell back, but Szabi caught me and helped me stand up, and we went over to one of the few benches that still had a back and a seat left on it, and we sat down. I was dizzy and my head was buzzing a little too, Szabi said he felt awful, but he thought this was only because of the water, because we drank so much of it so suddenly, but that this water wasn't cold enough to cause pneumonia after all, at most we'd just get diarrhea, and that wasn't worth shit, and sure enough my belly then began hurting and I had to press my palm against it, but when I hunched forward the pain slowly went away, and then I said to Szabi that this pneumonia trick was a bunch of bull, nothing would come of it, and if we wanted to get out from under what we had coming to us we'd have to think up something else, something that was sure to pan out.

Szabi said I was right, it would be best if we went and broke our legs, and I told him he was completely bonkers, you couldn't fake a broken leg, and he said, you sure couldn't, but we weren't out to fake pneumonia either, and if we really wanted to get out from under this mess about the money, then faking it wouldn't get us anywhere, not even the chalk was worth shit. Instead we should go up to where the woods began, to that abandoned construction site where they'd not only dug a ditch to put pipes in but had already laid this thick concrete pipe, and if we jumped on that pipe, our ankles would break for sure, and it's at least a week until you can walk even with a cast, but I said it was too dangerous to risk breaking your leg, it could lead to serious trouble, at which Szabi started laughing, he said I was chicken, his leg got broken twice already and one time his head was broken, and he'd have me know that it wasn't even so bad, the only thing that's not so good is when they set the cast, it's so hot when they do that it's like you're on fire, but afterward you can get out of all sorts of things, which is not to mention how good it feels to scratch yourself with a needle under the cast, and if it rains you don't have to go to school, and you can get out of running in gym class for six months because it's bad to strain your leg. And if I didn't do it he'd tell everyone what a chicken I was, that I was afraid of breaking my leg, and then I said, "Listen here, I'm no chicken," and then Szabi said, "All right, we'll talk it over after jumping," and we headed off toward the construction site.

We couldn't go too fast, our bellies were still so full of water, mine gurgled with every step I took, and one time we stopped because Szabi had to take a piss, and another time because my belly was so upset I almost puked, but finally we reached the construction site all the same. Szabi knew where we could get across the tall wooden fence because he'd been there once before to get some PVC pipes for blowguns and carbide for fireworks, so anyway, he told me not to be scared, no one had lived in the guard booth for a long time, and sure enough, finding that ditch with the pipe in it wasn't hard because the earth was thrown up high on one side. Szabi went first, we climbed all the way to the top of the embankment, from there we looked down into the ditch, which contained separate sections of thick concrete pipe that hadn't been cemented together yet.

Szabi said he truly regretted how we left our school comrades in the lurch like this, yes, he was really sorry that on account of us the others wouldn't be able to take part in the placard competition, especially because the class that made the nicest placard would win a two-week seaside trip, and I said I was sorry too, because I would have also really liked to get to the sea, but then I looked again at the sections of concrete pipe, and it occurred to me that nothing would ever flow through them, neither water nor sewage, because this new complex of apartment blocks would never be built, and I told Szabi he shouldn't worry himself over it, we wouldn't have won the competition anyway, some class from School No. 3 would win it for sure, because School No. 3 wins everything since that's where the children of Party activists go, and as for our own class, there was no reason to be sad because it just couldn't happen that the class wouldn't take part in the placard competition or in the parade if it's been told to do so, our head teacher would no doubt get enough material from somewhere, and they'd make a placard after all because our teacher didn't want to get in trouble either, and then Szabi asked if I was sure about that, and I said, "You bet I'm sure, and let's jump already, because if we stand around here for too long we'll get cold feet."

Szabi then said, "Okay, let's count out loud and jump on three," and then we both looked down into the ditch one more time and it looked pretty deep, from where we stood it must have been at least ten feet for sure, and then we both started counting at the same time, but Szabi stopped at two and said, "Let's shut our eyes and start again," and so we shut our eyes and started again, and then it suddenly occurred to me that if we both jumped and really broke our legs, then we wouldn't be able to climb out of the ditch, and I wanted to tell Szabi to wait, but by the time I said it Szabi had already jumped, and I opened my eyes just in time to see that he'd jumped so far forward that he almost cleared the ditch, but his jump still wasn't long enough, no, Szabi's shoulder struck the opposite wall and he fell straight into the ditch and onto a section of pipe.

Szabi let out a piercing cry and reached both hands toward one of his ankles, and he was lying there on his side beside the concrete pipe, and he kept on holding his foot, and he was screaming my name really loud, he was wailing and crying, and then I called down to him to wait because I'd climb down right away, and he looked up, his face was wet with tears, and he told me to go fuck my mother, that I was a chickenshit for letting him jump alone. But then I told him to shut his trap because I'd seen full well that he had wanted to clear the ditch and didn't want to jump in at all, and if I didn't have more brains than him there wouldn't be anyone left to go get an ambulance, but Szabi only kept swearing and saying over and over that his foot hurt like hell, and I called down to him again, saying he had it coming for wanting to play me for a sucker and telling him to wait right where he was because I'd go get an ambulance even though he didn't really deserve it. I started running back toward the apartment blocks, and meanwhile I already knew what I would say the next day in school, that the reason we didn't have the money was that I had to give half of it to the ambulance guys so they would take poor Szabi to the hospital and the other half to the doctors so they wouldn't set his fracture without anesthetics.

3

End of the World

.....

OACH GICA tended to us goalies specially, he made us show up at every practice an hour early and mainly had us do speed drills, plus we had to jump a lot and dive, jump and dive, jump and dive, and he had this goalie-terrorizing machine, he came up with it himself and the workers at the ironworks made it for him, a soccer ball was put on the end of this long iron pipe, the ball was filled with sand, and that's what he shot at us, the whole contraption was built onto an axle and revolved around it, throwing that sand-packed ball with no mercy, and Janika and I knew that if we didn't catch it, it would hit us in the head and break our bones. Other kids had already died in Coach Gica's hands, so they said, which is why he became a coach for the junior team, the adult players couldn't stand his heavy-handedness, one time they caught him and knocked half his brains out, and since then he wasn't allowed to coach the Ironworks' adult team but could work only with us eleven- and twelve-year-olds.

That May we were close to being dropped from the league,

so Coach Gica held practice every day, he got us passes so we didn't even have to go to school for the first four hours of the day, everyone knew that Red Hammer, the ironworks team, had to stay in the running, no way could we be dropped. Coach Gica even told us that if we didn't beat Breakthrough, the military team, then that's it, it's over, after the game he'd smash everyone's ankles with a crowbar, for him it would be all the same because coaching was his life, and if we fell from the running, that would be it, and from then on each and every one of us would be going to school on crutches, he even showed us the crowbar, and he took a swipe with it at one of the planks in the fence, the crowbar tore right into the wood and he said our bones would break apart just like that, in splinters, not a soul would be able to put them together again. We knew he wasn't kidding because by then he didn't have a family, he lived in the junior team's clubhouse, yes, we knew he was dead serious, and so we really did go all out getting ready for that game, everyone went running, no one dared skip practice, everyone was scared stiff about what Coach Gica would do to their legs. I went running too, as much as I could take, even though I knew I didn't stand a chance of playing anyway because I was just a backup goalie, Janika was the real goalie even though he was a Jehovah's Witness, a Jehovist, the truth is he shouldn't have been playing on the Ironworks' team at all because his father didn't let him be a Young Pioneer, but he was so good at keeping goal that Coach Gica paid a visit to the school and worked things out with the top comrade there, the principal, so Janika would be able to play all the same, and sure enough he kept goal in nearly every game because he had a much better feel for the ball than I did, even when he wasn't in top form. So we practiced really hard, seeing how we were afraid of Coach Gica, but we knew it didn't matter anyway, there was no beating Break-through, they had the backing of the army, their team was full of army brats, the armed forces gave them everything and gave the referees everything too, Breakthrough was unbeaten in the playoffs, and so we knew we didn't stand a chance, and we were scared stiff.

Even on the day of the game Coach Gica held a separate practice for us goalies, and as the two of us walked along toward the sports complex so early that morning, Janika, who was even more scared than I was, stopped all of a sudden while we were still outside in front of the complex, pressed a hand to his belly, then he started retching and puked, if I hadn't got a hold of him he might have fainted, and he said that only now, on seeing the entrance to the Ironworks sports complex, did he remember that he dreamed last night about Coach Gica, about Coach Gica smashing apart his ankles, and as he said this I handed Janika my canteen so he could rinse his mouth, and he said that in his dream Coach Gica took such a hard swipe at his ankle with that iron pipe that even Coach Gica was all in tears, even now he could recall the old guy's beet-red, glistening face, and Janika said he didn't care one bit, he was going home, he wasn't coming to the practice because he couldn't take it anymore, and that I should go along too, I shouldn't stay here all by myself, he didn't even care if the team was left without a goalie. "Soccer is only a game," he said, "it's not worth this much." He wiped his mouth, gave me back my canteen, and he said, "Let's go, let's get out of here before Coach Gica sees us."

"Okay," I said, "let's go," and right then I remembered that I had woken up last night too, I had heard a big, thundering bang, that's what woke me up, but then I just lay there all quiet, and for a long time I couldn't get back to sleep, so I now said to Janika, "All right, let's go," but then, right when I was thinking about my dream, we heard this rumbling sound, but it wasn't at all like in my dream, it was much quieter, and I knew exactly what it was, it was nothing but two trucks approaching the sports complex really fast. From a distance you could tell they were painted green, their canopies were camouflage patterned, we just stood there watching them come toward us, and then the drivers hit the brakes and stopped right in front of us, a soldier got out and came over and asked what we were up to here, and Janika was so scared he couldn't get a word out, so I explained, "We've come for practice, we're certified players for Red Hammer's junior team, Janika is the goalie and I'm the backup," but the soldier didn't even pay us any attention. "All right then," he said, "but what are you standing around here for, get going," and so we went into the locker room, but before we did we could see the soldiers unpacking all sorts of big instruments and devices from their trucks.

Coach Gica was there already, slicing and chewing away at his morning slab of roast bacon, he didn't say a thing but only showed us his watch and three fingers, and we knew this meant we were three minutes late and that we'd have to run fifteen extra laps at the end of practice, but I said, "We couldn't help it, we were late on account of the soldiers," and then Coach Gica asked, "On account of what soldiers?" and he told me not to lie or he'd slap me around so good I'd slide on my snot to the goalpost. But I said I wasn't lying, he'd see for himself if he didn't believe the soldiers were here, they must've come to observe the practice so they'd know what to count on, to see how ready we were to take on Breakthrough. Coach Gica then put away his knife and wrapped up the remaining bacon, and he stood up and said, "All right, get dressed," and he told us not to waste any more time or else he'd knock our brains out, then he went out and slammed the locker room door behind him.

We dressed in silence, not daring to say a word, scared that Coach Gica was listening in, he liked to know what was said about him behind his back. Janika was white as a ghost when we finally went out, and Coach Gica was there waiting for us by the edge of the field, he was talking with one of the officers, and as soon as he saw us he gave a wave of his hand. The pylons were already set up, and the two pairs of leaded shin-guards were out there too, they were made of leather but could be filled with lead tubes to make them heavier, Coach Gica had had these made too. Anyway, we got them on and then we began running the obstacle course, and after a while Coach Gica left the officer, came over, and began making us jump up and down. At one point Coach Gica hit Janika on the leg with his stick because Janika wasn't fast enough, and Janika fell and hit himself and his nose started bleeding, but Coach Gica didn't let him stop, he had to keep jumping up and down.

Meanwhile the soldiers were there the whole time, the officer was just looking at his men as they walked around the field in strange-looking clothes, pushing around machines full of wires and tubes, their hands also held all sorts of devices with wires and antennas. Just what they were doing was beyond me, maybe they wanted to broadcast the game on the radio, I'd never heard of such a thing, the machines were buzzing and rattling really loud, but we couldn't really pay attention, no, we had to keep running and jumping and diving.

The drills with the ball were the hardest, you had to dive for the ball blindfolded to get a feel for the direction, at one point I fell on the goalpost and Coach Gica kicked the ball right into my gut and I started heaving. Since Janika was always jumping in the wrong direction, I won the diving contest, by then Janika was pure white, he knew what this meant, it meant that today I would be the first one to give a kickoff, because Coach Gica had us practice kickoffs by setting up eleven balls in a row, one of the goalies had to stand ten feet away while the other goalie ran up to each ball and tried to kick it onto the other's head, and you weren't allowed to jump clear of the ball, no, you had to catch it, clutch it, or deflect it, and if we didn't kick it hard enough then Coach Gica took our place kicking off. So you really had to kick, and the one to kick first was better off because by the time the other goalie had his turn he was so beat that he couldn't really kick hard. The fourth ball I kicked sent Janika's nose bleeding again, I didn't want to kick the ball hard but there wasn't any choice, I had to run up to the ball from four steps away, and the balls always let out this huge snap, and by the end of my turn Janika didn't even reach out his hands anymore, he simply jumped right out in front of the ball and fell to the ground together with the ball. The grass was all bloody in one spot, he could hardly get to his feet, it was obvious he wouldn't be able to kick, he was all worn out. Coach Gica came over to him, he was holding a towel and he handed it to Janika, and he said, "All right, wipe your face, for once we're taking a break, get yourselves into the locker room because that comrade over there, the officer, wants a word with you two in private."

Janika pressed the towel to his nose and that's how we went, the officer really was there, I could tell from his epaulet that he was a colonel, my grandfather taught me the ranks a while back, so anyway, this colonel was sitting there on the bench in the locker room, and he motioned with his hand for us to shut the door and then he told us to sit down, and he asked what grade we were in and if we were good students, and I had to answer the questions because Janika's nose was still bleeding. The officer took an apple and broke it in two, he gave one half to me and the other half to Janika, and he said, "Fine then, you're clever boys," he could see how hard and honorably we worked, we could be proud of ourselves, we'd proven through hard work that we sure had earned the Young Pioneers' red cravat. Then he asked us if we loved our country, and of course we nodded, even Janika, though Janika was a Jehovist and Jehovists can't be Young Pioneers and can't love their country, and then the colonel asked if we knew what radioactivity was, and I said, "No, we haven't yet studied physics, but in Homeland Defense drills we learned that if there's an atomic flash you're supposed to cover your face and climb under the table or under the bed, and then you have to report to the Chemical Defense Command for protective gear, and in the Homeland Defense textbook they write about radioactivity too, they write that radiation rays go through everything and cause damage to living organisms." Anyway, after I said all that the officer nodded and said he had two sons just as big as we were and that's why he was telling us what he was about to say, but if we dared talk to anyone about it we'd wind up in reform school for rumormongering, and they'd send our moms and dads to prison. "Do you understand?" he asked, and we nodded, but he said he wanted a proper answer, and then we said, "Yes, sir, Comrade Colonel, we do understand," and Janika even took the towel away from his face and he said it along with me, that's how scared he was.

And then the colonel said that last night there was an accident in an atomic power plant in the Great Soviet Union and that the wind brought the radioactivity here, and the fact of the matter was that the game shouldn't even be allowed to go ahead, but they didn't want people to panic, so it would be held after all, but he advised us goalies not to dive and to avoid contact with the ball because the ball picks up radioactivity from the grass, and anyway, we should watch out for ourselves because we were handsome, healthy little lads, and then he gave us each this white pill, saying we had to swallow it here and now. "It's just iodide," he said, "don't be scared," and only after we took the pills did I remember once seeing a movie about the Germans, about how they'd poisoned themselves with white pills like this, and maybe Comrade Colonel wanted to poison us too because he was sorry about telling us about the accident, and I could tell that Janika was thinking the same thing. But then we didn't die after all, the pill did have a bitterish taste but not like almonds, no, I knew poison was supposed to taste like almonds. Then the colonel patted me on the head and said, "All right then, everything will be okay, take care of yourselves," and he turned and wanted to leave, but then Janika called after him and asked, "Comrade Colonel, if we can't touch the ball or even dive, how are we supposed to keep goal?" And then the colonel turned back around and looked at us and he didn't say a thing, I thought he was about to yell or give us a good slap, sometimes Coach Gica turned all quiet for a second too, before coming at us, but Comrade Colonel only shook his head and said, really quiet, that he didn't know, so help him God he didn't know, and then he bowed his head and went out without a word and left us there in the locker room.

Janika had taken only two bites from his half of the apple, so I told him to give it to me if he didn't want it, and he gave it to me without a word, and I was just swallowing the last bite when the door opened and Coach Gica came in. One of the balls was in his hand, he stopped, and he asked us what Comrade Colonel had wanted with us. Janika and I looked at each other again, and then he pressed the towel to his nose and I replied, "Nothing," but Coach Gica stepped over and without a word he slapped me so hard that the apple core fell right out of my hand and I got all dizzy, I had to grab onto the coat rack to keep from falling, and then Coach Gica told me not to lie to him, he'd heard every word, besides, he knew everything about us, he knew we wanted to skip out on practice, and he'd heard full well how the colonel had lied to us, and he could tell that we believed the colonel, how could we be such idiots, we'd deserve to have our brains knocked out, to have the coach hammer out what was left of our brains. He'd have us know that the soldiers had come only because that's how they planned to guarantee we'd get creamed, they wanted to scare us so we wouldn't dare keep goal properly, what did they mean by saying avoid contact with the ball? And as Coach Gica said this he got so angry that he kicked one of the benches right up into the air, and the coat rack above the bench fell over and almost broke the window, and then Coach Gica got all quiet and shook his head and said, "Get it through your skulls that the colonel was lying, if there really had been an accident in that reactor, you wouldn't even be alive anymore, besides, the Party wouldn't let the game go on, everyone knows that the country's future is its youth, yes, that's the country's greatest treasure, there's no way the Party would expose this treasure to danger."

Janika then sat down on one of the other benches and took the towel away from his face, his mouth and his chin were smeared all over with blood, and he said, really quiet, that his father had told him the end of the world would come and that it would begin with a nuclear war, with a nuclear strike, and he knew that the colonel wasn't lying because the colonel had said "So help him God," and soldiers were atheists, they could never say the word "God" aloud, and if they did, why then, even they must sense that the end of the world had come and that nothing mattered anymore.

Coach Gica went over and stood in front of Janika, he snapped the ball to the floor and caught it with both hands, and he ordered Janika to stand up, but Janika didn't move, he only shook his head, at which Coach Gica snapped the ball to the floor again and shouted, "I won't repeat it, stand up, for Jehovah's fucking sake," and then Janika stood up and threw the towel to the floor, and Coach Gica said all right, he understood if what the colonel said scared us, but we still couldn't be such cowards, and if Janika apologized he wouldn't be angry at him, the others would be here soon, they had to get ready for the game, but Janika shook his head and said that the end of the world was here and that he wouldn't apologize, at which point Coach Gica snapped the ball to the floor yet again, and he reached a hand into his pocket and said he'd wanted to give this to Janika only right before the game, that this here was a pair of real leather goalie's gloves that did service on the national team. Coach Gica said that he himself kept goal with them when he was chosen one time for that team, and then he reached out with the gloves toward Janika. "Here, put them on, these will protect you from the radiation."

Janika shook his head and shouted that he didn't need them, and he spit on the gloves and I could see that his spit was all bloody, and then Coach Gica shouted something really loud, you couldn't even make out what it was, and with all his might he slapped Janika across the face with those gloves, and then he stepped back and kneed the ball right into Janika's gut and Janika doubled over, and as the ball snapped back I saw that Coach Gica wanted to knee it again, but instead of hitting the ball this time he kneed Janika's face, I heard something crack, and Janika fell onto the coat rack and slid to the floor. And Coach Gica bent down and picked up the ball, and as he looked at me I saw that his face was all red and glistening with moisture, and Coach Gica shouted, "All right, then you'll keep goal," he was shrieking, you could hardly make out his words, and he shook his head and suddenly he kicked the ball at me, straight at my face, and I jumped forward, reaching out both hands, and I caught the ball, it struck my two palms hard and stung my skin, and when I sprang to the floor and instinctively clutched that ball tight to avoid giving the attacking player an opportunity, just as Coach Gica had taught us, I saw Janika lying on the floor next to the bench, he wasn't moving and there was blood flowing from his ear.

The ball was a little slick, which I knew was from Janika's blood, and as I stood there holding the ball I thought of the radioactivity, but except for that slipperiness the ball felt exactly the same as always, for a moment I shut my eyes and just stayed there holding it in my hands, and when I opened them again, Coach Gica was still standing in the door and Janika was still lying there and not moving, and I thought, maybe he hadn't really died, maybe he'd just fainted, because if he had died there wouldn't be a game and I wouldn't keep goal, and I looked at those real leather goalie's gloves there on the floor next to Janika, and then all at once my tears began to flow, and the ball fell out of my hands, bouncing once and rolling into the corner, but by then Coach Gica was no longer in the locker room.

4

Pickax

■ ■ ■ ■ ■

THE EXCAVATORS ARRIVED on Sunday morning, we
were playing soccer with the guys from the other
street, they were leading four to two and the game
went to five, it was almost certain we'd be beat, but I didn't
mind since I wanted to go home already. I was always at
home on Sundays waiting for Father because when they took
him away to the Danube Canal, he promised he'd come get
me and take me with him to the sea. True, Mother said I
shouldn't wait for him because after eight months of hard labor I might not even recognize him anymore, besides, we'd
know beforehand if he was coming home, but I didn't completely believe he was really in a labor camp even though
we'd already got a couple of prewritten camp postcards, no,
I thought that maybe Father wasn't in a labor camp at all but
only working in a secret research institute, just like he told
me when they took him away, and I'd also read that when the
Americans were making the atomic bomb in Los Alamos, no
one was allowed to know where the researchers really were,

and so I knew that Father would come home, all right, that he'd come get me and take me with him, that he'd take me to the sea, and even if he didn't recognize me I'd sure recognize him because his picture, which I'd taken out of his old military ID holder, was with me all the time. Anyway, there we were playing soccer, and I wanted to go home, yes, I could hardly wait for them to kick another goal against us and for the game to be over.

We were on the offensive, Big Prodán had the ball, and when the excavators drove off the road right onto the soccer field, they came all the way to the middle and one of them drove right toward Big Prodán and almost hit him, Prodán just barely jumped out of the way, and then both excavators stopped in the middle of the field, they were buzzing really loud, the air was full of this smelly blue smoke. Then the two drivers turned off their engines at the same time, you couldn't hear a peep from anywhere, we were quiet too, we went over and stood around the machines, they were painted yellow and rusting in a lot of places, but the teeth of the scoops were sparkling just a little bit.

One of the drivers then climbed off his machine, stood right where he was, looked at Big Prodán, and said, "Get over here." Prodán went over really slow, first he threw the ball over to his kid brother and then he stopped in front of the laborer, he was only fourteen years old but he was big for his age, he was almost as tall as the laborer, and by then he hadn't been going to school for a year because his dad had sent him to work on a construction project, you could tell he wasn't scared of the laborer, yes, he stopped right in front of the guy and said, "Whaddaya want."

The laborer just grinned and drove a fist into the pit of Big Prodán's belly, and Big Prodán doubled over and the laborer said to him without yelling at all, "I'll knock your brains out if you keep talking to me like that," and then the laborer stepped back and looked on, smiling, as Big Prodán brought a hand tight against his belly and kept holding it there and asked, "What would you like, sir?" The laborer nodded and said, "That's better, so you can talk nice too, huh," and he looked at the other laborer, who was still sitting there in the seat of the excavator, "Hear that, Traján? The kid can talk nice too," at which the other laborer nodded and spit on the ground and said, "Good, glad to hear that."

The laborer reached into his pocket, took out some money, gave it to Prodán, and said, "Get going, bring three packs of no-filter Karpacis, get running already, you know where to go, The Elk Restaurant, which is open on Sundays." Prodán nodded, turned, and started off toward the paved road, but then the laborer called out, "Hold on, there's this pockmarked working man who might be there having a drink, he's called Pickax, anyway, if you see him, tell him that Traján and his partner here say he can bring the shed, got that?"

Prodán nodded and headed off again, and the laborer at first just watched him go, but then called after him, "I said get running already, if you're not back here in five minutes I'll knock your brains out, you hear," and then the laborer turned around, reached under the seat of the excavator, and pulled out a big paper bag and a monkey wrench, his eyes passed over us and he said, "Come closer, all of you, don't be scared."

None of us moved, I was staring at the laborer's work boots, one of the laces was red, a genuine bootlace, but the other lace was just some homemade, twine-twisted thing, but anyway, none of us budged as the laborer then unfolded the top of the bag, which he held toward us. "Real caramels," he said, "go ahead, all of you, dig in."

The others stepped closer, it was a really big bag, at least six pounds of candy, I could see the caramels' colored wrapping, which meant it really was caramel inside, and the laborer again held the bag toward us. "Take some," he said, "no need to be scared," and then Áronka, the smallest one of us, took a step forward, he reached a hand into the bag and pulled it out heaping with caramels, and he popped one of the caramels right into his mouth and chewed it up without even taking the paper off first. "Thanks," he said with a full mouth, and the laborer just nodded and held out the bag toward the rest of us. "Here you are," he said, "take some, take some."

One after another everyone reached into the bag and took some, everyone except me, but there were still a lot of caramels left, and the laborer finally looked at me and asked, "Whatsa matter, don'tcha want some?" and he stepped toward me and held the bag right in front of my face. "Don't you go offending me, take some," he said, and then I shook my head and said I couldn't eat sweets right now, even though I really did like candy, and I explained that the day before I ate so many peppermint candies that my stomach couldn't handle any more sweets, but the laborer shook the bag. "Oh come on," he said, "sure you can have some," and he reached into the bag and pulled out a piece of caramel, he held it out to me pinched between two of his fingers and told me to hold my mouth open, he had a really big hand, his fingers were greasy, I saw, and I wanted to turn around and run away, but then someone grabbed my shoulders from behind me, it was the other laborer, he'd sneaked up on me without my even noticing a thing, he held my shoulders tight and told me not to move or else he'd rip me apart and he told me to hold my mouth open at once, and then he grabbed my neck from behind with one hand while squeezing my jaw from the side with the thumb and index finger of his other hand so I'd open my mouth, but no matter how I tried to shake my head and bite him, his grip was too tight, and then I heard one of the laborers shout, "Not like that, pinch his nose shut, Traján," and in no time I wasn't getting any air, I shut my eyes and I wanted to shout at them to let me go or else my dad would knock their brains out, no way was I about to open my mouth wide, but then my ears started buzzing and all of a sudden that piece of caramel somehow ended up on my tongue. Using two fingers the laborer stuffed it right into my mouth, his fingers had this stale tobacco smell that stirred up my belly, but no matter how I tried to spit that candy out, they pressed my mouth shut and again pinched my nose tight, and I couldn't even taste the caramel, which was coming apart between my teeth, wrapping and all, and then they let me go and I fell to the ground and I tried spitting it out, but by then there was nothing in my mouth, only the stale taste of tobacco, and my heart was up in my throat, but I wasn't about to cry if I could help it, no, I shouted at them that my dad was going to kill them for this, but the laborers just smiled, and then the one called Traján said they'd smack my father's kisser good, and he told me to shut my trap or else he'd stuff it with caramels, and then he looked at the others. "All right then, boys," he said, "you've had your candy, but it's best you know you didn't get it for free, nothing in this world is free, you've got to work for everything," and as the other laborer gave a nod, Traján continued. "And he who doesn't work shouldn't eat, but all of you have already eaten, so now it's time to work," and as he said this he went over to an excavator and took a big felted wool sack off the back and threw it on the ground in front of us. "Here you are," he said, "open it up," and the bag rolled right up to our feet, it was tied with a belt, everyone stepped back, no one wanted to touch that bag, we just stood there and stared at the workers and they stared back at us, but by now Traján was staring only at me, he was looking right in my eyes, and I saw him lick his lips and I knew he was about to call on me to reach for that bag and undo the belt, but then all of a sudden Traján turned away and so did the other laborer, they looked out toward the road. Big Prodán was just getting back with the cigarettes, he came running up to Traján and handed him the cigarettes and the change, Traján stuffed two packs along with the change into his pocket, and he threw the third pack over to the other laborer. "There you go, Feri, you go poison yourself too," he said, and then he looked back at Prodán. "Didn't you meet up with that pockmarked guy?" Prodán shook his head, and the laborer called Traján then spit on the ground. "Fuck it, Pickax, fuck your motherfucking mother," he said under his breath, and then he looked again at Prodán. "All right, but what are you standing there for, go ahead and hand out the shovels," and he gave that felted wool sack a good kick and said, "There's enough here for everyone, so let's get a move on, we don't have all day."

Big Prodán bent down and opened up the bag, which was full of short iron-handled shovels, lots of them, at least forty, both the blades and the handles were painted with black enamel. Prodán picked one up and looked at the laborer called Feri and asked, "What do you want to do with them?" The laborer gave a nod toward the woods and said, "Not us, you're the ones who want to do something with them, a whole new neighborhood is being built up there by the woods, you know, and one of the sewage lines will run right by here, and you will all dig part of that line as community service work so you can save the state some diesel oil."

Big Prodán looked up and asked, "Where? Here, on the soccer field?" The laborer called Feri spit on the ground and said, "You bet, and in a sec we'll measure out exactly where."

After looking at the shovel and not saying a thing for a while, Big Prodán finally did speak after all. "But this is our field," he said. Traján stepped over to him. "Sure," he said, stopping in front of him, "that's exactly why you all want to help do the digging, you're the ones who asked for it, your school, we got shovels just because of you, so enough gabbing, everyone take a shovel, the sooner you start the sooner you'll finish, you're kids, you don't need to earn your bread, so you got the time." Right then Big Prodán took a step back and said, "I don't go to school, I work at a construction site, today's Sunday, so sure as hell today I'm not taking no shovel into my hands." Traján then swung back his arm, but he wasn't able to hit Prodán because the other laborer, the one called Feri, stepped up next to him and grabbed his arm. "Wait," said Feri, "this here's a smart boy, no sense being rough with him," and then he reached out that bag of caramels toward Prodán and said, "You didn't get any candy, go ahead, take some."

At first Big Prodán didn't want to take any, but then he stuck in his hand anyway, and when he pulled it out I saw clearly that it was packed full of caramels, and as he stuffed all that candy into his pocket he almost dropped one, and meanwhile the laborer called Feri was still holding the bag toward him. "Don't be shy," he said, so Prodán stuck his hand in one more time and again put the candy into his pocket, and then the laborer called Feri folded the bag shut. "All right, then," he said, "you'll get more later, now help hand out the shovels, meantime Traján will measure out where the ditch will go," but Prodán didn't move, he looked at the excavators and then back again at the laborer called Feri and asked, "Can I sit up on the excavator too?"

The laborer called Feri shrugged and said, "All right, if the work goes well then I don't care, you can sit up there, you can even start it up if you want, but now go ahead and hand out those shovels, it's time to start digging, don'tcha worry, your school principal knows all about this, he okayed all of you working here every afternoon, all of you attend School No. 12, right? Tell the others that as long as they're working here, they don't have to do their homework, you'll see, they'll even be glad."

Big Prodán nodded and said, "Okay," and he picked a shovel

up off the ground and gave it to Áronka, and then he handed one to each of us, one at a time, to me too. "Here you are, Djata, use it in good health." Of course he didn't give his little brother a shovel, only a caramel, and he looked at the laborers and said, "That's my brother, he's gonna help me," to which the laborer called Traján gave a grunt, but the one called Feri just nodded. "All right," he said, "you two will be the brigade leaders, but if the work isn't going well, we'll find others to take your places, you'll see just how nice voluntary community service work can be, what a good feeling it is to build the country, you can all be proud of yourselves that even being kids you're able to take part in this, besides, if you do decent work you'll finish the whole thing in a week, and that's nothing, you should just see the Danube Canal, now that's real digging for you."

A fiery heat came over me when he said that, I reached into my pocket and touched my father's picture, I'd never met anyone who'd worked at the Danube Canal, and I looked at that laborer called Traján and saw him pull a folded sheet of paper from his pocket, unfold it, and look at it a bit before picking a shovel up off the ground, walking to the end of the field, and thrusting the shovel into the ground by one of the goalposts. "I've done it," he shouted to the laborer called Feri, "I've measured it out, it goes straight exactly from here." Then Big Prodán and the laborer called Feri lined us up, we didn't have to stand according to height like we did at school, the point was only to stand in a nice neat line not too far from each other, and then, once everyone had stood up, the laborer called Traján gave Prodán a shovel too. "All right, you don't have to work, but show the others how to use the tool, so get to it, drive it into the ground."

At first Prodán didn't want to do it, no, I could tell from the way he was holding the shovel that what he really wanted was to knock their brains out, but then he started digging all the same, flinging the dirt behind him, and then the others also got down to work and so did I, the shovel's handle had a really bad grip, it broke into the skin of my palms, and the dirt was so hard that I had to push the shovel into the ground with my feet, but the shovel was so short that I had to stoop over, and in no time my back was hurting. Anyway, the work wasn't going too well, not just for me but also for the others, and while digging I kept thinking of the Danube Canal, of how hard it must be to divert an entire river, and of just what my father was really doing there, because he'd written only a couple of times, and even then all he said was that he was doing fine and he didn't really say anything else, so that's what I tried thinking of, and meanwhile my back was hurting even more, along with my palms, but I didn't dare stop working.

Of course by then Big Prodán hadn't been working for a while, no, he was walking back and forth behind us, telling us to keep it up, he even gave Áronka a good kick on the ass, but then one of the laborers yelled at him not to do such a thing again or else he'd knock his brains out, it was enough to keep an eye out for anyone not putting his all into the shoveling, they'd take care of the rest, so from that point on Prodán didn't bother anyone, he just walked back and forth behind us and kept an eye on how we worked.

At one point I turned my head and noticed that the laborers had meanwhile spread a blanket on the ground by one of the excavators and laid down on it, the one called Traján was puffing a cigarette and the one called Feri began to eat something, and then Prodán sat down there too, and by then only his little brother was walking back and forth behind us, and when I looked back again, I saw that those guys were playing cards.

Áronka was just about to try driving his shovel into the ground when his foot suddenly slipped off the blade and came out from under him, and he flopped on his side and just lay there with one foot in the ditch as if he didn't want to get back up at all, and when that happened all of us stopped working and wiped our foreheads and gathered around Áronka, and Prodán's kid brother asked what the problem was, but Áronka didn't say a thing, he just shook his head.

One of the laborers, the one called Feri, stood up and came over and looked at Áronka and said, "You weaklings wouldn't last even a day at the Danube Canal," and then he said, "All right, time for a break," and he said we could take fifteen minutes and try to pull ourselves together, but he was otherwise satisfied with us, we'd been doing decent work, and we shouldn't worry, we could go home for lunch, but everyone had to come back for the afternoon, the work would last till dark, and he added that they'd written down everyone's name and address on a sheet of paper, so they'd go after anyone who didn't come back, no one was allowed to sabotage community service work.

The laborer then turned away and went over to one of the excavators while the rest of us sat down on the ground by Áronka, everyone was resting, Janika was the only one still moving, he was juggling the soccer ball with one of his feet, yes, he had such a feel for soccer balls that he could have kept that up all day long. I just sat on the ground like everyone else, looking at the ditch I'd been digging, it wasn't deep at all, and at all those tiny pebbles and white roots of grass along the sides, and then I pulled out my father's picture and also looked at that, it was smudged on account of my touching it all the time, but his face was still clear as day. Everyone used to say how much I looked like my father, one time I looked at myself a long time in a pocket mirror while holding his picture up to it, and I really could tell that my chin and my mouth were just like his.

So I was sitting right there and looking at the picture when all of a sudden one of the laborers stopped next to me, I could tell from his bootlaces that it was the one called Feri, and he leaned down and tore my father's picture right out of my hand. "Whatcha looking at?" he asked, and then he held the picture really close to his eyes, like someone who couldn't see well. "Who's that," he asked, "your old man?" But I didn't answer, I only nodded, and this fiery heat passed from the top of my head all the way through me, and my ears were practically on fire and I couldn't say a thing, I couldn't say yes and I couldn't say no, all I could do was nod, and my stomach was in knots, it felt as if a lump had begun moving up out of my belly toward my neck, and when it reached my throat, somehow I did speak after all. "Do you know him?" I asked, but my voice was shaking terribly. "He's there too, at the Danube Canal, you guys also came from there, huh?"

The laborer held an index finger in front of his mouth, bent down closer, hissed *shhh,* whispered that this was a state secret, and gave me a wink, and then for a long time he didn't say a thing, no, he just kept looking at the picture, turning it in his hands as if he couldn't see it right, and meanwhile he kept biting his lips, and then he shook his head and stood up straight and called out to the other laborer, "Get over here, Traján, get a load of this, you won't believe it!"

The laborer called Traján then put down on the blanket the piece of bread he'd been chewing, stood up, and came over. When he got there, the laborer called Feri put the picture into his hand without a word, but then he said, "Look at it good, at first you won't be able to tell, but just look at it extra careful." The laborer called Traján looked at the picture for a long time too, turning it in his hands, but then he shook his head and asked, "What am I supposed to see? Because I don't see a thing." Feri bit his lips again and said, "That's because you're blind," and he poked an index finger at my father's face and added, "Just look at that mouth and you'll see plain as day that this is none other than Pickax."

Knitting his brow, Traján just stared at the picture for a while before suddenly breaking into a grin. "Holy Jesus, well I'll be, damn me if that's not Pickax." Now Feri started nodding and tore the picture out of Traján's hand, "Pickax it is," he said, "and get a load of how young he was, get a load of how nice and smooth his face still was, I wouldn't believe it if I didn't see it," and then Feri got all quiet and looked at me. "So then, you're Pickax's son, are you?" and he reached out a hand, and as I took it he patted my shoulder with his other hand and said, "You can be proud of your dad, he's a really decent guy."

He shook my hand tight but it didn't hurt, and so I asked, "You two know him? You really know him?" Traján nodded. "You bet we know him, he'll be here in no time, he's bringing the shed we'll be staying in," and then Traján put the picture back in my hand. "Here it is, put it away," he said, and I asked, "Is he really coming here, you swear?" Even I could hear how much my voice was trembling, and I could feel my whole body shaking, like when you get the shivers from being cold. The laborer called Feri then looked at me again and asked, "What did you say you're called?" When I told him, Feri nodded. "Yes, he mentioned you, he sure did, you remember too, Traján, huh? He said he hasn't seen you in a long time, and he'll come look you up and bring something for you."

On hearing all this I got so dizzy all of a sudden and looked down at the ground, at my shoes, everything seemed to be turning round and round, the chunks of earth and blades of grass and pebbles too, everything was spinning and I almost fell, but then the laborer called Traján put an arm around me. "It's all right," he said, "get a hold of yourself." But I was still shaking as I then remembered my father's postcards, and how Mother had at first waited and waited for him to return, and how she always shuddered whenever the doorbell rang, thinking that my father had finally been allowed to come home, and then I said to the laborers, "You two are lying, if my father really came back he would have looked us up for sure, he would have come home to us, to Mother and me, besides, my dad isn't called Pickax, my dad isn't friends with you guys."

The laborer called Feri then grabbed both of my shoulders and turned me toward him and said, "Get a hold of yourself, how long has it been since you've seen your old man?" "Almost nine months," I said, and he nodded. "Nine months at the Danube Canal is a real long time," and then he asked, "Do you know what smallpox is?" and I said, "Sure I know, it's a disease that's been wiped out already," and then the laborer said, "Yeah, yeah, sure," and he leaned even closer to me and started whispering, but so I could hardly hear what he was saying. And he whispered that he for one had seen men die of smallpox because that disease still flares up here and there along the Danube Canal, especially in the reeducation camps, but no one's allowed to talk about those camps, and that that's where my dad caught it too, and it almost killed him, but he was lucky that on account of this they let him go, that they didn't do the whole reeducation thing with him because then he wouldn't remember a thing about his former life, which is why only his face had changed, from the pockmarks, that is, but so much so that you couldn't even recognize him anymore, and he was real ashamed about this, and that's why he didn't write to us anymore, and that's why he didn't dare look us up, because he was scared of what my mom and I would say to him, he had to gather up the courage and the strength. But when he finally got here with that shed, why then, I'd see him for myself, and then the laborer called Feri told me again not to be scared, and he held out that bag of caramels and said, "Go ahead, take some, don't be scared, you'll feel the call of blood kinship anyway, and if you're brave enough, everything will be A-okay."

The two laborers then sat back down on the blanket, but not before Traján slammed two shovels together and shouted that break was over and that we had another hour of work left, and then everyone could go home for lunch, and we'd have to come back only two hours after that. Even though I was still dizzy when we got back to work, the shovel seemed to move by itself in my hands, yes, I kept flinging more and more dirt behind me, and the whole time I was watching the road, but no one came, and I didn't want to be looking that way all the time, but no matter how I tried I just couldn't stand not to look, so I shut my eyes because I didn't want to see that empty road, and I opened them only when I drove the shovel into the ground. But not even that helped, because even with my eyes shut I could see my father's face before me, and as the earth crumbled I thought of the smallpox, and I didn't want to imagine the pockmarks. And then all of a sudden I heard a cowbell, I looked up and saw the shed approaching, it was being pulled by two donkeys, and one of them had a cowbell tied around its neck, the shed was really big and it was painted gray, and someone was sitting up front on top of it, someone all wrapped up in a blanket and driving the donkeys with a long stick, and then the shovel fell out of my hands, and I kept looking at that figure, there was a peaked cap on his head, a miner's cap, and even though I couldn't see his face, the way he sat there wasn't familiar at all. Then the shed came closer and closer, it drove onto the soccer field, and the driver's face still wasn't visible, and then I climbed out of the ditch and I stood there at the edge and waited, and I felt my legs shaking and my hands shaking too. Then the man yanked at the reins and the donkeys stopped, and he jumped off the driver's seat, I could see only his back, but the way he now moved really did seem like how my father moved, at least the way he held his head, and by then everyone was looking at me, the laborers and everyone else, and I took a step toward the person on top of the cart, and then suddenly he turned and looked right at me and threw the blanket off himself, which is when I saw his face. It was nothing but pockmarks, I couldn't make out his features at all, the pockmarks were really deep and they flowed together, besides, they were spread thick with some sort of whitish cream that gave his whole face a greasy glitter, and when he saw that I was looking at him, he smiled, and I wanted to look only at his eyes and at his mouth, and by then I knew he wasn't my father, no he wasn't, no way could he be my father, but I took a step toward him all the same, and my mouth opened up and I cried out, "Father," even though I knew it wasn't my father I was looking at, I knew the laborers had lied, but I said it anyway, and because I'd said it, for just a moment I thought maybe, just maybe, I was wrong, that this was my father after all, because he was still smiling at me, and that made me even more scared, and I felt a chill come over me, and then suddenly everyone around me burst out laughing, Traján and Feri and the Prodán brothers and all the others, and even the pockmarked laborer, who, I was now certain, was not my father, and as that blaring laughter came at me from all directions, I reached inside my pocket and felt my father's picture, and I knew I was about to cry, and I clenched my teeth and turned away and took off running toward our apartment block, and I could still hear them laughing at me, and although I had no idea what I would say to Mother, I just ran and ran toward home, wishing I would never ever get there.

5

Jamming

■■■■■

I WAS SITTING on a bench behind our apartment block, up by the path on the hill, hammering away with a brick at my new pocketknife, it was a classic, with a fish-shaped metal handle, except the blade had come loose, it snapped shut nearly every time I stuck it into a tree or something, and I was scared it would cut my fingers. So that's what I was trying to fix, except the brick wasn't hard enough, it did no good slamming it down really hard on the rivet, it wasn't worth a damn except to get my school pants and my hands covered with brick dust.

Not too many people took that path in the afternoons, I'd been sitting there a half-hour already and only old Miki went by on his way to the waterspout, and I said hello, I wasn't scared of him even though others told stories about the things he did during the war before he went blind, but what did I care, he was always nice to me. Even now, when I said hello, he stopped and waved his white cane toward me and said, "Hey there, Djata." He recognized everyone right away from their voices, he may have been blind but he sure did know which way he was going better than lots of other folks. Anyway, he had a huge three-quart jug with him that he was holding by the handle, and I knew he was taking it to the spout because someone once lied to him that if he drank three quarts of water from the King's Well every day, he'd see again.

Except for him I didn't meet anyone at all, no, I just sat there hammering away at my pocketknife, thinking how bad it must be, being blind, living in darkness forever, seeing only with a cane, and right when I thought this, all of a sudden someone put his hands over my eyes from behind me.

I was waiting for whoever it was to ask me who I thought it was, and I even tried figuring it out, but he held my eyes shut really tight so I couldn't see a thing, he had pretty big hands, I felt that right away, and also the fingers smelled of cigarette smoke. It couldn't be Janika, he never smoked, and it couldn't be Feri either, he'd gone away to his grandmother's for a week. "All right, Laci," I said, "let me go. I figured out right away who you are, huh," but the two palms were still stuck to my eyes, it seemed like he was pressing his hands harder and harder. "All right," I said, "you're not Laci, but don't go cheating, because if you don't ask me who you are, how am I supposed to figure it out?"

But he still didn't say a thing, all he did was start pulling my head back nice and slow until my neck was really strained and my back was pressed tight against the wood board of the bench. "Go to hell," I said, "go to hell, fuckit, don't cheat or I'll knock your brains out," but not even then did he let me go. I tried pulling my head out of his grip, but he held it tight, and I told him to watch out because I had a knife with me, and then all of a sudden I felt his breath against my neck as he leaned really close to my ears and whispered, "That's right, Djata, you got a knife with you, that's just the problem, because it's not your knife, you cheated my kid brother out of that knife," and by then I knew who it was, yes, I'd heard his voice, so I knew it had to be Big Prodán.

"Okay, Prodán," I said, "I'll give it back, I'll give it back right away, but let me go already," and by now I was really scared because Big Prodán was the strongest kid in the neighborhood, after he was kicked out of school his dad sent him to do construction work, and he got even stronger doing that, he could beat up anyone and he wasn't scared of a soul, so anyway, Prodán then took his palms off my eyes, but as he did so he hooked one of his arms under my neck and pulled my head back, so I got hardly any air, and meanwhile with his other hand he reached down and took the pocketknife out of my hand. "I should beat you up good," he said, and then he let go of my neck, went around the bench, and stopped in front of me. This big boxlike knapsack hung from his shoulders, it looked like our school knapsacks only it was bigger, he took it off and put it on the edge of the bench next to my knapsack and meanwhile he wiped the knife on his pants to get the brick dust off. "Look what you did with it," he said, shaking his head. "I should beat the shit out of you," he said, but he didn't hit me, he just sat down beside me on the bench and said, "Okay, maybe I won't touch you this time, but if I find out again that you played cards with my kid brother, why then I'll knock your brains out, got that, this time I only want your money, so go ahead and empty your pockets," and I didn't say a thing back, no, I only shook my head because I knew full well I didn't have any money on me. Sure, I poked around in my pockets anyway, but I really didn't turn up a thing, and then I said to Big Prodán that I didn't have any money on me, but if I did, I'd give it to him, cross my heart, and if he waited a day, then maybe I could get my hands on some, even though I really didn't have any right now, but Prodán shook his head. "Don't go lying to me, Djata," and then he waved the pocketknife, signaling for me to get up from the bench, and he even showed me where to stand, there, in the middle of the path, and he said, "Now we'll see if you got a jingle and a jangle to you or not, so get to it, hop around a bit in one place," and he waved his hand for me to start, and he kept waving, up, down, up, down, but I really didn't have any money on me, so I could keep jumping up and down as much as I wanted, yes, I knew that nothing was about to jingle or jangle in my pockets, and Prodán must have known too, but he made me keep hopping for at least two more minutes, I was all hot and sweaty by the time he finally waved for me to stop, and he said, "All right, I can see you weren't lying, you can come sit down now."

"I can't stay," I said, shaking my head, "I've got to go home," but Prodán just gave another wave of his hand. "Fuckit, Djata, I said you can come sit down," and then he slammed his fist down on the bench, and so I sat down, but I didn't look at Prodán, no, instead I kept my eyes lowered, staring at the rips in my sneakers, waiting to see what would happen, and for a while Prodán didn't say a thing, but then he spoke after all. "Djata," he asked, "is it true you spent two years learning how to play the piano?" I thought I heard wrong, but I didn't ask him to repeat what he said, I just nodded, and I thought of my piano teacher and her reed cane, and how she sometimes hit my shoulders or my hands when I didn't hold myself like I was supposed to. I looked at Big Prodán and said, "It wasn't even a year, we had to sell our upright piano when they took my father away because we needed the money," but Prodán just slapped me on the back and said, "Fuckin hell, Djata, you studied piano playing for a year, so you gotta know it really well, so you'll teach me too, because the good summer weather will be here in a month, the weddings will be starting up, and by then I gotta learn, I really gotta know how."

"Impossible," I said, shaking my head, "one month is nothing, and anyway, it's not like I know anything anymore, even back then all I knew was 'The Flea Waltz,' but I didn't even know that properly," and right when I said that, I almost broke out laughing, I mean, Big Prodán had big, shovel-like hands, and his fists were all scratched up from laying bricks and fighting all the time, anyway, I tried sucking in my gut to keep from laughing. "Your hands are too big for piano playing," I said, but meanwhile the corners of my mouth kept wanting like hell to curl up, but I didn't want Prodán to sock me in the gut, and so I didn't laugh after all, no, I just said, "You need at least three years for the piano." Prodán smirked and said, "Stop kidding around, Djata, a guy can learn to ride a bike in three days, and anyway, it's not piano playing I'm after, where am I supposed to get a piano, hell no, I want you to teach me with this thing here"—and he hit his elbow hard against that big black bag he'd put down beside him on the bench just before—"with this fucking accordion," and again he hit his elbow against the bag, and then he took that bag by the strap and put it on his knees, he opened it up and removed an accordion that was all scrunched up. "Here it is," he said, "my father got it from somewhere, and now he wants to take me off construction work and send me to play music at weddings because he says there's a shitload of dough in that, and it's not like playing music is work anyway, so we can get rich real easy."

I looked at the accordion and didn't feel like laughing at all anymore. "You must be glad," I said, "because it's not too good for you doing construction," but Prodán just shook his head and said, "At first I was glad about this music thing, you can imagine, but the problem is, I don't hear the notes, I can't hear the difference no matter what, and today the teacher said I didn't practice and that I shouldn't go there anymore, even though he was teaching me in the first place only because we slipped him a little dough, you know, because when they kicked me out of school they took away my red cravat and ever since then I haven't been allowed to go to the Young Pioneers center, and that's where the accordion classes are at, and that's why you're gonna teach me now instead of him, unless you want me to beat your brains out, of course. And don't go teaching me chords, just show me how to move my fingers and show me when I have to press which button so I can get the sound out of it, I can learn that for sure, I'm really good with my hands, besides, I gotta learn, I gotta, you understand, huh, Djata?"

By the time he finished saying all this he was almost yelling, but not the way he shouted when making me jump up and down, no, it was different this time, not so loud, but a lot more scary, and I had no idea what to say, I just looked at that accordion, it was really big, with a whole lot of buttons and keys, and I knew that Prodán would put it in my hands in no time to have me play him a little something, play a tune, something entertaining, some nice wedding music, and then it would turn out I couldn't play, and Prodán wouldn't believe that I really couldn't, no, he'd think I was doing it on purpose because I didn't want to teach him, and then he'd beat me up really good, he'd use his brass knuckles on me, and I knew Prodán was waiting for me to say something already, but my heart was up in my throat, and I was still staring at the accordion, at those black folds on the part that can be pressed together, and the metal corners on the folds, and then I finally spoke after all. "Whew," I said, "this accordion is big, it's really big," that's just what I said, and I was surprised too at what I was saying. "It's a real adult-size instrument," I added, and Prodán nodded and said, "That it is," and he wanted to say something else too, but he cut himself short, he must have seen something because all of a sudden he brought his hand to his mouth so I'd keep quiet too, even though I didn't want to say anything anyway, but I slowly looked back because I wanted to see what made Prodán go quiet all of a sudden.

Well, it was just old Miki on his way back from the spout, tapping out the path ahead of him with that white cane of his.

Prodán grabbed my arm to let me know not to move, and suddenly I remembered where I'd seen this accordion before, around old Miki's neck, yes, it was old Miki's accordion, the one he made music on in the summers in the main square, in front of the statue of a guy on a horse, and by playing like that he collected enough in his hat to buy himself some beer, wine, and plum spirits. I motioned my head toward old Miki, and meanwhile I raised my eyebrows in a way that asked Prodán, without my having to say a word, if this really was old Miki's accordion, and from the way Prodán shook his head I knew right away that it was, and then, as Prodán moved just slightly, the accordion's fastening clip snapped open and the accordion filled up with air and gave out a soft boom, and then old Miki stopped and turned around, and I saw him tip his head and listen, and in the meantime the accordion almost dropped, and when Prodán grabbed it to keep it from falling it gave another boom, and then the old man headed toward the bench and he stopped in front of us. "Let me have it back," he said, "let me have my accordion back," and he reached out with his white cane toward the accordion like he wanted to give it a tap, but then Prodán grabbed the end of the cane and yanked it out of the old man's hand. "This accordion here ain't yours no more," he said, "my dad won it off you, you shouldn't have played backgammon with him." The old man waved a hand in the air. "That's really something, huh, to beat a blind man at backgammon, when I've got to tell from the sound what number I threw. Your dad cheated as much as he damn well pleased, you know that full well too, so go ahead now and give me back my instrument," he said, stepping toward the bench, but then Prodán jabbed him in the back with the end of the white cane. "Be careful not to trip, else you'll fall right over and knock your head on something, and then who knows what'll happen," he said, and now the old man turned toward me and scowled. "Djata, my boy, you're still here," and I said, "Yes," but I didn't say "It's too bad I'm still here," I only thought that part, and then old Miki said, "All right, then be a good boy and bring my accordion over here," but of course I didn't take it over, and I even said I couldn't, but old Miki shook his head. "Whatsa matter, are you scared of this shit Prodán?" But I didn't answer, Prodán answered in my place. "You bet he's scared. Why, ain't you scared?" and old Miki didn't say a thing back, he just took a step toward the bench and took off his black glasses and said, "I'm not scared, I was a soldier, I've faced death a couple times already, that I have."

Never had I seen old Miki without his black glasses, and I didn't want to either, no, I didn't want to see what the deal was with his eyes, but somehow I just had to turn toward him anyway, all I saw were two black holes, even his eyelids were missing, it was just like a skull, both of his eye sockets were pitch-black inside, like really deep holes, and Big Prodán looked at him and the white cane fell out of his hand and he didn't say a thing, and then the old man reached out a hand and tapped around a bit until he found the accordion, which he took from Prodán's lap, then he put the jug of water on the ground and got the accordion on his shoulder, and he put the glasses back on his nose, and then Prodán was finally able to speak again. "Give it back," he said, "or else my dad'll knock my brains out," but old Miki didn't say a thing back, all he did was put his two hands on the buttons and keys and pull the accordion open, and he squeezed it together and started playing. To me it looked like his hands weren't moving a bit, but the accordion blared really loud, he was playing a crackling wild sort of music, and it's like I felt my hands move to the rhythm, and my legs started moving too, and I was tapping out the rhythm with my feet against the ground, but then all of a sudden old Miki squeezed the accordion back together and everything went quiet. "What did you do with this poor accordion?" he asked Prodán. "It doesn't play the way it used to."

Prodán just shrugged. "Maybe it's just you who forgot how to play on it," he said, "but you still got what it takes, all right. But now you're gonna give it back to me all the same because if you don't, I'll go tell my dad, and maybe you're not scared of me, but you're sure as hell scared of my dad, because everyone's scared of Dad."

Old Miki shook his head and said, "Your dad's a chickenshit and you're no better than him, and anyway, why do you need this instrument, you can't do anything with it, after all, it's not like you can play on it." Prodán turned beet red. "Then you'll teach me, you will," he said, and he looked at me. "I wanted to ask Djata, but you'll do a lot better. Then I'll be the one making folks dance, they'll go crazy wild for my tunes, they will." Old Miki shook his head and said, "So you think you have it in you, huh, you think you could learn how to play," and he shook his head again. "So let's see, boy," and he waved a hand at Big Prodán to go on over, "let's see if you're cut out to be a musician."

At first Prodán didn't move, but then old Miki snarled, "Whatsa matter, are you chicken about this too?" and Prodán stood and went over to the old man, who took the accordion off his own shoulder, and then, once Prodán was there in front of him, he reached out, grabbed Prodán's shoulder, and held Prodán up close to him. "Don't be scared," he said, stepping behind Prodán and putting the accordion into his hands, "go ahead and put it on your shoulder," and Prodán did put it on, and then old Miki stood right up close behind him, put his two hands on Prodán's hands, and he said, "Let yourself go, loosen up," and then one on top of the other their hands pressed the buttons and the keys, yes, old Miki began moving Prodán's fingers, and then suddenly the accordion made a sound, then another, at first the sounds were all weird, but then little by little a sort of melody took shape, at first I didn't recognize it, but then I realized what it had to be, it was a soldier's song, when I was little my father used to sing it, but I didn't remember the words, only the melody. So that's what they were playing, but not exactly, the sounds somehow slipped out of place and the rhythm was different, and the whole song slowed down, it didn't have as much of a crackle to it, and old Miki leaned up close to Prodán and whispered something in his ear, and for a moment the accordion got almost all quiet, bellowing a single note that kept up for a while, and then old Miki leaned his chin on Prodán's shoulder from right behind Prodán, and Prodán shut his eyes, and then all at once they began a new tune, one I never heard before, it was a really complicated tune full of sudden chord shifts, it sounded like a mix of two different tunes, I didn't think one accordion could do that sort of thing, I'd never heard anything like it before. Old Miki began moving his head to the rhythm, and then Prodán also began slowly tossing his head, and the tune kept speeding up, and I saw how Prodán's fingers and old Miki's fingers were making their way over the buttons and keys, sometimes I couldn't tell whose fingers were whose, it seemed like Prodán was already playing on his own, that old Miki wasn't even guiding him anymore, and it seemed like they were dancing too, by now they were moving their whole bodies to the rhythm as if they were jumping in place, old Miki's black glasses almost slipped off his nose, and the tune got even louder. Then all of a sudden Prodán opened his eyes and his face twisted up, and he yanked his hands away from the keys and he shouted something, the music was too loud to hear what he said, but it must have been a swear word because he gave a backward kick and even tried hitting old Miki with his elbow, but the old man sure must have been holding him hard because Prodán couldn't free himself from his grip no matter what, he stepped forward and tried turning with the accordion still on him, and when he finally managed to get free, things didn't get all quiet, not yet, the accordion was still moaning away, but by now I could hear what Prodán was shouting, he was swearing, calling old Miki a motherfucking son-of-a-bitch and a dirty bastard too, and the old man nearly fell down when Prodán pushed him away, old Miki was also shouting, he was calling Prodán a chickenshit and saying he'd never learn to play the accordion, never in his life, because he couldn't stick it out, and then Prodán lunged at the old man. "I'll kill you, you filthy faggot," that's what he yelled, and I saw him reach into his pocket and pull out that pocketknife with the fish-shaped handle, and old Miki must have sensed what was happening because he tried stepping out of the way, he was beating the air with his hands, but Prodán jabbed the knife straight into old Miki's belly, and then both of them cried out at once. Old Miki stooped over the accordion for a moment before stepping back, tripping on his jug and almost falling down again, and Prodán then put his hand into his own mouth, his fingers were bloody, I saw, but I couldn't see the pocketknife anywhere, and only when Prodán then turned toward me did I notice that it was there all right, stuck into one of the accordion's folds. And then I knew right away what had happened, the knife had snapped shut on Prodán's fingers and cut his hand, and then, when old Miki stooped forward, it had pierced the accordion, yes, that's what must have happened.

Old Miki grabbed his jug and crawled on all fours toward the path, and when he found it he stood up and headed off toward the apartment blocks so fast that he was just about running, and Prodán was gasping as he then sat down on the ground and rubbed his wounded hand on his shirtsleeve, he looked at me and said he'd beat my brains out if he got wind of my telling anyone what I'd seen, and I said all right, I wouldn't tell anyone, and that's when Prodán took the accordion off his shoulder and he too noticed the knife stuck in it, and he said a swear word and pulled out the knife and stood up. Old Miki's white cane was still there by the bench, and Prodán leaned down and picked it up before sitting back down beside me, looking in the direction old Miki had gone. "I'll never play a decent cocksucking note," he said, and then he broke the cane in two on his knee and threw the pieces on the ground behind the bench.

6

Numbers

■ ■ ■ ■ ■

ACCORDING TO the roll book, Szabi and I were supposed to be the monitors that week, but Szabi fell into the ditch at the construction site back in May and his ankle broke so bad that it had to be operated on three whole times, so anyway, he was in the hospital, and every day another one of us had to take the lesson in to him, and on account of that, Iza and I were the weekly monitors, because her name came next after Szabi's on the roster.

Before then I never spoke to Iza, who wound up in our class only in fourth grade and became the best student in no time, but since playing with her was impossible, no one liked her, and she didn't really have any girlfriends either, the teachers always told us to follow her example. "She's such a diligent orphan and always winning academic competitions," that's exactly what the teachers said. Iza's parents died in a car accident when she was little, and she was raised by her uncle, everyone in town knew he was a brute, he was even kicked out of the fire department because he got so angry one time that he almost beat someone's brains out, but it did no good asking Iza about it, she never said a thing about her stepparents or about being tortured by her stepfather even though the girls in class said her back was always covered with black and blue spots and streaks. But Iza never ever said a thing about it, so these days we never really asked her about this, and I was pretty down about being a weekly monitor with her because with Szabi I'd play tag and throw chalk, and I knew that with Iza I could thank my lucky stars if she didn't go tell the head teacher that I wasn't cleaning up.

The two weekly monitors had to stand up front at the start of each class, right beside the raised platform with the teacher's desk on it, and wait for the teacher so they could report out loud who was absent. Anyway, Iza and I were waiting there for the math teacher when the class bell rang, and then all of a sudden some kind of sweet smell hit my nose, it was like a flower smell but not completely, at first I didn't know what it was, but then I looked at Iza, and Iza just happened to be adjusting her skirt and tucking her white Young Pioneer shirt back under her belt because it had come loose, and as she did so a little sliver of her waist showed clear as day, and I could have sworn I saw a blue spot, but maybe it was just where the elastic of her tights squeezed against her, and in the meantime I could still smell that smell, and then I thought to myself that it must be a big-girl smell because Feri said girls grow up when they get to sixth grade, their boobs get bigger and their smell changes on account of becoming big girls, and indeed Iza's boobs really were pretty big already, almost as big as little peaches, and then I thought to myself that Iza had become a big girl and that was what I was smelling, her being a big girl, and right when I realized this, that's when our math teacher came in. We called him Sir Uclid, and the whole class stood up, and Sir Uclid went to his desk and slammed down the roll book with all his might, as usual, and then he looked at us and waited for our report, and although it was my turn, I couldn't think of what to say, I just stood there all tongue-tied, but luckily Iza then stepped forward, she saluted and then she spoke, just like we were supposed to, "I report to Comrade Teacher that class attendance today is . . ." But somehow I wasn't even paying attention, no, I was just staring at Iza's neck from behind her, at how her long black hair hung loose and only her headband held it in place, never before had I even noticed that she had earrings, but now I saw that she had a tiny little stone set in one of her earlobes. So anyway, Iza then read out the absences and said the usual closing words, and Sir Uclid told us he accepted our report and said we could go sit down.

As we went back to our seats I smelled that big-girl smell again, it wasn't as strong anymore, but when I sat down and opened my notebook I still smelled it a little, and then I thought of Iza, and I looked up front to where she was sitting on the model students' bench, and it occurred to me that ever since Father had been taken away I was half an orphan too, and then all of a sudden I wondered what Iza looked like naked, whether she really had black and blue streaks and what her thighs were like, because the other day Feri said, "Naked girls are really interesting," but I said, "No, they're not, I don't see it that way at all, they're all the same," and Feri told me I was full of it, he gave a big laugh and said I didn't know a thing, I was dumb, it was obvious I'd never had a lover, why, he'd seen naked girls three times already, and one of his cousins even let him look between her legs, and that cousin was already all hairy down there.

And I was still looking at Iza, at how she held her head a bit to the side as she wrote, but I couldn't imagine that thing between her legs, under her panties, even though when Feri and I had talked about it he asked if I ever saw a pussy, and I said, "Sure I have, of course, and not just one," though really I had never seen a pussy at all, only the illustration in the seventh-grade anatomy book, which the older students would show us younger ones for money, and when Feri asked, "Whose pussy?" I said, "One time when I was eight years old I went with my dad to the swimming pool, and I noticed that you could crawl under the wall of the changing cubicle to the ladies' side, a regular grown-up man wouldn't have fit, but I just barely squeezed through, and then I hid behind a curtain in the ladies' shower room, and there I saw at least fifty ladies, and then when I crawled back they almost caught me, but luckily I was soaped up good and so I slipped out of their hands," and then Feri asked me if I saw blond women and redheads too, and I said, "You bet I did," and he asked if their pussy hair is the same color as their head hair, and I said, "Sure it is, it's exactly the same," but Feri didn't believe that.

But even as I thought about this I kept looking at Iza the whole time, and meanwhile Sir Uclid had started explaining something, some example, he even drew a triangle on the blackboard, an isosceles triangle, he wanted to prove that the bisector divides the sides into equal parts, but when I tried imagining that isosceles triangle, all I could think of was a pussy because I knew that pussies are triangle shaped and that drawing a pussy is exactly like drawing an isosceles triangle, and then I carefully turned my notebook because the triangle was pointed the wrong way, and now that I'd turned it, there was just enough room above it for two semicircles, which I drew as boobs, because Feri said that anyone who can draw a pussy can draw a whole naked woman too, and then I tried drawing the curves of the body, the way the waist thins out toward the middle, but the drawing didn't turn out too well, no, it wasn't at all nice, so then I began shading in the triangle a bit, and meanwhile I kept looking at Iza, the way she was copying down what Sir Uclid was writing on the blackboard, but from the middle of the bench where I was sitting I couldn't see her boobs at all, only her back and her arms and the side of her face, and as I sat there looking at her she almost turned around one time, she must have sensed that I was watching, and then I thought for sure that she'd turn around and look at me, and I felt myself blushing, and I turned my head right away and noticed that Sir Uclid was approaching from behind.

He was in the habit of giving anyone he thought wasn't paying attention a whack on the head, so I quickly turned the page from my drawing and started copying the last line from the blackboard as if I'd begun a new page, and when Sir Uclid got there he just barely swatted the back of my neck, it wasn't a real whack, and so I figured that was all I had coming to me, because by then Sir Uclid had passed by my bench, but then he reached back and grabbed my ear without so much as looking back, and he jerked it so hard that it felt ready to rip right off, and I cried out from the pain, and then I heard Sir Uclid suck in air through his teeth and tell me to bring along my notebook, and so I did, and he pulled me by the ear right up front toward the platform and he said, "Maybe you didn't notice that this is math class and not drawing class, but I'll make you notice, don't you worry about that," and he yanked the notebook right out of my hand and opened it, and he held my drawing up in front of the class for everyone to see, and he told me I should be ashamed of myself, and as he passed by the platform he yanked my ear so hard I almost fell right on the platform, and I heard the others laughing at me, and Sir Uclid still didn't let go of my ear, no, he took me straight over to the trash can and then let me go and kicked over the can, all that paper and all those apple cores and pencil shavings poured out onto the floor, and then I knew what my punishment would be, and indeed Sir Uclid really did announce that starting now until the end of class I'd be a pillar saint, and he said, "Power of two," which meant I had to stand on top of the upside-down trash can, and until the end of class I had to balance there like just that, on one leg and with my arms straight up in the air, and meanwhile I had to count in my head two times two and always multiply the product by two, and again and again and again, and by the end of class I had to come up with a number at least ten figures long, because if I didn't, Sir Uclid would automatically slap a failing grade on me for each digit short of that ten-figure number, and doing that was really hard, no one was ever able to complete it, because everyone got to four thousand ninety-six, no problem, but after that it wasn't easy keeping the numbers in your head.

Anyway, I stepped up on the trash can and stretched out my arms above my head with my fingers all spread out, just the way we were supposed to, because Sir Uclid always said that pillar saints had to hold their hands like that so birds could make a nest in their hands if they wanted. As I did this I noticed that Iza was looking at me because the trash can happened to be right there in front of the model students' bench, and meanwhile Sir Uclid leaned against the lectern on his desk and went on explaining when triangles are called similar, and that similarity is not the same as uniformity, and I tried counting, I even managed to double four thousand ninety-six, but the whole time I was looking at Iza, she had on thick brown tights and black shoes fastened with straps, and as I watched her I felt myself getting all warm, and my back started to itch and my school shirt was squeezing my neck even though my red cravat definitely wasn't pulled too tight. I tried multiplying thirty-two thousand seven hundred sixty-eight by two, but then I noticed what nice handwriting Iza had, how neat and orderly her letters were, and how she was sitting there all alone on the model students' bench, and then I saw that she'd filled up the page, and when she turned it I noticed that the next page didn't yet have a margin line, only all those little squares on account of its being graph paper, so she pulled out her ruler and put it on the page, just the way you're supposed to, four squares from the edge, and before drawing the line she looked right up at me and gave a smile, which ruined my counting. I didn't know two hundred sixty-two thousand what, and I felt myself blushing, and as Iza then drew the margin line, the ruler slipped to the side, and the tip of her pencil went right off the page, and then I noticed that she was blushing too, and she lowered her head, and as I stood there on the trash can with my arms held up high, all of a sudden I thought that maybe I was in love, and then I almost fell off the trash can, and I quickly went back to sixty-five thousand five hundred thirty-six and tried starting from there again, but by now my arms were hurting, it was getting hard to hold them up, and I didn't know how much time there was left in class. I tried not looking at Iza but at the others instead, so in the meantime I could think of the multiplying, but somehow my eyes went right back to Iza, and I wanted to know if I was really in love because never before had I really been in love, not even once, and Iza then stretched one of her legs, and I noticed that her blue school skirt had slipped a bit to the side, and one of Iza's knees showed through, along with just a sliver of her thigh, and then I thought again of what Feri told me about pussies, how he saw a black woman naked one time and her pussy hair was pure white, like when someone's gone all gray, but it's not like I believed him, so anyway, Iza then looked at me again, but this time she wasn't smiling, she simply looked up, that's all, and that made me all ashamed about the things I'd been thinking, and I tried counting instead, but by then my arms and my shoulders were really beginning to hurt, and I got hungry and thought of my midmorning snack, an apricot jam sandwich, but Sir Uclid just kept explaining away about triangles, and again I messed up the multiplying, the last number I remembered for sure was one hundred thirty thousand seventy-two, I really wished I could let my arms down already, and I saw that the guys were fidgeting a lot, which meant the class bell would ring in no time. I knew I didn't have to keep it up for long, and so I'd stick it out, I would, just like the great Communist hero Filimon Sirbu, who kept pulling that siren through the whole strike, and at the end, when the imperialists' volley cut him down, with the last of his strength he tied himself to the siren using his handkerchief, so that even with his lifeless body he would inspire his beloved comrades to strike, but unfortunately I didn't have a handkerchief with me, and it's not like I would have had anything to tie my wrists to anyway, and so I just kept holding my arms high and I tried counting, but it was no use at all anymore, and then all at once Sir Uclid looked at me and said, "The bell will ring any second now, so it's time to see what product divine inspiration has given our house saint, I can see that the storks haven't built any nests in his hands, but that doesn't mean miracles didn't happen in his head," and he told me to wipe that asinine look off my face because he'd kick the trash can right out from under me, instead I should be a good boy and say the number I'd reached, but by then my arms were hurting so bad that I couldn't even remember the end of sixty-five thousand whatever, and so I didn't say a thing, but then from the corner of my eye I noticed that Iza was looking at me again. She was silently whispering something, and I even managed to read the words on her lips, one billion seventy-three million seven hundred forty-one thousand eight hundred twenty-four, but her whispering it to me that way made me blush so hard that I couldn't say it, even though I really had read the whole thing on Iza's lips. I only stood there on the upside-down trash can with my hands held high and didn't say a thing, the skin on my face felt really hot all over, and then Sir Uclid said this would do, he'd given me a chance, but if it wasn't going to happen, well then, it wouldn't, and as he said that he smiled and suddenly kicked the trash can out from under me, and then the class bell rang.

I took a pretty hard fall, back and to the side, mainly I hit my butt and my elbow, and my school clothes got messy from the trash, and from down there on the floor even the ringing of the bell sounded a lot louder. Sir Uclid looked at me again and said what a good little weekly monitor boy I was, and right before sticking the roll book under his arm and leaving the classroom he told me to get ready to be called up front for an oral quiz during the next class, but I didn't care anymore about that because Iza was looking at me again, and I saw she was smiling.

It being the main recess, everyone left class pretty fast, Feri came over and said that if I wanted, he'd stay in and we could play the coin-toss game, but I said I didn't have any money on me, and he said that's no problem, I could sell him my snack for one twenty-five and then we could play with that money, but I said I wouldn't give it to him, I was hungry, and so he left too, and then only two of us stayed there in the classroom, Iza and I.

Iza opened the windows while I put the trash can back where it belonged, my pants were still covered with pencil shavings so I tried dusting them off, but then Iza came over and told me to be careful, that I had a lot left even on my back and that I should turn around, and then she began dusting my back, and when she did that I could tell I was turning red again, so I told her it was fine already and I stepped aside, but even through my school jacket I could still feel how warm her hand had been, and I thought to myself that it didn't do any good being in love because I wouldn't dare touch her hand, and then I said to her, "Thanks for whispering me the answer," but she looked at me like she didn't know what I was talking about and said she hadn't whispered a thing, she never did that, but I said I'd seen it, I'd seen her whisper to me "One billion seventy-three million seven hundred forty-one thousand eight hundred twenty-four," but Iza just shook her head again and said it wasn't true, and I said it was, and she said again that it wasn't, and then she turned and went over to the coat rack to get the broom and the dustpan, and as she turned I noticed that one of her ears was all red, and I said, "Let's not clean up yet, let's eat first instead," to which Iza said she wasn't hungry but I should go ahead and eat if I wanted, and so I went to my seat and got out my apricot jam sandwich and unwrapped the napkin around it, but before taking the first bite it occurred to me that I'd never seen Iza snacking at all, and then I thought that her stepfather must be starving her, and I looked at my sandwich, it was pretty big, I could give half of it to her. Meanwhile Iza had begun sweeping up the trash scattered in front of the blackboard, so I stood up and went over to the platform, and I wanted to ask her if she liked apricot jam sandwiches.

As Iza crouched to sweep the trash into the dustpan, her skirt slipped all the way up to her knee, and for a split second I thought I even saw her panties, and my mouth felt all dry, and I thought that maybe I should give her the whole sandwich, and even though I realized right away what a dumb idea that was, I took a step toward Iza all the same, and I even reached out the sandwich toward her, and meanwhile I said, "It's got apricot jam on it," but all Iza said was for me to be careful, one of my feet had just landed in a little heap of trash she'd swept up, but I just kept standing there because I still couldn't decide if I'd really seen Iza's panties or not, and Iza leaned forward, which is how she tried pulling away the little trash heap from in front of my foot before I stepped all over it even more, and she told me again to be careful, and as she reached out with the broom, suddenly I smelled that big-girl smell again, and then I knew I should tell her I like her, and not just that, but that I love her, and again I felt myself blushing, and I didn't say a thing, and then, right when Iza was pulling the broom toward herself, one of her shoes slipped and she almost fell, and as she tried to keep her balance she leaned way back and her knees went up in the air and her skirt slipped up completely, and then I really did see between her legs, and along the inside of one of her thighs there was a run all the way up her tights, and I noticed these long bluish streaks in zigzags on her skin, I saw them clearly, and I even saw her panties through her tights, yes, there was a white trapezoid-shaped spot right between her legs, and then I heard her say to me, "You pig," and I knew she knew what I was looking at, and I also knew it from how she then tried locking her legs, but the motion really did make her lose her balance.

And she fell back and I stepped forward to catch her, but as Iza flung her arms about she knocked the apricot jam sandwich out of my hand and one of her legs kicked me in the ankle, and I could tell I was about to fall right on her, and while keeling over I still saw only her panties before me, and as I then fell on Iza with my arm out in front of me, it was as if my hand took off on its own, and in no time all I could feel were her panties and then her pussy too, I could tell just how soft it was and how hot, and then Iza screamed really, really loud right into my ear, my body filled up with that piercing cry and I smelled that big-girl smell again, it was stronger than ever, and I noticed that my apricot jam sandwich had fallen in two pieces and the jam-spread side was face-down in the dust, but I didn't care because I was still holding Iza's pussy, and I knew I would never, ever let it go.

7

Valve

▪ ▪ ▪ ▪ ▪

THE CLASS BELL had rung two whole minutes earlier,
but Iron Fist flat out pretended not to notice, he just
kept drawing the mountain ranges on the blackboard,
which was really obnoxious of him because the two weekly
monitors always had to erase the board by the next class if
they didn't want the physics teacher to slap them around, and
all of us in Iron Fist's class had to stay in the classroom during recess so we could copy the outline of the map after Iron
Fist left the room because the textbook still had the mountain
ranges with their old names, but we weren't really supposed
to say those out loud ever since they were renamed in memory of our homeland's heroes two years earlier on the birthday of Comrade General Secretary. So anyway, we would have
told any other teacher that the bell had rung already, but no
one dared to say a thing to Iron Fist because no one wanted
him to smash their nose in, like he did to Szövérfi when he
shot off his mouth while Iron Fist was telling us about tec-
tonic plates, and when Iron Fist finally put down the chalk

and stuck the roll book under his arm, there were only seven minutes left in the break, and when he reached the door he stopped and without even looking back he said, "Djata is coming with me."

That made me really scared, never before had he called me by my nickname, so I knew he'd somehow figured out that two weeks earlier it was me who'd filched the valve from his motorcycle's front wheel, which I did because I was still really angry with him on account of his dropping me from the Homeland Defense team when it became official that Father had been taken away. So I was now really scared, and I looked at Feri, who'd helped me steal the valve, and Feri turned so pale I thought he'd faint right away, and I too felt my face go cold, and when I stood up I was afraid I wouldn't be able to let go of the edge of the bench, that's how terrified I was, but then somehow I must have let it go after all, because I saw my boots taking steps across the wood floor and then the concrete hallway, and I saw that one of my laces was half undone, and finally the knots tied at the frayed ends kept winding up under my foot, but I didn't feel it, it was almost like I couldn't even feel my feet.

Iron Fist wasn't in a hurry, he was taking relaxed, easy steps, and when he passed by the stairs leading to the faculty room without going up, I knew right away that we were going to the science supply room and I could feel my heart in my throat, and if he'd asked me something then, for sure I wouldn't have been able to say a thing, so I tried taking deep breaths to calm down, and when we reached the supply room I was hardly trembling anymore, my mouth was still pretty dry but I was able to swallow again, but when Iron Fist then opened the door and waved a hand for me to go in ahead of him, I got scared all over again because I knew that that's when he starts pounding away at you, by punching you from behind, right in the kidneys. Szabi pissed blood for four days

73

after Iron Fist took him in there, so when I stepped in the door I was waiting for the blow, and I was thinking that if I lunged forward at the very moment he hit me, then maybe I'd lessen its force, and if I pretended it really hurt, then maybe I'd pull through with just a couple of kicks on top of that, but then nothing did happen after all. I stepped right over the threshold and didn't stop, I just went ahead straight toward the window, and I was already in the middle of the science supply room, and his not hitting me scared me even more because I didn't know what would happen. And then Iron Fist finally spoke, he told me not to be frightened, he wasn't going to knock out my kidneys, and he was talking funny, and when I looked at him I saw why, there was a cigarette in the corner of his mouth and he was just putting his lighter away, and then he looked me in the eye and blew that smelly smoke on me, but I wasn't about to start coughing if I could help it, and he said he wouldn't give me a beating even though I deserved it, and he waved a hand toward one of the chairs and told me to go sit down.

As I went over to the chair I kept my eye on Iron Fist's face the whole time, his mustache was cut really short but was still pretty striking, and he was clean-shaven everywhere else, so anyway, he waited until I sat down, and then he slowly came over and stopped in front of the chair, and while standing there he leaned against one of the glass cabinets, I could see the colored plastic models of the heart and internal organs behind him, we hadn't studied those yet, human anatomy was taught in seventh grade, and then Iron Fist said I didn't have to lie, I could be honest with him.

I nodded but didn't say a thing because I knew that until you get questions fired at you, you don't really need to say much of anything, no, that can only spell trouble, so I waited for him to ask me something, but Iron Fist didn't say a thing, he just kept puffing his cigarette, at least he wasn't blowing the smoke on me anymore, and at last he spoke. He asked if I really did like those Homeland Defense competitions because he remembered well how angry I'd been when he dropped me from the team, and I just sort of half nodded and half shook my head, I didn't know what the proper answer was, if I said yes, that's why he'd slap me around, and if I said no, then that would be the reason, but I had to say something, because if I didn't I'd get slapped all the same, so finally I told him that what I really liked was shooting, not that I told Iron Fist why, I didn't say it's because when I was little my dad taught me to use an air gun and took me to the shooting gallery a lot, where the two of us always hit everything right on target, one time I even shot out a candle's flame. Anyway, all I told Iron Fist was that I liked to shoot, and he nodded and said he could tell that from the way I held a gun, which was just the way you're supposed to, I was a natural born talent, and he was really sorry when he had to drop me from the team, but he had no other choice, Comrade Principal told him flat out that on account of what happened to my father, I wasn't allowed to be on the team because I too had become unreliable from a political point of view, and what they teach at Homeland Defense competitions is a highly classified state secret, and it's best for me not to even know that stuff because I might get into trouble on account of it. And Iron Fist really was right about that, one time I almost got into big trouble because of what we learned about radioactivity, but that didn't matter a bit, I would have been angry at him all the same for taking me off the team, but I knew that these questions were just meant to soften me up and what he really wanted was for me to admit that I had taken the valve out of his motorcycle wheel, and so I didn't say anything else, I didn't even look into his eyes, no, instead I looked at those plastic models behind his back, the seventh graders said there was even one of the female genital organ and that it looked just like the real thing, but of course I didn't see that model anywhere, it must have been locked away in the lower cabinet.

So anyway, I was looking at those models and not saying a thing, Iron Fist was smoking his cigarette and not saying a thing, and I had no idea what he was planning, so I began getting more and more worried, and then I heard the bell ring, and I knew that physics class was about to begin, and I wanted to stand up, but Iron Fist told me to stay right where I was because he'd arranged for me to be let out of the next class, and that's when I really got scared because he'd never done that before with anyone, and I must have gone pale because right away Iron Fist asked, "Whatsa matter, why do you look like you're about to shit your pants?" and I said, "It's nothing at all," but Iron Fist just smiled and said, well, my face was pretty white, even though it really wasn't necessary to be scared of him because he'd never bothered anyone, and he didn't want to do me any harm, he just wanted to ask me for a little favor, but if I talked about this to anyone at all, I really would have something to be scared of because I wouldn't survive that, the same thing would end up happening to me as happened to my dad, and then I almost spoke up, I wanted to say that it's not true, my dad hadn't died, he was still alive, because if he did die, I'd know about that, but I didn't say anything after all, and then Iron Fist said that Horáciú, the boy who took my place on the Homeland Defense team, had been hospitalized on account of falling down the stairs and breaking his nose, and the city finals were being held today, and he needed someone to put in Horáciú's place, someone he could trust, and so he thought of me, but he didn't say that this was because I was the best shot in school, no, he said it was because I looked the most like Horáciú and we were going to the competition at School No. 16 just as if I were Horáciú, but he'd have me know again that I wasn't to speak about this to anyone, and he didn't ask if I wanted to do it or was willing to do it, no, instead he said it as if he was certain that this was how it would be because I had to do what he wanted, and he said that the city finals had already been held in cross-country, the 3,000-yard obstacle course, map reading, politics, and military history, the only thing left was shooting, and although we'd done pretty well in other areas, the competition in shooting was really stiff this year, we now had only a theoretical possibility, a mathematical one, he said, of getting through to the next round, and to do that I had to shoot at least 117 points out of 120, but even then, no more than two shooters on other teams could shoot better than me, true, with those cheap Czechoslovak air rifles this was hopeless anyway, especially since we had to save on ammunition, and everyone got no more than three practice shots, but still, there was a mathematical possibility, and then I said, "That means that if I shoot a perfect score, 120 points, the team will definitely get to the next round," and Iron Fist nodded, and again he blew the cigarette smoke at me, and he said, "Oh sure, that's all I need, for you to shoot a perfect score, how could you even think such a stupid thing," and he got really, really nervous, his mustache was quivering, I saw, and he was taking only little puffs on his cigarette, but I said didn't he think I could do it, because if not, he sure didn't remember how well I used to shoot, because I do know how to shoot, I do, I know how to feel the gun, how to become one with the bullet the moment I pull the trigger, I know how sharpshooters think because my dad taught me that, and I told Iron Fist that if he didn't believe it, he should go ahead and take me to that competition, I'd show him, I'd show him where those holes would be once I was done with the target because if I wanted, I sure could shoot 120 points if necessary, or even 130, because my hands had what it takes to switch one of the practice pellets for the tip of a ballpoint pen since if you need to, you can shoot with that too, yes, that's how I'd get my hands on an extra pellet, and then I could shoot even 130 points if I wanted because no one would notice that I'd taken not twelve shots but thirteen. And as I said all this, all of a sudden I got such a big slap that I almost fell off the chair, Iron Fist hit me so suddenly that his cigarette dropped right out from between his fingers and I had to grab hold of the back of the chair from the side, and the cigarette fell to the rug, I saw, where it was still giving off smoke, and I felt dizzy, that's how big a slap I got, but luckily my mouth just happened to be open when he hit me because I was still in the middle of a sentence, and so I didn't bite my tongue and nothing happened to my teeth, and then Iron Fist said I should be ashamed of myself for daring to talk to him in such a tone of voice, it was best if I didn't forget that we weren't born the same day, and he must have noticed that while he was talking I never once took my eyes off that cigarette smoldering there on the rug because he suddenly said he wanted his cigarette back, so I crouched down nice and easy and picked it up, and as I started putting the cigarette back in Iron Fist's hand I thought I should press the burning end right into his mouth, he was such a beast that he deserved it, and I knew he was about to make me apologize, but I decided not to if I could help it, not if I didn't need to, I would not apologize, and then Iron Fist snatched the cigarette from me and stuck it back in his mouth, and he took a big drag, except he didn't blow the smoke on me like he had at first but into the air. Then when he did speak again, he told me to get it through my head that we had to lose the competition because our school's team must not go on to the next round, and if one thing was for sure, it was that I mustn't say this to anyone, I shouldn't even know about this, and by telling me he'd put his head through the noose, and as he said this he poked at his neck with the hand that was holding the cigarette, almost getting ash all over himself, and then he said, but that didn't matter because now the noose was around my neck too, and I didn't need to know any more about this anyway, and he told me to get it through my head that no way should I shoot more than seventy points, for if I did so I'd put my school's future at risk because at the city finals it was School No. 3 that had to get through to the next round, and not our team, so I should promise to do as he told me, that I'd shoot sixty points, or no more than seventy-five, and that was it.

While he was talking I kept looking into his eyes, but after a while he stopped looking at me, and my eyes also drifted away, back to those plastic models again, the ones there behind the glass. Two thick tubes stuck out of the top of the heart, one of them was painted blue and the other was painted red, and when Iron Fist got all quiet I looked at him again, straight into his eyes, and he asked me to promise, but right this instant, because we really did need to get going right away or else we'd be late for the competition. And then with one hand I grabbed the back of the chair, and I said, "No, I won't promise, no way, that wasn't what my dad taught me, sports are supposed to be fair, there's no room for cheating in sports, everyone who participates starts with an equal shot, it's only about how every single person performs," and I said I didn't care, he could go ahead and take me to the competition, but I was going to shoot as well as I could all the same, I'd give it my all, and while I was talking I got really scared from hearing my own voice, it was almost like it wasn't even me talking, and then my hand started really hurting from gripping the back of the chair so hard, and I knew I'd get slapped around in no time, I tried relaxing my mouth, but I was gritting my teeth so much that the pain shot right up into my temples, and I knew that this was it, that Iron Fist would beat my brains out, but not even then could I keep my mouth shut, no, try as I did to swallow my words, not even then could I stop talking. But Iron Fist didn't hit me, instead he just stubbed out his cigarette and put one of his index fingers in front of his mouth and hissed *shhh,* but that wasn't what made me shut up, it was when I saw him put his other hand in his pocket, because that meant he was about to pull out his brass knuckles, and that would be the end of me, I'd be lucky if I only ended up in the hospital, and in the meantime Iron Fist pulled his hand out, and he didn't have brass knuckles on it, instead he was holding something in his hand, I couldn't tell what it was, and then he held his fist right in front of me, he was wearing a really wide gold ring, I saw my own face reflected in it, and then he asked if I could guess what he had in his hand, but by then I was so scared that even if I figured it out, not even then would I have dared to say a word, that's how terrified I was, and so I only shook my head. Meanwhile I looked again at the heart behind the glass, and for some reason it occurred to me that cold blood flows from the heart through the blue tube and that hot blood flows through the red tube, but when I thought of that, I knew right away it was dumb.

And then Iron Fist said, fine, he could tell that I was giving up, I shouldn't rack my brains anymore because I'd get muscle fatigue doing that, and he opened his hand, and I saw right away what was on his palm, it was the valve of his motorcycle wheel, yes, that's what he was holding right there under my nose, and as soon as I saw it, I felt myself turn pale, I felt my body filling up with ice-cold blood, so cold that my skin would turn blue, and I felt almost as if my heart was about to stop altogether, that's how scared I was, and then Iron Fist said he knew everything about this little prank of ours, Feri had told him everything, that's right, Feri had more brains than I did, the day after our prank Feri realized it would be best to go ahead and fess up completely, because then maybe he could get out of this in one piece, yes, Feri was smart enough to realize that if Iron Fist figured out for himself who was responsible for his having to push his motorcycle up the hill he lived on, whoever it was would be a goner for sure, and then I thought of Feri, so that was why Feri had looked white as a ghost, and while Iron Fist went on talking, the whole time he held the valve right under my nose, and as his hand moved I could see that little ball moving in the valve, it was almost as big as an air-gun pellet, and then Iron Fist put the valve back in his pocket and turned his back to me as if he was looking out a window, and he stood there just like that as he said, "You know what you did, don't you. That wasn't just some school-kid prank, it was an act of sabotage, sabotage against the state." And he said that if he wanted he could not only kick me out of school but also see that I wound up in reform school, and the only reason I wouldn't end up in prison was because I was still under fifteen, "But don't you worry," he said, my mother was older, so I could rest assured that she'd wind up in a real prison and I'd never see her ever again, and then I thought I was about to cry, but I didn't want to cry if I could help it, so instead I only said, really quietly, "All right, I'll do it, I'll shoot as many points as you say, if need be, sixty, and if need be, forty, just like you want," and then I stood up and said we should go, that we should get it over with, and Iron Fist slapped me on the back and said, "Now that's talking," and then we left the science supply room and went all the way down the hall and down the stairs, and we went out the teachers' entrance, and the student monitor clicked his heels and saluted as he opened the door, but Iron Fist didn't return the gesture, and even I just barely raised my palm to my temple.

Comrade Principal let Iron Fist borrow his car, so we went in that, and Iron Fist let me sit up front, never in my life had I sat up front in a car, but I wasn't able to enjoy it, not now, because I kept thinking more and more about Feri, and Iron Fist kept smoking the whole way, and he didn't say a thing.

School No. 16, where they were holding the competition,

wasn't far, so we got there fast, but before we got out of the car Iron Fist showed me the valve one more time, not that I was about to say anything if I could help it, and then we went into the school and out to the yard, which was decorated with pine boughs and panels of red felt with pictures and all sorts of quotations on them about the armed forces and about the nation's youth and about the Party General Secretary and about peace, and we got there just in time because the woman commander of the school's Young Pioneers was already greeting "all those assembled here today," she even gave a little speech, not that I paid much attention, no, I had my eyes on the firing positions. Judging from the blankets that had been laid out, it looked like we'd have to shoot lying down, but the targets hadn't been put out yet, and so I couldn't estimate the distance, and in the meantime the Young Pioneers commander was saying something about solidarity and peace, and then all of a sudden her speech ended and everyone saluted, and then we sang the national anthem, not only the first stanza and the last, as usual, but all the way through, I didn't even know the middle stanzas so well, they said something about some plows and, I think, some swords, but then that ended too, and then the school principal wished everyone much success, and then the competition really did begin.

First we drew lots for the weapons, all of us had to pull a number from out of a gas mask to decide which weapon we'd get to fire with and in which half, I pulled the number thirteen, but that didn't worry me because thirteen always brought me luck, besides, it now meant I'd be shooting in the second half with rifle number three. There were ten air rifles and ten ranges in all, and on purpose I didn't look to see how the person using rifle number three in the first half shot, although that would have given me an idea of how accurate that rifle was and which way it would take my hand, but I figured, what the hell, it didn't matter anyway, and so I didn't look there at all, no, instead I just walked around the yard and took a good look at the Corner of Peace, the word *peace* was written there in a whole bunch of languages, and it also said that the world's children wanted peace, and at the top were the pictures of the Party General Secretary and the commander in chief of the armed forces, and underneath there were pictures of war heroes and generals, and a couple of pictures of tanks and airplanes and of the armed forces' May Day parade, of all those tanks and mortars and missiles passing by the grandstand, the picture of the generals seemed strange, and when I took a better look, I noticed that it had been cut to pieces and taped back together again, which was pretty obvious because of how the wall behind the generals looked, and then it occurred to me that I knew this picture because it was in the appendix at the end of our fifth-grade textbook, but back then the picture still had seven generals on it, and now there were only five, meaning two generals had disappeared from the picture, and it wasn't like I'd even heard anything about them being traitors, and in the meantime I saw that everyone had just about stood up already at their firing positions, which meant that they were done shooting and our round was coming right up, so I began moseying back there, and I noticed the teachers standing around and chatting away by the school entrance, Iron Fist was there too, he was still smoking, and he must have sensed it when I looked that way because he turned toward me and gave a smile and a wave of the hand, with the same hand that was holding the cigarette, and the whole time his other hand was in his pocket, and I knew he was holding the valve, and then all of a sudden I felt this heat surge through me, and as I stood there someone behind me said, "Horáciú," and I got really scared, but I turned around all the same and saw that it was the woman commander of the Young Pioneers, and when I noticed that she was reading my name from a sheet of paper

I calmed down a bit because I figured she didn't know the real Horáciú, and so it wouldn't turn out that I wasn't really him, so I said, "Yes, that's me," and then she asked me what I'd been looking at in the Corner of Peace, and I said, "Nothing, Comrade Commander, it's just that before competitions I always look at the picture of the commander in chief of the armed forces, to bring me luck, I mean, because he's my role model," and then the commander of the Young Pioneers nodded and said, "It's just such patriotic thoughts that take the country forward on the path of peace," and then she jotted something down on a notepad and wished me much success, and I went over to my firing position and got down on the blanket.

One of the competition officials quickly handed out the three practice pellets because by then the practice targets had been set up, and I took the rifle, it was Czechoslovak, sure enough, but in really good condition, it was really easy to close, and on purpose I didn't aim for the center of the target but for the white line between the circles worth five points and six points, and as I squeezed the butt of the rifle to my shoulder, the rifle's weight was enough to calm me down, and when I aimed I didn't even need to pay attention to my breathing because everything just took care of itself, I fired the shot right when I exhaled, and when the competition officials then handed out the twelve competition pellets and gave us the practice targets to look at, I saw that every one of my shots really had gone right where I'd aimed it, so I knew I really could shoot a perfect score if I wanted, and then the other competition official set up the official targets, and I was really surprised because never before had I seen any like them, they were much bigger than plain targets, and each one looked like a human torso, and you had to aim for the left side, where the heart is, and I thought of the plastic model of the heart behind the glass, and it seemed to me that the bull's-eye, all ten points, was right between the two arteries, between the red and the blue blood vessels, and as I then took aim, somehow all I saw before me was that plastic model, and it did no good trying to aim at the circle worth six points because all I saw were those two holes, the red hole and the blue hole, and somehow it seemed like those two holes were Iron Fist's eyes, and then as I pulled the trigger for the first time, I knew the pellet would go there, right between Iron Fist's eyes, and that if I was in the Wild West, he'd drop dead just like that, and then I could also make out the tiny black hole in the middle of the bull's-eye, it looked only as big as a pinprick from where I was, but I shot there a second time, right into the circle worth ten points, and a third time and a fourth too, and even without looking at the target I knew that my every shot was there inside the bull's-eye, all ten points each time, and at the end I looked at the target, after all, and I saw that they really were all there, right beside one another, I'd shot 120 points, or 119, and as I set down the rifle I knew that meant big trouble, and I thought of the generals and I thought that Mother and I would now also disappear, and I would be removed from our class picture.

I was all dizzy when I stood up, luckily we couldn't look at the targets because I didn't want to see the shot-up bull's-eye close up, the judges took every target away immediately for evaluation, and then as we waited for the results Iron Fist came over and said all right, judging from how pale I looked he could tell I'd done what must be done. "Such is life," he said. "Smart people go with the flow," and then he reached into his pocket and took out the valve and put it in my hand, and he said, "Here, go ahead and put it away, you worked for it, you did," and as I took the valve it felt really hot, like it was burning my palm, and then the woman commander of the Young Pioneers called out, "Comrades, the results are about to be announced," and everyone went over to hear them, and when they got to our school, Iron Fist put an arm around my shoulder and just held me there like that, and I had my eyes on the mouth of the Young Pioneers commander, it was as if I saw that mouth in slow motion as it formed the words, and I didn't even hear the sound of her voice, I only read her lips saying "Sixty-three points," and I wanted to cry out, "That's a lie, that's cheating, I shot a perfect score," but that piece of metal was still heating up my hand, it felt like a real bullet, and then for some reason the names of the mountain ranges came to my mind, both the old names and the new ones, and I didn't say a thing, all I did was swallow, and meanwhile I heard them say that School No. 3 had won the shooting competition with 107 points, and then Iron Fist again pounded my back and said, "Don't be down about it now, you need to know how to lose."

8

Gift

■ ■ ■ ■ ■

EVERY TIME I saw my grandfather, his chest was covered with medals, he had so many that they didn't even fit on his coat, and besides the ones he wore, he had at least twice as many at home in a china cabinet where he kept his old sport-shooting trophy cups, but those medals on his chest sure did jangle when he leaned down to peck me on the cheeks. I didn't like it when he kissed me, his face was all oily from this cream he made himself, and he was always spreading it all over me too, and for days afterward I smelled that disgusting lavender smell, true, we didn't meet often to begin with, and practically never since my father was taken to the Danube Canal because my grandfather and grandmother didn't like my mother too much, they called her a screwed-up slut who couldn't get it through her head what a good world we lived in and that she was the one who made my father lose his senses, that this whole big affair with the Party was because of her, yes, he wound up at the Danube Canal because of her, and so they didn't even talk to my mother, and when they passed her on the street, even then it was like they didn't know her at all, they looked right through her and didn't even say hi, and if I was with her at such times, they were just the same with me, but twice a year I got to go visit them after all, on my birthday and my name day.

On those occasions my grandfather used to come by in his car to pick me up, he would wait for me down in front of our building in his sparkling black car, and when he saw me coming he always got out and opened the car door, but he didn't say hi and he didn't kiss me either, no, all he said was, "Do get in," and then all the way to my grandparents' place he didn't say a thing, just as if he was a genuine chauffeur, and only after we arrived and got out of the car did he say how glad he was I'd come, and only then did he peck me on the cheeks, as if the drive there didn't count, as if we'd met only there, in front of their house. My grandfather always sent the invitation a month ahead of time, and he always wrote the same words with his snaky handwriting, "I await you with love for a pleasant afternoon on the occasion of our mutual name day," that's exactly how he wrote it, he had the same name as my father and I, but I was not allowed to call him by his first name, and never Grandfather either, only Comrade Secretary, everyone except my grandmother called him that, though I think my grandfather was already retired, so he couldn't have been a secretary anyway.

That year the invitation came only two days before my name day, I was already thinking that my grandfather had forgotten all about it, but then I found the usual cream-colored envelope in our mailbox, just like always, addressed to me, and I told Mother right away and asked her if she'd let me go, and Mother broke into a sad smile and nodded the way she did when I asked her something she wasn't happy about, and she said, sure, she'd let me go, but like always, on one condition, of course it was nice of my grandfather the way he remembered me at least twice a year, and then she asked me if I still remembered what the condition was, and I nodded, and I said right away that I wasn't allowed to accept the gift I would receive, meaning I was allowed to accept it but not to keep it, I could play with it there as much as I wanted, but I'd have to give it back at the end, I couldn't bring it home because there was nothing in our home from my grandfather, and if it was up to my mother then there wouldn't ever be anything either, and then Mother said she knew how hard this was for me, that this was really a very strict rule, but once I got bigger I'd understand that it was the right thing to do, and I'd see, I'll even be glad, and of course I nodded, but I didn't say a thing because I thought of that electric train I got three years earlier for my birthday and how I wasn't able to try it out properly ever since, and I knew that Mother couldn't be right.

Mother also insisted that on these occasions I had to dress up, that no matter how hot it was, I couldn't go in plain shorts and a T-shirt, I had to get on those scratchy wool trousers she made from one of father's suits, plus a white shirt and a knit sweater and my Young Pioneers cravat, luckily I'd just grown out of those disgusting high-legged patent-leather shoes, so it was only my boots I had to shine, and I was done too when of course Mother then told me to comb my hair, but at least she didn't mat my hair down with a wet hand like the other times, and then she looked me over one more time, adjusted my cravat so it would be right in the middle, pecked me on the cheeks, and I was free to go.

Sure enough, there was that black car out front as soon as I stepped outside our apartment block, my grandfather was never late, he was always telling me that punctuality was extremely important, and as soon as he saw me he smiled, but he didn't get out of the car this time, no, he just reached back and lifted up the latch on the rear door, so I even had to open the door, but this time when I sat down inside he said, "Hey there," which really surprised me because he never said that sort of thing, he was much more formal, but as usual I said right away, "I kiss your hand, Comrade Secretary," and my grandfather nodded and started the car, and we hadn't even turned out of Long Street when he spoke again, he told me how big I'd grown since the last time he saw me, pretty soon I'd be a regular grownup, not that I knew what to say to that, only when we reached the church everyone just called Small Church did it occur to me that I should have said, "And you don't look a day older, Comrade Secretary," but by then it was too late, so instead I kept quiet, I could just barely see my grandfather's mouth in the rearview mirror, there was a little wound above his lips on one side, he must have cut himself while shaving, and it must have hurt because he licked it more than once, and through the whole ride I kept looking at his mouth because I wanted to know beforehand when he was about to say something, but my grandfather kept quiet for a long time, but when I saw him break into a grin I noticed that his mouth was exactly like Father's, and I almost told him so too, but luckily I remembered in time that I wasn't allowed to mention Father at all, and so I cupped my hand quickly over my mouth as if I'd only yawned, and then my grandfather spoke again, he said he could tell I was uneasy about talking to him the way I used to, it seemed I'd grown up, addressing him in formal terms didn't come naturally to me anymore, but I shouldn't let it get to me because before long we'd have ourselves a toast to celebrate finally being on friendly, grownup terms. Well, that surprised me even more, and when he asked me if that would be all right, I said, "Quite all right, Comrade Secretary," but my grandfather didn't say a thing, he just frowned and shook his head. Meanwhile we drove through the main square and turned onto Heroes' Avenue, which was lined with great big trees, and finally we reached the side street where my grandparents lived.

After stopping in front of my grandparents' house we got out, and after locking the car my grandfather shook my hand, but this time he didn't say how glad he was I'd come, he only leaned down and gave me a peck on each cheek, so I got that face cream of his all over myself again, and when he stepped to the door to open it I wiped my face with my shirtsleeve as best I could, but that disgusting lavender smell was still really strong.

There was always a big mess in the yard, before the Party gave the house to my grandparents some sculptor lived there who used the garage as a studio, and a couple of half-finished statues were still there in the yard along with these big white dismantled sculpture molds, you always had to step around the stuff, some of it was completely overgrown with ivy, and as we went toward the door, something moved back in the yard, I saw it only out of the corner of my eye, but I turned my head right away in that direction, all I saw was a flickering shadow, my grandfather also looked over there and he saw it too, that's for sure, because I heard him say under his breath, "Those fucking cats, they shit all over the grass."

We then went into the kitchen, where my grandfather pulled out a chair and told me to sit down, he said he'd go get some pastry and that it would be best to also do that toast right away, and he went into the pantry and brought out two glasses, a decanter, and a plate full of walnut crescents, and he put the plate and one of the glasses in front of me and said, "Don't be shy, go ahead, take some," and he took a walnut crescent and began chewing, and meanwhile he uncorked the decanter and poured himself a glass of red wine, and I also took a walnut crescent, but it wasn't at all as usual, it was a lot harder, I could hardly chew it all the way, sure, it was sweet, but it had a sort of stale taste as if it had been sitting around in the pantry a long time, and I was still eating it when my grandfather filled my glass too, all the way up, I wanted to tell him I'd never had wine before and that I didn't even think I was allowed to have any, but my grandfather had already picked up his glass and was holding it in a way that told me he was just waiting for me, and so I picked up my own glass, and then my grandfather said, "Hey there," and he clinked his glass against mine, but I didn't say a thing because I didn't know what you're supposed to say, and then my grandfather told me that this wouldn't do, and he told me to say "Hey there" too, and again he clinked his glass against mine, and he repeated it, but this time I said it back, and then my grandfather said, "Bottom's up," and he drank his whole glass of wine in one gulp, so I too lifted my glass to my mouth and began to drink, I thought the wine would be bitter and would burn my throat, but it didn't, it was just really sour and it tasted a little like beef, but it wasn't bitter, and so I was able to drink it after all, and when I put down my glass it didn't have a drop of wine in it either, and my grandfather smiled at me and said, "All right, from now on we're chums, happy name day," and then he asked me if I knew what my gift would be, and I too wished him a happy name day and said, "No, I don't know," and meanwhile I took another walnut crescent and bit into it carefully, figuring it might not be as stale, but sure enough it was, and so I ate it really slowly, and then my grandfather said he knew that my mother didn't like him and my grandmother, and he also knew how bad it was for me not being able to take home my gifts, so this year I'd be getting something I wouldn't even have to take with me, and did I want to guess what it was, but I said, "I don't like guessing games, I prefer real surprises."

My grandfather then said, "All right, if you don't want to, you don't have to guess," and he nodded toward the inside room and told me to go in and say hi to my grandmother, and in the meantime he'd get my gift ready, but I should be careful not to tire out my grandmother because she wasn't feeling well, and I wanted to ask him what was wrong with her, but my grandfather just waved his hand toward the door of the inside room and said, "Go ahead now, we'll talk more after."

The inside room was pretty light even though the see-through drapes were drawn shut, and the table was covered with flowers, white hyacinths and lilacs in crystal vases, the flower smell was really thick, and there was my grandmother, lying in bed, her long blond hair hanging off the pillow, one of her legs stretched out from under the blanket, and I saw her toenails were painted red.

When I shut the door from behind me, my grandmother woke up and looked straight at me, and I greeted her as usual, "I kiss your hand, Grandmother," and she just asked, "You don't say, is it you?" as if she didn't even recognize me, but then she said right away, "Come over here, my little grandson," and then she really did reach her hand out toward me, she held her arm so straight that only the back of her hand was hanging down, like in the movies when ladies hold out their hand for a kiss, and I didn't know what to do, so I went over and with my right hand I took her hand, like I'd seen in the movies, and when I leaned down toward her I thought, now she'll yank away her hand for sure, but then she didn't yank it away, so I didn't have a choice, I really had to give it a kiss, and then my grandmother gave me another smile and waved a hand toward the armchair by the bed. "Sit down," she said, and she told me she could see I'd become a real grown-up gentleman, so I sat down, I stared at the embroidered wall hanging above my grandmother's bed and the jeweled rings on her hand, and she said that unfortunately she wasn't feeling well nowadays, that this agonizing headache had kept her in bed for a while already, and then she asked me how school was going, and I said fine, and meanwhile I noticed that down by the roots her hair wasn't blond after all, but a grayish brown, and then Grandmother said she was glad I was a good student because at least I, for one, wouldn't bring shame on my grandfather, and then with her ring finger she pointed toward the glass pitcher on the table by the vases, and she asked me to pour her a glass of water, and I said, "Yes, ma'am," and I stood up and brought over the water. Grandmother drank by holding her glass in both hands and taking big gulps, and in the meantime I kept looking at how wrinkled her skin was, and I was wondering if that pointy stone on her hand really was a diamond, and if it was, then whether it could cut glass. Meanwhile Grandmother at last drank down all the water, and when she gave me back the glass I noticed that its edge was smudged with lipstick and that Grandmother's eyes were watery, and at first I thought that this was only from exerting herself, because drinking had been so hard for her, but when she then looked at me and asked if I could keep a secret, and her voice was shaking as if she was about to cry, that's when I saw that she really had gotten all sad, and she didn't even wait for my reply, she said that Doctor Csidej had come by to examine her, and what she'd suspected for years was now certain, she had cancer, she was terminally ill, she wouldn't live to see the summer. She said all this at a whisper, and by the time she finished, her tears were really trickling down, and while crying like that she reached out and took my hand and said, "For the love of God, you mustn't say a word of this to your grandfather, he mustn't know about it," and I was just in the middle of promising I wouldn't, and I also thought of asking her where the cancer hurt, but Grandmother didn't pay even a bit of attention to what I'd begun to say, no, she just whispered to me to be a good boy and leave her be because I'd really tired her out, and then she told me again to be a good boy, and when she said that her eyes shut right away, so I stood up and headed toward the door, and just as I stepped out of the room I noticed that my grandmother was pulling her leg back under the blanket.

My grandfather wasn't in the kitchen, and at first I didn't know where he might be, but then I sat down and heard someone puttering about in the bathroom, and I looked at the walnut crescents but I didn't take any more, I was more thirsty than anything, the taste of the wine was still strong in my mouth, I thought of standing up and pouring myself a glass of water from the tap, but then the bathroom door opened in the hall and my grandfather came back into the kitchen and put a little package on the table, something wrapped in an oily cloth, and then he poured each of us a glass of wine and meanwhile asked me what my grandmother had said, and I said, "Oh, nothing, she only asked me about school," but my grandfather gulped down the wine and told me not to lie, because my grandmother must have told me that story about her being sick, and then I said she had, but I'd promised her not to talk about it, and my grandfather nodded and said, "Fine then, a promise is a beautiful thing," and he poured himself another glass, so I also took a little gulp of wine, but this time it wasn't good at all, and in the meantime I had my eyes on that oily package on the table, and I was wondering what could be in it, and my grandfather noticed that I was looking at it, but this time he didn't say a thing, he just kept gulping his wine nice and easy, and then all of a sudden he asked me if I still played soccer, and I said no, and whether I still took part in Homeland Defense activities, and I said I didn't do that either, and then my grandfather got all quiet, and after he finished the rest of his wine he asked if I remembered the time he promised to take me hunting, and I said yes, even though I didn't remember, because he never did promise me any such thing, and then my grandfather pulled that oily package close to himself and began unwrapping the cloth and he said, "Well then, the time has come," and he pulled out a big pistol.

Never had I seen a pistol like that before, it was much bigger than what policemen wear, its barrel was longer and its stock had a different shape, my grandfather snapped out the magazine and put the empty pistol in my hand, and he told me to hold it knowing it's a Luger, and that no living person had seen this weapon in twenty-five years, and to be careful with it because this was not a child's toy, and then he stood up and said, "Let's go out to the yard," he'd teach me how to aim, besides, the wine would steady my hand, but I didn't pay a bit of attention to what he was saying, no, I just kept holding the weapon, it was heavy and really cold, before then I always thought pistols were a lot lighter, I couldn't imagine how someone could do a quick draw with this sort of pistol, and then my grandfather asked something, but just what he asked I didn't hear because I'd aimed the pistol at the clock on the wall and I was imagining what would happen if I shot a bullet right in the middle of that clock, and then my grandfather yanked the pistol out of my hand and said really loud that he'd told me once already that this was not a child's toy, I should get it through my head that this wasn't some crappy air gun like we clown around with at Homeland Defense activities, this was a real pistol, a genuine Parabellum, and then he looked at my glass and asked, "Aren't you going to finish your wine?" and I wanted to say, "Yes, I'll drink it" because I was scared he'd be offended and give me a good slap, but by then he'd already taken my glass and downed the remaining wine in one gulp, and he said, "Fine then, let's go, time is passing by."

When we went out to the yard, my grandfather gave me back the pistol and told me to aim at the watering can hanging from a nail on the garage wall, and then I lifted the pistol, but it wasn't the watering can I aimed at, no, I aimed at one of those white statues leaning against the garage wall, its face wasn't carved out properly, but I aimed right between its two eyes all the same, and my grandfather told me to lower the weapon and take aim again, and I pointed it right there one more time, at the statue's head, and then my grandfather stood behind me and slightly adjusted my grip, he told me not to hold my arm so stiffly and he told me to aim at the watering can, that I mustn't direct a loaded weapon at a human being unless I planned to kill him, and I wanted to say, "It's just a statue," but without a word I turned my arm away so the barrel of the gun really was now aimed at the watering can, and my grandfather then went off to the side, and at first he told me to lower the gun and then raise my arm and take aim, but then he didn't say it anymore, he just kept waving his hand, up-down, up-down, the gun was pretty heavy and really different to hold than an air gun, but I finally got really good at taking aim, and twice I even pulled the trigger, and I did so right when I breathed out, like I learned to do with the air gun, and I knew that if there had been a bullet in the pistol, I'd have shot the watering can to smithereens.

After a while my grandfather didn't even wave his hand anymore, he let me raise the gun to my own rhythm, and then he said fine, I was talented, I was holding the pistol just the way I was supposed to, sure, he could tell it was a little heavy for me, but nothing could be done about that, this was a serious weapon, not some measly air gun like we shoot with in school, and then he took the pistol from me and inserted the magazine and adjusted something on it, and when he gave it back he told me to be careful because the safety was now off and the gun was loaded, so I should pull the trigger only when he said to. "So, come on," he said, "let's stand by the pear tree because if we don't move they won't notice us, and don't be scared, because we won't have to wait for long," and I didn't understand why he was saying this and who it was that wouldn't notice us, and I was just about to ask him who he meant when my grandfather put his hand over my mouth and pulled me along with him to the pear tree, and meanwhile with his other hand he pointed to the top of the stone fence, and that's when I saw this big black cat standing there, and suddenly I knew what it was we were going to hunt, I felt my hand tighten around the pistol and I wanted to raise it and aim, but my grandfather gripped my shoulder and whispered, "We should wait," and then the cat jumped off the top of the wall, and with its tail held up high and its legs looking all stiff it stepped slowly over the grass, it stopped twice and hunched up its back, and it sniffed about for something, and one time it even looked our way, but either it didn't notice us or it wasn't interested because then it squatted on its two hind feet and started doing its business, I wanted to take aim again, but I could feel my grandfather gripping my shoulder even harder, and then the cat finished doing its thing and started scratching at the grass with its paws, and then my grandfather whispered, "All right, take aim," and I began raising the pistol nice and easy, holding it with both hands just like my grandfather taught me, but the pistol was a lot heavier on account of the magazine, and when I finally aimed it at the cat I could feel my hands trembling a little, but by then my finger was on the trigger and my grandfather said, "Now," and then I pulled the trigger, the cat looked at me as soon as my finger moved, its eyes were all yellow and I imagined what it was seeing, me standing there by the tree in my knit vest and trousers, and then suddenly the shot rang out and the cat jumped up, all four of its paws left the ground, but it wasn't a jump after all, it was just the force of the shot that lifted it off the ground, I'd hit only its side, not its head, even though I'd been aiming for the head, and then I lowered the gun, but the shot was still echoing around the stone walls of the yard, and then Grandfather put a hand on my shoulder and said, "Nice shot, let's go take a look," and we were only three steps away when I saw the cat stir, at first only its tail began to curl up and snake around in the grass, and then the cat began meowing, and I saw its side was bloody and the grass around it was also drenched in blood, and then I looked at my grandfather and he said, "Quick, shoot it in the head already, don't let it suffer," and sure enough, the poor cat was somehow keeping its head up, and as if it wanted to bite the air, it whimpered really loud, plus its tail was still twitching in the grass, and so I raised the pistol one more time, with both hands, just the way you're supposed to, and I aimed right between the eyes and pulled the trigger, and again the pistol almost jumped right out of my hands, the sound of the shot crackled back and forth between the walls of the yard like with the first one, and finally there was silence, the cat wasn't moving anymore, and I saw that nothing was left of its head, and the grass all around it was soaked with blood, and then my hand began shaking so hard that the pistol almost fell right out of it, and my grandfather put an arm around my shoulder and took the gun out of my hand and said, "Such is life, we all die, don't be down about it now, you have practically a whole life ahead of you yet," and then he ripped a medal off his coat and pressed it into my hand and told me it was his favorite award, the Gold Veteran Star, but he was giving it to me because I'd really earned it, and as he spoke I could smell the wine all over his breath.

Once we got back to the kitchen my grandfather told me to wait, and after putting the pistol on the table he pulled open the sideboard drawer and took out a safety pin, and then he stepped in front of me, took the medal out of my hand, and he leaned down and pinned the medal on my vest, on the left side above my heart, but he couldn't manage to click the pin shut, it even pricked me a little, not that it hurt, and as he went on pressing the pin I kept looking at the top of his head, he was going bald, never had I noticed that before, but I now saw clearly that a saucer-sized patch of his hair was already gone, and after finally clicking shut the safety pin he adjusted the medal on my chest and gave me a peck on each cheek and he said, "Happy name day, live long," and I said, "You too, Grandpa," and then all of a sudden my arm felt really tired from all the aiming, and I thought of the cat, and I felt like sitting down.

My grandfather looked at his watch and said the time had come for me to go, he couldn't take me home just now, he said, he was waiting for someone, but I was a big boy, I'd find my way home alone no problem, and I said, "Of course, I go to the cinema on my own too," and my grandfather picked up the decanter and poured himself the rest of the wine and said, "Take care of yourself, goodbye," and suddenly I got really thirsty, and although I didn't want to ask for water, I turned my head while opening the kitchen door to leave and asked my grandfather one more question all the same, I asked him if my grandmother was really going to die, and without even looking at me my grandfather just said I should know well enough not to believe everything I'm told and that there was nothing the least bit wrong with my grandmother except that she was old, true, that was enough of a problem as it was, and then he waved his hand at me to get going already, and while shutting the door I noticed him sniff at the empty glass of wine.

It wasn't even getting dark yet when I went out the front gate, no, I knew that if I hurried I'd get home in a half-hour, so I stopped for a second and took the Gold Veteran Star off my vest and gave it a look, it had a crooked sword and a machine gun set across each other over the star, plus my grandfather's name and a year engraved on the back, and then I took out my handkerchief and wrapped it around the medal and also the safety pin, and I stuck the little bundle in my pants pocket and I thought, no way would Mother ever find it there.

9

War

■■■■■

PUJU AND I were lying on our bellies in the wheat field,
and it was hot, really hot, sweat was pouring from us
in buckets, it flowed right down my face and washed
off the black war paint we'd made from burnt corks, the sweat
flowed salty and bitter into our mouths but we couldn't spit
it out and we couldn't rinse our mouths, no, we didn't have
any water with us, neither one of us thought of bringing a
canteen along with our weapons. The sun was beating down
something fierce, it had been a lot warmer ever since that
atomic power plant accident we weren't allowed to talk about,
even the wheat matured much sooner, it was still the middle
of June when the grains wafted out of the ears, but no matter
how long we chewed on those grains we couldn't make wheat
gum out of them anymore, they didn't stick together at all,
they were as dry as sawdust, but anyway, Puju said harvesting
would soon begin, he knew that because his dad was a trac-
tor man at the collective farm, and he said the collective had

already put in a request for the necessary gasoline, and they'd be getting it too, so the harvest would begin any time now.

By now we figured we were definitely close to the little wooden watchtower that hunters used, which had a ladder leading up to a roofed blind with a waist-high wall all around it and which was where the Frunza brothers had set up their headquarters. We were exhausted from all the crawling, the wheat stalks and leaves had chafed our arms and palms, Puju was wearing leather gloves but not even that helped much, the gloves only made him sweat more, which left thin streaks of gray on the war paint on his face, and I knew I looked exactly the same, not scary at all, just ridiculous. Anyway, we crawled slowly ahead through the wheat, and Puju whispered for me to take a peek up over the stalks to see how far we actually were from the watchtower, and I said no, he should look himself because it was his turn, I'd looked up three times already, so Puju then really did stick his head up out of the wheat, he didn't stand up all the way, he just rose up on one knee, that's how he did it, and afterward he got back down on his belly right away, and even under his war paint I could tell he was white as a ghost, and I asked him what it was, what did he see, and then Puju made the sign of the cross and said that those Frunza brothers weren't kidding around, they really had gone and killed someone, he saw clear as day that a spear was stuck in the ground in front of the watchtower, and jammed on top of it was a child's head covered with blood, and then I told him I didn't believe it and that he'd better not go lying to me, but Puju said that if I didn't believe him, I should take a look for myself, so I got up on one knee and peered out, I saw pigeons flying in circles above the watchtower, and there really was a spear stuck in the ground, but just what was fixed on its point, that part I couldn't make out because a thick plastic fertilizer bag was pulled upside-down over it, and the bag was tied up so not even the shape of whatever was inside was easy to make out, but the moment I brought my head back down into the wheat I remembered seeing something else too, that down there at the bottom where the bag was tied something was flowing thick and red all the way down the spear, and by the time I got back down on my belly next to Puju I felt sick to my stomach, I looked at the wheat stalks we'd flattened while crawling and I wanted to tell Puju we hadn't seen it right, no way was that blood on the spear, but when I opened my mouth to speak I could feel my hand hurting, and that's when I noticed that I'd dug my fist into the earth and was squeezing the soil really hard, and when I yanked out my hand, a big clump of wheat roots came up along with the soil, and then I looked at Puju and saw that the edge of his mouth was quivering with fear, and I let the soil-filled roots fall from between my fingers and I thought to myself that I shouldn't have come to this battle after all, no way would I be able to climb up the watchtower to get Prodán's leather ball.

The whole thing started when it turned out that the new sewage line would pass right through the middle of our soccer field, which meant we had to go over to the soccer field used by the kids one street over whenever we wanted to play. At first their field was supposed to be dug up too, but then one day the workers left and never did come back, even though their tool shed was still there by the ditch. Anyway, the other-streeters, which is what we called those kids, let us play there until the day the Frunza brothers, orphans who moved there to their grandfather's place, beat up Zsolt, who until then was the strongest other-streeter, yes, the two Frunzas took over their gang and said we couldn't go there anymore, meaning we could go only if we paid, and when Big Prodán laughed in their faces and said, "What do you think this is, a soccer field is public property, you can't just take it over," then Romulus Frunza said, "Folks don't go talking back to my big brother," and then Remus Frunza flicked out a switchblade and stabbed Big Prodán in the shoulder so fast that Prodán didn't even have time to pull out his own pocketknife, and right when he put a hand to his shoulder, the leather ball his cousin sent him from Yugoslavia fell out of his hands, and Romulus Frunza leaned down and picked up the ball and said that from now on the ball was theirs and that Prodán could thank his lucky stars they hadn't stabbed him in the belly, because that shoulder wound was nothing, it would heal in a week, his big brother hadn't stabbed deep, no, he'd given Prodán just a little taste of his knife. Romulus Frunza then started bouncing the ball on the ground and said, "Well, that's that," and if we didn't like it, we could go to war with them, they'd send us a declaration of war with all the details written down precisely, and just so we'd know, the battle would be up on top of the hill in the wheat field behind the apartment blocks, and it would be life or death, our side would have to attack, and if we got as far as the watchtower at the edge of the woods and then escaped with this here leather ball, then we'd have to get the ball only as far back as the Big Tree, and if we did that, we'd win, and then we'd not only get back the ball but we could also use their soccer field for free whenever we wanted. But they knew that nothing would come of this, we were such scaredy-cats that even the declaration of war would make us shit our pants, no way would we be brave enough to stand up to them, said Romulus Frunza, no fucking way, that much was obvious on account of how Prodán just stood there without a word, letting them take his blood.

At first Big Prodán didn't say a thing back, he just took his palm off his shoulder, his whole hand was drenched with blood, I saw, and not only his palms but every one of his fingers, and then he looked at his palm as if he was seeing it for the first time, and suddenly he said, "Blood can be washed off only with blood," and he took one step forward and he gave Romulus Frunza a helluva slap on the face, so hard that Romulus staggered back against his big brother, and Prodán's bloody palm print stayed right there on Romulus's face, and then we all turned around at once and started running back toward our street, we were scared they'd come after us, but the other-streeters just threw some big rocks our way and luckily they didn't hit anyone, and meanwhile we could hear Romulus Frunza yelling really loud about how we were good-for-nothing sons of bitches and half-blooded sissies.

The next morning the declaration of war did arrive, a bloody beheaded pigeon was stuck in the mailbox at Prodán's place along with a sheet of notebook paper that had a declaration of war supposedly written in pigeon's blood. Prodán asked Jancsi to read it out loud, it said the battle would be on Sunday in the wheat field, and they'd have us know that what everyone was whispering about them really was true, the two of them, Romulus Frunza and Remus Frunza, had both fought in the civil war, so it would be best if we all got ready for certain annihilation because anyone they got their hands on wouldn't be getting any mercy and they wouldn't even have a goddamn rock around here to crawl under and call home, and besides, we were fucking losers, every last one of us, and we were motherfucking assholes too. When Prodán heard this, his face got all red with rage and he tore the declaration of war right out of Jancsi's hand, crumpled it up, threw it on the ground, and stepped on it good, and he said that those Frunza brothers wrote stuff like that because they didn't even have a mother, their father raised them until the old man hanged himself out of despair on account of having sons like that, everyone knew that's why they ended up here with their grandfather, because they didn't have anyone else in the whole world, and besides, their saying that they fought in the civil war was a bunch of crap, the civil war was seven years ago, they couldn't have been past eight years old back then, and not to worry, come Sunday we'd show them, and until then every one of us should go make blowgun pellets, bend lots of nails, collect stones for slingshots, and put feathers on arrows, so we'd be properly armed, and we shouldn't be scared of the Frunzas, no, we'd show them they can't go fucking with us.

No one said a thing, we all just stood there tongue-tied, looking at Prodán and the bloody pigeon and the crumpled declaration of war by his feet, and then Prodán made a fist and punched an arm toward the sky three times and cried out, "Hurrah!" The nails rattled on his wide leather wrist-guard, and all of a sudden everyone else started shouting "Hurrah!" and I joined in too, but when I looked at Prodán's face I could tell that flailing his arms like that made his shoulder hurt.

Starting then, the whole week we went all out getting ready for the battle, everyone knew it would be a hard struggle because even if the Frunza brothers hadn't fought in the civil war, they were really dangerous all the same, before ending up here they lived in a village somewhere up in the snow-capped mountains to the west, and supposedly they lived there like Indians, hunting and snaring birds until their father died, and no one knew exactly how old the two Frunza brothers were, both of them were in sixth grade but Remus looked even bigger than the ninth graders, while his kid brother, Romulus, was so short he would have counted as little even among the fourth graders, but both of them were really strong and equally good at fighting, plus they knew a thing or two about weapons, their slingshots weren't made of cut-up bicycle tubes but of real upholstery rubber, for example, and we heard that the other-streeters had made themselves all sorts of secret weapons, which is why all of us made sharp pellets for our blowguns, the sort with a pin on the end. I made myself armor out of cardboard and tinfoil to protect my back, I even tested it to see if it would fit under my T-shirt and I asked Puju to shoot me in the back so we could see if it worked, but he didn't want to, he told me to remember the time we wanted to test if I could catch an arrow like the Indians do in the movies, but I told him I was younger then, a nine-year-old little runt, so it was no wonder my reflexes weren't as good, and luckily the nail on the end of the arrow wasn't too sharp so it went less than an inch into my arm, all it did was pierce my skin, the bone in my forearm stopped it no problem, sure, the tetanus shots afterward hurt a lot, but this wasn't going to be like that because we were bigger now, almost twelve years old, and besides, this armor didn't depend at all on reflexes. But not even after I said all that did Puju want to, no, I had to give him four caramels before he finally agreed to shoot me in the back three times, and of course the armor really did do the trick, it stopped the pellets just like it was supposed to, the shots felt only like mosquito bites, and I decided to make armor for the front of me too, I'd already cut out the pieces of cardboard, the only things left to do were the sewing and the gluing, around half a day's work in all, but then I just ran out of glue, so I couldn't make that extra armor after all.

While working on my armor I thought a lot about that declaration of war, about the beheaded pigeon, and about how this wasn't going to be just another game but a real war, a fight to the finish, and when I thought of that bloody pigeon, my heart always sank a little, but I figured I wasn't the only one thinking like that, no, even Puju said maybe he wouldn't be at the battle after all since his dad didn't want to let him go, and when I then asked him why he'd told his dad there was going to be a battle, because if the workers at the collective farm, the collectivists, found out that we were all set to trample the wheat, not only wouldn't they let us but they'd give us a good beating to boot, but then Puju got really mad and said he hadn't told his dad a thing, and anyway, it was easy for me, my dad was off at the Danube Canal so I could do what I wanted, no one was going to kick my ass, and then I told him that he's a scaredy-cat, a crybaby, and that he'd better not mention my dad because I'd kick him good, and I also said that if he didn't come to the battle, he'd lose his Young Pioneer's honor forever, but then Sunday morning came and even I was thinking that maybe it would be better to stay at home, sure. After breakfast I got out my blowgun all the same, and I put on my two ammo belts in a crisscross over my shoulders, I'd filled the belts with rolled-up, dried-up blowgun pellets, and then I told Mother I was going down to play, but I thought how good it would be if she said I wasn't going anywhere, that she needed me at home, except Mother didn't say a thing, she didn't even stand up out of the great big armchair by the window where she was sitting around a lot nowadays, she gave only a nod that meant "All right," and so I headed off after all, I went up the hill to the Big Tree because I knew the others would soon be there too, so we could talk over our tactics and our strategy.

By the time I got there, they already had a fire going in the old combat helmet, almost everyone from our apartment block was there and everyone had their weapons with them, Jancsi and some others had lathed themselves real throwing stars and tomahawks, I had my tin knife with me, sure, I knew it wouldn't be worth much in hand-to-hand combat, but I brought it with me all the same, figuring that when you're lying low in the wheat field in a war, it feels good to have your hands on a knife. Anyway, when I got there to the Big Tree, Csabi was just throwing two handfuls of corks into the combat helmet, and that made the smoke even smellier, and just about everyone was there, everyone except for our commander, Big Prodán, who was the biggest of the our-streeters, before the Frunza brothers came along no one had ever managed to beat him up, and he was the one who got us the combat helmet, saying he dug it up out of a civil war soldier's grave, not that anyone believed it, no, Janika once told me that it wasn't a combat helmet at all, only a stew pot, but anyway, by the time the corks were all burnt up Prodán got there too, he had a quadruple-barreled blowgun with him, it was really something, every single one of its PVC pipes had electric tape all around it, he even made it a stock and a grip, it looked completely like a genuine machine gun, plus he found a strap for it so he could wear it around his neck, and he had a mace tied to his waist, he'd made that using a dumbbell, and the combat wrist-guards on both his arms reached almost all the way to his elbows and were studded with square brass clamp nails, the sort used on ships, and along with the mace a knife was also tied to his waist, one with a long black handle, never had I seen a knife like that before, it looked really warlike, and when Prodán reached the combat helmet, he took the canteen off his belt right away and poured water over the smoldering corks, which caused a lot of hissing and smoke, and the black liquidy soot that remained in the helmet was like pitch, that was our color of battle, that black stuff. Prodán was the first to paint himself with it, he spread it all over his face and his forehead until you could hardly recognize him, and then he let out a war cry, and one after another we each painted our face, and I did too, but I was careful not to touch my mouth with the stuff because I knew cork ash had a really bitter taste, of course right then it didn't occur to me that the sweat would make it run into my mouth, anyway, the others also painted their faces nice and black, and once everyone was done Prodán stood in front of us and said that this would be a big battle and a difficult one, and that we should get it through our skulls that the enemy's main headquarters were at the other end of the field, at the watchtower by the edge of the woods, we had to get all the way there and get the leather ball, but that wouldn't be enough for victory, no, to do that we had to bring the ball back here to the Big Tree, and Prodán said the best tactic would be to begin by scattering apart as much as possible, as quietly as we could, so when he gave the signal, all of us would attack the other-streeters from as many directions as possible, and then he told me and Puju to go up close to him, we'd be the special reconnaissance force, we'd be getting our very own assignment, and when we then went up to him, he said that when he gave the signal and everyone on our side all started shouting hurrah, we shouldn't attack along with the others but instead stay down in the wheat and try to get as close as possible to the watchtower, we shouldn't even go shooting anyone in the back if we didn't need to, and when we heard Prodán shout the war cry three times, that's when we should break cover and try to get our hands on the ball, and when we had it, then we'd run like friggin' hell back toward the Big Tree and he'd come after us, and at the end he'd be the one running with the ball, and they wouldn't catch up to him, and that's how we'd achieve victory, and then he looked at us and asked if we understood, and Puju and I said we did, but I also said I didn't like the idea of lying low that way, why didn't he send his kid brother instead, and couldn't we be in on the hand-to-hand combat too, and Prodán said, sure we could if we wanted to lose and to defy our commander's will, and we should get it through our skulls that we were too weak for real fighting, and besides, how dare we even bring his kid brother into this, and how dare we shoot off our traps about hand-to-hand combat when both of us were chickenshits, he knew we'd shit our pants right away, that's how scared of the Frunza brothers we were, and we'd better watch out because one more word out of us and he'd take away our weapons and hound us right into the wheat field, and while saying that he shook his head like he was all teed off and he pulled out that big knife I'd never seen on him before, and he held it there in front of us and told us to take a good look, this was a real bayonet he'd dug out of the same grave as that combat helmet there, and that long groove by the tip of the blade, why, that was the blood gutter, and if we didn't obey his commands word for word, then we shouldn't be surprised to see our own blood flowing down that gutter because he swore he'd stab us in the belly himself, and after doing that maybe he'd scalp us too, and then Puju and I didn't say a thing, and Prodán asked if we understood, and we said we did, and meanwhile I wished his shoulder wound would tear right open so he'd get blood poisoning, and then Prodán put away the bayonet and turned to the others and said, "Prepare for battle," and then we all stood in a circle and stretched out our right arms and put our hands on top of one another's, all at once we let out our war cry, which went, "Justice and brotherhood, the revolution will triumph!" and then we all started running toward the wheat field.

When we got there, we all dropped right down on our bellies and started crawling through the wheat, we had to be careful to press down the stalks in as narrow a row as possible because whatever we scrunched down stayed like that, and if we flattened too wide a path, it could be seen from far away, which might easily mean a mud bomb on our necks, and since getting hit by a piece of clay the size of two fists can hurt pretty bad, we crawled carefully, but the wheat stalks and leaves chafed our legs and our arms a lot all the same, the lucky thing was that Puju and I didn't have to really hurry because Prodán said the important thing was to crawl as slowly as possible, in the meantime the others scattered good, and after a while we couldn't even hear them anymore.

As we slithered ahead, all of a sudden I felt something sticky, and although I pulled my hand back right away, it was too late, my palm was full of this gooey black stuff, pitch or maybe tar, and when I looked I saw that it was poured in a long line between the stalks of wheat. I called over to Puju to stop and be careful not to stick his hand in it too, and then with my other hand I tore a big clump of wheat out of the ground and used the rough stalks to rub the stickiness off my palm, it wasn't easy, I had to rub my hands against the earth, and when we then went on crawling I was extra careful where I put my hand.

We must have crept another hundred feet at least when Puju suddenly grabbed my elbow and whispered to me really quietly that we should take a little rest, and then right away he put a finger to his lips to signal that I should keep my mouth shut, as if I didn't know well enough that we weren't supposed to talk, and then for a while we didn't move, and I looked slowly around for any signs of movement in the wheat field, but the rows were pretty thick, we couldn't really see anything at all, and so we just waited a little, we knew the assault had to begin soon, but since it was pretty uncomfortable leaning with our elbows on the ground, I waved a hand to Puju to signal that we sit up against each other's back because I figured waiting that way would be easier. So that's what we did, I even stuck my head up out of the wheat for a split second but didn't see a thing except swaying stalks in all directions, and then I tucked my head right back under and waited, it was really, really quiet, you couldn't tell at all that the field was full of kids, the sun was even shining strong by now, you could tell it would get warm. I grabbed my blowgun and stuck in a pellet, and for a moment I imagined that it wasn't a PVC pipe in my hands but a genuine wood blowgun and that the pellet didn't only have a pin stuck into it but also frog poison, because we were in a real war, a fight to the finish, get a scalp or get scalped, so I grabbed my knife and imagined that it was an authentic scalping knife, yes, I'd cut around my enemy's skull just under the hairline with the razor-sharp blade, and then with a sudden movement I'd tear the scalp off the skull, but my tin knife didn't have a real blade, no, I felt bad about not having my pocketknife anymore, the one with the fish-shaped handle, not as if that was very sharp either, but at least it had a proper steel blade. Suddenly I felt Puju nudge me in the side with his elbow, I thought he wanted to tell me something, but all he'd done was push himself away from my back and spring forward onto his belly in the wheat, I thought he'd been hit by some secret sort of ammunition, but he turned right around and held out his cupped hands and whispered for me to get a load of what he caught, and so I leaned really close to his hands, and then he opened his palms just enough for me to see in between the black leather fingers of his gloves, and I saw that this time he wasn't out to pull one over on me, like at other times, because there really was something in his hands, a little mouse, it wasn't moving, it was like a gray ball of fur, its tail was hanging out from between Puju's fingers, and Puju whispered that we should dissect it, but I said we should skin it instead, its fur would be just like a tiny scalp, but not even Puju had a decent knife, and we didn't even have a razor blade, at most we could have stabbed it with a blowgun pellet, Puju took one out and was just handing it to me so I'd do the job, but then all of a sudden we heard Prodán yelling really loud, and even though he was too far away for us to make out his words, we knew he was saying that the revolution would triumph, and then everyone on our side started shouting hurrah really loud from all directions and sprang up out of the wheat and started running toward the opposite edge of the field to where the woods began, and as Puju and I got up on our knees to see which way we had to go, the mouse slipped out of Puju's hand and disappeared into the wheat.

By now the other-streeters were also jumping up out of the wheat, it was easy to tell who they were, all their faces were smeared with red war paint, they were standing in two rows, the ones with slingshots were up front and the archers were about thirty feet behind them, I didn't see blowguns with any of them, they all began shooting at our side as Puju and I got back down on our bellies in the wheat and went on crawling ahead, meanwhile we could hear the rocks from their slingshots swishing all around us, and as we kept going forward I even found two arrows, they were stuck right in the ground, I pulled one of them out, it was a proper arrow with feathers and a nail hammered into its tip, with the head of the nail sticking out so it was blunt, but no doubt it would have had a pretty good punch to it if it hit you in the head, and sure enough I heard everyone yelling all over the place, you could hear a lot of the guys wrestling in the wheat, and although back when we used to play soldiers anyone who got pinned by both shoulders had to stay just like that until the battle was over, since they counted as dead, now it seemed like they were fighting harder because everyone was yelling and swearing really loud, so by the time Puju and I started getting close to the thick of things we were completely on our bellies, and I got all tired out from creeping forward over the ground, my knees and my elbows were hurting and the cardboard armor was pressing against my back, I wished I hadn't even made that getup in the first place, but I didn't want to take it off either, because I knew that Puju would laugh in my face about that.

There was nothing else we could do, so we just crawled on ahead, the shooting had stopped and all we could hear was the fighting and everyone shouting all sorts of things, someone really close to us cried out that he surrendered and that you're not allowed to mistreat the wounded, and then he started shouting even louder, "That's cheating, you can't do that." I didn't recognize his voice, I looked at Puju but he just shook his head, and we went back to creeping forward, we didn't even know how far we might be from the watchtower, but we didn't dare get up to look, I was covered with sweat and was really sorry I hadn't brought along my canteen, Puju didn't have water with him either, and from the way he was panting I could tell he was thirsty too, but at least the field had gotten a bit higher, yes, I could tell we were going uphill, which meant the watchtower couldn't be too far, it was there at the edge of the woods where the wheat field ended, and then all of a sudden we heard this really loud scream from somewhere in the wheat behind us, as if someone was being killed, it really gave me the creeps, Puju looked at me and said, "Let's turn back because those other-streeters really did go and kill someone," but I told him I didn't think so, and to wait, that I'd look up to see how far away we were, and I stuck my head up out of the wheat for a split second, and sure enough, there was the watchtower right in front of us, not too far away even, no more than 150 yards, and I got back down on my belly in the wheat and whispered to Puju not to worry because we were crawling in the right direction, and it wasn't worth turning back from here, and he should remember what Prodán said, and Puju said he didn't give a flying shit about Prodán, but we kept inching forward in each other's tracks all the same, except by then we were so exhausted that we weren't crawling at all the way you're supposed to, like we learned during Homeland Defense activities, no, it was more like we were just going on all fours, and again I was up ahead, I was leading the way, but by then it was really warm, and I could feel myself sweating, feel the water flowing from me all over, but we didn't stop, we just kept creeping straight ahead, and in the meantime we heard the fighting still going on behind us, now and then an arrow whizzed above us, and we got thirstier and thirstier, and we sweated more and more, and when I figured we had to be really close to the edge of the wheat field I got down on my belly, and Puju crawled up to me and also got down on his belly, and when we then looked up out of the wheat we saw the watchtower and the child's head staked on the spear in front of it, and we got even thirstier than before, and Puju said he didn't care, he was turning back to get his canteen because his mouth was all bitter on account of that stupid war paint, but of course he didn't move, the edge of his mouth was quivering, I saw, and I too was so scared that I didn't even want to look up out of the wheat anymore.

For a while we just stayed there motionless on our bellies on the ground, and when I finally leaned up on my elbows I could feel the sweat and the war paint flowing all the way down my neck and into my underarms, and then it occurred to me that if I had to lie here for long in the sun, then in the end I'd look completely like a zebra, and that made me have to laugh so bad I could hardly hold it back, and when Puju grabbed my elbow and asked me in a whisper what was up, why did I have to go and laugh, I just shook my head and waved a hand, and then I crawled up ahead and again looked up out of the wheat, the pigeons were still circling around the watchtower and the wheat around it was stomped down in a semicircle at least a hundred feet wide, but I didn't see a sentry anywhere at all, as if that spear alone was enough of a sentry, and then I looked back toward where the fighting was, but all I could see was the wheat swaying this way and that as the guys were wrestling inside it, and then all of a sudden someone sprang up out of the wheat right up to his waist and started running toward the watchtower, at first I thought it was Little Prodán, but then I recognized him, it was Jancsi, but he took just two steps before someone caught up with him and must have dragged him back down, because Jancsi cried out and fell back down into the wheat with his arms stretched out wide, and then I got back down on my belly and told Puju that no one was guarding the watchtower, maybe it would be best to just go ahead and climb up there for the ball, yes, it would be best if he started off for it right away, but he shot right back that this whole war was a bunch of crap, it was cheating because we weren't allowed to climb up the watchtower at all, it was the property of the state hunting association and you needed a hunting permit to go up there, his father said the collectivists kept an eye on it with binoculars on account of poachers, and the whole time he was talking I saw that he was still white as a ghost, and the sun was beating down so hard that I could hardly talk, that's how dry my throat was, and then I spit that bitter black saliva out of my mouth and I thought of Prodán's bayonet and I told Puju I'd had enough, if he was really that much of a chickenshit, why then, I'd climb up there just because, and Puju asked what I was fussing about when I knew full well I couldn't start off until Prodán gave the signal, but then the taste of that disgusting cork ash shot right back through my mouth and I didn't have even enough saliva to spit it out, and I said Prodán could go to hell along with that bayonet of his, and I got up on my knees and threw my blowgun and ammo belts on the ground and I stood up, and I started off toward the watchtower, running as fast as I could.

As soon as I stood, I told myself I wasn't about to look at that spear close up, but then when I got next to it I couldn't resist, I just had to take a look, and that's when I saw that the handle really was soaked in blood, and blood was even pooled fist-deep in the upside-down, tied-up plastic fertilizer bag, but you couldn't tell what was really stuck on the tip of the spear, I turned away my head because I was scared that if I saw it clearly, I wouldn't be brave enough to climb up into the watchtower, but then I thought it had to be just a pigeon or a rabbit up there on the tip of the spear, something the other-streeters had poached, and meanwhile I reached the foot of the watchtower and started climbing the ladder.

It wasn't even a real ladder, just a pole with strips of wood nailed to it crosswise as rungs, and it swayed a lot and the rungs creaked as I began climbing, I had to hang on tight to keep from falling, and then I looked up between the gaps in the floorboards of the blind and saw someone there, it was Remus Frunza, which really surprised me, because until now I thought he was down in the wheat field fighting along with the others, but no, he was right up above me in the watchtower, crouched in one of the corners of the blind on a bunch of coiled rope and smoking a cigarette, his face was all red from the war paint, and all of a sudden he looked right at me, and I was so scared that I couldn't say a thing, even my hands just stayed there on the top rung, and Remus Frunza didn't say a thing either, he just kept staring at me, and when he blinked I saw that his eyelids were also smeared with red war paint, plus his eyebrows were highlighted in black and there were black stripes on his forehead and his face, he looked so scary that my heart shot right up into my throat and I thought I should climb back down, except that I still couldn't move, no, my hands just squeezed that top rung tight, but suddenly someone told me not to stop, to go on climbing, and that someone was Romulus Frunza, Remus's kid brother, who was sitting up there on the tiny bench even though I hadn't noticed him at first, and then Remus Frunza finally gave a nod, but he still didn't say a thing, no, he just took another drag on his cigarette and blew the smoke out through his nostrils.

Somehow I then moved, edging my way slowly to the top rung, my legs felt like dead weights, they did, but all at once Remus Frunza reached out and grabbed one of my wrists and yanked me up into the watchtower without a word, and meanwhile I heard Romulus Frunza ask me my name, and I told him, and he nodded and asked, "So are you that orphan kid?" and I said, "No, my dad's just at the Danube Canal," and Romulus gave a wave of his hand and said, "Oh, that's all the same," and then he said, "Congratulations," he wouldn't have thought one of us would get so far, and then he asked me what I was doing there, and Remus Frunza also looked at me as if waiting to hear what I'd answer, and he crushed his cigarette in the upside-down top of a tin milk can, and I didn't dare say a thing, and all of a sudden Remus Frunza took out his switchblade, but instead of flicking it open he just turned it around in his hand, and Romulus said he was asking me one last time what I was doing there when I knew that the watchtower was off limits to everyone, and of course I didn't dare turn the question right back on them and ask them what they were doing there, no, I just said, "I came for the ball, I'm here to take it away," and Romulus Frunza said, in a jeering tone of voice but without the slightest grin, "You don't say, I would never have thought," and then he said, "All right, as long as you're here, take a seat, but careful, everything in here is full of pigeon shit." And then I looked up and saw a bunch of beams nailed crosswise under the watchtower roof and a whole lot of pigeons sitting on them, at least forty, preening their feathers and stretching their necks, and of course there was nowhere at all for me to sit down, Romulus Frunza took up all of the tiny bench, and although there would have been a little room next to Remus Frunza on the rope, I didn't dare sit down there, even though by then he'd put away the switchblade, so I said, "Thanks, but I want only the ball, and if possible I'll be on my way already," but Romulus Frunza then said only that I wasn't going anywhere, and he asked if I saw a ball around here, and I said no, because I really didn't see it, and I bit my lips and added, "That's cheating, the ball is supposed to be here, that's not fair," but Romulus Frunza said I should get it through my head that war is never fair, because it's all about victory and not about being fair but that he recognized my courage in saying this to his face, and soon it would be clear if I really was brave or if my mouth was just too big for my own good because he was about to give me the chance to prove it, and when he said that, Remus picked up a piece of wooden board near the coiled rope and laid it on the floor, there was a brownish spot in the middle of the board that looked just like a person's palm spread open wide, and Romulus told me to kneel down and put my right hand on the board, and only after I put my hand down did I suddenly realize what was about to happen because I'd seen this one time in a movie about the partisans, and what I wanted most was to pull away my hand, but by then it was too late because Remus had again pulled out his switchblade, and in the same motion with which he flicked open the blade he'd already jabbed it into the wood between my index finger and thumb, and as the knife kept quivering I felt the face of the blade touch the skin of my index finger again and again, and meanwhile Romulus said his big brother's hands were pretty steady and that I'd better not try to take my hand away from the board because then who could say if the knife might slip out of place, and Remus didn't say a thing, he just grabbed the switchblade handle and pulled the knife out of the wood and started jabbing it nice and easy between my fingers, the blade pierced the wood with a thud every time, and then Remus plucked it out of the wood and the board gave a creak, so I kept hearing a thud and a creak, a thud and a creak, and I looked down at my hand, my fingers looked really thin all spread out like that, but then I thought that they weren't thin enough, because sooner or later Remus would stab one of them for sure, and I felt goose bumps form on my arm all the way up to my shoulder, and I didn't want to look at my hand, I didn't want to see the knife making its way between my fingers, instead I tried raising my head nice and slow so I wouldn't have to look that way, and right when I did so I saw that Romulus Frunza was staring at me and smiling and nodding too, and then he said, "All right, all right so far," and I heard the thuds and the creaks pick up pace a little, but I still didn't look down at my hand, no, I just kept looking at Romulus instead, and then Romulus asked me if I was sure I wanted to take away that ball, and I wanted to say, "No, no way, I don't want a thing, to hell with Prodán's ball, just let me take my hand away from there," and I felt the board shaking under my palm from the jabs, but then I didn't say a thing, all I did was give a nod even though I knew I should be shaking my head instead, and then Romulus said all right, but I should get it through my skull that this pigheadedness of mine would spell trouble not just for me but for all the other guys on my street, but if I could stand it until he told his big brother to stop, then he'd tell me where the ball was, and if I couldn't take it anymore, there wouldn't be any trouble then either, all I had to do was say, "Enough, I give up," and the knife in his big brother's hand would stop that instant and I'd be free to go, but then I thought of the spear stuck in the ground, and of the blood oozing slowly from that fertilizer bag, and I knew it was now all the same to me anyway, and so I spoke, I said this would be fair if Romulus put his palm down there next to mine, but Romulus didn't get angry on account of my saying that, he just said that here, he got to say what was fair and what wasn't, and I didn't say anything back, I didn't even look at Romulus but behind him instead, at the watchtower's wind-breaking wall, and that's when I noticed a bunch of pigeon feathers nailed beside each other on one of the boards, and I could feel Remus moving his hand even faster, and suddenly Romulus asked how long it had been since we'd gotten word about my dad, and my hand almost moved, that's how shocked I was to hear him ask that, and I wanted to tell Romulus it was none of his business, but then I spoke anyway, "A pretty long time," I said, and then Romulus said he'd have me know that no doubt I too was already an orphan, just like him and his big brother, and I said, "It's not true, I'm not an orphan," and I looked back down at my hand, by then Remus's hand was moving so fast I couldn't even tell which two fingers of mine the knife was jabbing between, the thuds and the creaks flowed together, and the board was shaking terribly by now under my palm, I could practically feel the ice-cold blade against every one of my fingers at once, as if they'd slipped a big, quivering iron glove over my hand, my whole body was covered with goose bumps by now, and I thought my hair must be standing up like that time they switched the electricity on me in physics class, so anyway, my left hand was clenched tight in a fist, and I knew that any time now my right hand would try clutching at the board, and I also knew what would happen then, the tip of the knife would go through one of my fingers like going through butter, which is also why I didn't want to move my hand, I knew I must not. I looked at Remus Frunza, his tongue was sticking out a little, I saw, he was squinting and he was staring hard at his own hand, but then he must have sensed that I was watching because now he looked right back at me and the knife started going even faster between my fingers, and I knew that this was it, that he couldn't do it any faster, that he'd call it quits any time now, and then Remus suddenly broke into a grin and shut both his eyes, his teeth were all painted black, and I saw his eyelids were red from the war paint, and a big black pupil of an eye was drawn with coal on each one, and when I saw that, I felt the sweat start flowing again, and I knew this was it, now that he was doing it blind he'd slip up for sure, he'd stab that knife into one of my fingers any second now, and I knew I wouldn't be able to take it anymore, that in no time I'd cry out and ask him to stop, so I clenched my teeth to keep from screaming because I knew that if I did cry out, he'd slice that knife right into the middle of my hand, it was the same in that movie about the partisans, that was the punishment for cowards, but the scream had already started up my throat, and then

while still clenching my teeth I began hissing and then letting out this long wordless scream, and my face cramped up
completely, so much so that I could feel its every single muscle throbbing with pain, and the whole time my hand was still
pressed against the board, and I still hadn't said, "Enough,"
true, it's not like I could have said anything anyway, on account of my screaming, and then Romulus Frunza gave me a
smirk, and suddenly he also opened up his hand and put his
palm right down there on the board next to mine, Remus
didn't even open his eyes, but he must have known what had
happened because by now he was passing the switchblade in
and out between his kid brother's fingers too, his hand was
so fast you couldn't even see it anymore, and the board was
vibrating so hard under my palm that it felt as if the whole
watchtower was swaying, I wasn't screaming anymore, just
hissing really loud, and then Romulus Frunza spoke. "All
right," he said, he didn't think I could take it so long, all I
needed to do now was admit the truth to myself, that I was an
orphan and I didn't have a father either, all I needed to say
was that I knew he died and that he'd never come home, and
then he'd tell me right away where the ball was, but I still
didn't say a thing, and then Romulus spoke again, he told me
to believe him that it would be best even for me if I said it out
loud, it would be a relief, I'd see, and when he shut his mouth,
in that instant I figured out where the ball was, the only thing
I didn't get was why it didn't come to me earlier, and I shouted,
"No, no way, both of you should go drop dead," and suddenly
I snatched away my hand, and in the same motion I kicked
the board toward Remus and lunged for the ladder and I saw
Remus open his eyes, but he was already jabbing down the
switchblade right where the middle of my hand would have
been, but because the board had slipped, it wasn't my hand
but Romulus's that was now there, but whether or not Remus
stabbed into that hand with the knife I didn't see, because by

then I was already climbing down the ladder, all I heard was one of them let out a cry so loud that the pigeons on the beams overhead all flew off at once, and meanwhile I was climbing down as fast as I could, and one of the rungs slipped out of my hand at the end and I fell on my rear end right there in front of the watchtower, but luckily I didn't land too hard, and I looked up and saw Remus Frunza leaning out of the watchtower up to his waist, and then Remus told me in a harsh, rasping voice to go ahead and run as hard as my lungs could take it because I could kiss my life goodbye, and that they'd catch up to me even if I got two hundred yards ahead of them, and then I felt the air biting at my hand, and I looked and saw blood flowing from it in a bunch of places, the switchblade had caused a bunch of tiny wounds on both sides of my fingers, which was why the ladder rung had slipped out of my hand, yes, my palm was slippery because of the blood, up to that moment I'd wanted to leave the ball right where it was, but then I thought I wouldn't after all, not if I could help it, and I stood up and ran over to the spear and yanked it out of the ground and tore the fertilizer bag off the tip, and I threw down the spear, and with the bag in my hand I started running back toward the Big Tree.

The blood flowed in a thick stream from the bag as I ran, which made the plastic so slick it almost slipped out of my hand, but from its weight I could tell it had to be the ball inside, and by then I also knew that the blood could only be pigeon blood. All at once I saw Puju spring up out of the wheat, and I shouted, "I have the ball here in my hands, so let's run," but Puju just stood there at the edge of the wheat field, staring at the watchtower, and when I got up to him I also turned around to look, Romulus was leaning out of the blind with a Young Pioneers bugle in his hand and Remus was climbing down the ladder lightning fast, even though he was hanging on with one hand only, because there was a lit torch in his right hand, and then the bugle blared, Romulus was playing some march, I didn't recognize it but I knew he had to be sounding the alarm, and now I saw the other-streeters leap up out of the wheat all over the place and start running toward the watchtower, and I was sure they wanted to catch me, to knock me off my feet and get back the ball, but I looked back again and saw Remus Frunza reach the edge of the field and stop and lower the torch to the ground. And suddenly I remembered all that pitch poured between the rows of wheat, and in no time I heard it crackling into flames and I knew what would happen and why they said I should run as hard as my lungs could take it, but by then the flames were right beside me as they raced along between the rows of wheat, at first the wheat itself didn't go up in flames, only the pitch was burning in a long winding band between the stalks, and then everyone began shouting at once, the our-streeters and the other-streeters too, everyone had already sprung up out of the wheat as the band of flame split in two and then branched off in all directions, and by then the wheat was on fire too, the stalks were burning with high yellow flames, they didn't give off too much smoke, but even so there was enough smoke so you couldn't see the apartment blocks or even the city, I could hear kids start coughing all over the place, and by then even the our-streeters were getting the hell out of there, not in as orderly a way as the other-streeters but all over the place, out toward the Big Tree or the watchtower, and in the meantime I was still running straight for the flames, clutching the fertilizer bag with all my might and shouting for Prodán to come already and take the fucking ball, even though I knew the battle was over, that I should turn around and run out of the field because by now the stalks and even the grains were roasting like fat, but I still couldn't bring myself to turn around, I just kept going right toward the flames, and by then my mouth and even my lungs were full of stinging black smoke, I could feel a coughing fit erupting in my throat, and then someone I didn't recognize ran past me shouting and beating at the air, but I went on running at the fire anyway. I knew I should stop and I also knew I wouldn't, that I'd run right through that sea of flames even though I knew I wouldn't get across, and then I saw someone flailing his arms in the smoke, and suddenly I thought of Puju and wondered where he could be and what happened to that mouse we wanted to scalp. And by now I was closer than ever to the flames, the wheat stalks were crackling exactly like machine-gun fire in the movies, and I knew I was about to fall down and the ball would go flying out of my hands straight into the middle of the blaze, the flames before me were still really high and yellow, and then all at once I heard Romulus Frunza calling out my name really loud, shouting that I was now about to die, and I looked behind my shoulder and saw Romulus sitting there on his big brother's shoulders as if he was on a horse, Remus was running straight toward me and screaming that I was done for, and Romulus was spinning a lasso above his head, I heard the swishing of the noose and then all at once I threw myself toward the flames, but as soon as I left the ground I felt the noose fall on my head and tighten around my neck, it yanked me so hard that I fell back and the fertilizer bag dropped from my hands and rolled, along with the ball, into the burning wheat. I brought my hands to my neck to grab the rope and I heard Remus screaming at the top of his lungs, "Hurrah!" and he started running back toward the watchtower, his kid brother was still there riding him, they were dragging me along behind them at the end of the rope, I turned to my side to try taking the noose off my neck or at least to stand up, but my hands hurt too much, and as they hauled me along my feet kept coming out from under me and the flames got even higher, by then the fire was crackling louder than ever, and suddenly a great big thunderous boom came from the direction of the collective farm. I remembered what Puju had said about the harvest and the gasoline, and I knew the fuel must have caught fire too, and again I saw someone moving in the flames, and I wanted to shout, "This way, run this way," and the booming was getting louder, it was like thunder only much more powerful, and as the Frunza brothers dragged me along behind them, my T-shirt slid up and the cardboard armor turned and came halfway out, and I reached a hand down to take it out, but that just made the rope tighter around my neck. I felt like I was about to faint, but right then I saw someone jump up out of the wheat to my left, it was Big Prodán, he'd tied his T-shirt over his mouth and nose, and with that machine-gun-shaped blowgun held out in front of him he ran straight for the Frunza brothers, the bayonet was fixed to the end of the longest PVC pipe, and I figured he'd use that to hit Remus on the back, but instead Prodán turned to his side and body-checked Remus really hard from behind, which made Remus fall flat on his face and sent Romulus flying off his big brother's back and tumbling into the wheat, and I reached for my neck and pulled off the rope, my right hand hurt so much it felt like the skin had come off completely. I got up on my knees and coughed, and I saw Prodán thrusting his bayonet toward Remus and then all at once I heard a loud hissing, everything was covered by thick black smoke much more bitter than even our war paint, I wanted to stand up and run back to the watchtower so I wouldn't have to breathe it in, and meanwhile the booming got louder, but by now I heard the fire crackling all around me, and I knew for sure that I wouldn't have the strength to get up, that I'd wait there on my knees for the flames to swallow me whole.

By now the noise was so loud that I thought maybe I was just imagining it, that my head was buzzing from all the smoke I'd swallowed, but suddenly I thought I heard Puju's voice, Puju shouting my name, and as I again tried standing up, the smoke lifted all at once and I saw these huge machines slowly approaching, combines with flatbed trailers hooked up behind them, the collective farm's fire truck was coming too, one of the collectivists was standing on its edge and hosing the wheat with water, and then came two pickup trucks with their loading platforms full of barrels, the collectivists were up there bucketing water from the barrels and splashing it onto the burning stalks, Puju's dad was driving one of the combines, as he passed by me I could hear him swearing like crazy, and suddenly I had another coughing fit and my eyes got all watery, and only now did I see that the trailers hooked up to the combines were full of kids, Puju was up on one of them and shouting my name, and when they got up to me I saw that Prodán's dad was also up there, and when he saw me he leaned out and yanked me right up onto the trailer, and I could hear him saying that he'd give me a war if that's what I wanted, and I was still busy coughing when he gave me two full slaps on the face and said that if I was his son, he'd beat my brains out, and that's when I noticed Little Prodán sitting next to a barrel, his face all swollen and red, and then Mr. Prodán asked if I knew where his Niku was, and I told him where I saw him last, but I didn't think Mr. Prodán understood what I was saying because I was still busy coughing, and I felt my mouth bleeding a little on the inside from the slaps, and by then we'd almost reached the edge of the wheat field, and Prodán's dad was shouting left and right for his son, calling out, "Niku, Nikusor," but we didn't see Prodán anywhere at all, by then the fire wasn't burning anywhere, at least a third of that big field was history, all you could see was scorched wheat and black puddles and stomped-down, petrified grains of wheat, in a couple of places the wheat was standing just like normal, and in some places the blackened stalks were still giving off smoke.

The combine stopped when we reached the watchtower,

and I heard Puju's dad say it was lucky the woods didn't catch fire, Puju handed me a tin cup full of water and told me to drink and to wash off my face, and I said, "Thanks," of course the water was bitter because of the soot, but I drank it anyway, and I thought to myself that it was good after all that Puju had told his dad we were having a war, and then I was just wiping my face with my T-shirt turned inside-out when I heard Prodán's father again start shouting really loud, and right away the others began shouting too, everyone was calling Prodán's name, I looked where they were pointing and saw Prodán climbing slowly up out of the wheat around fifty yards away from us, and then Prodán looked back and saw the combine and the trailer at its back, and he must have seen his dad too because he stood up and started running with a limp toward the woods, and his dad started yelling even louder, telling him to stop, because if he didn't, he'd beat his brains out, he'd skin him alive and turn his back into boot leather, he'd cut his fucking balls right out, and meanwhile Puju's dad started up the combine, and that's how we went after Prodán, it was obvious we'd catch up to him in no time, Prodán looked back while running and finally he stopped and turned toward us and just waited there with his arms hanging down, and you could tell he knew what was going to happen next, and sure enough, his dad then leaped off the trailer and took off after his son, and when he reached him it was like he didn't even stop, no, Mr. Prodán still seemed to be running at full tilt as he gave his son a helluva slap so hard that Prodán fell practically under the combine, but he stood back up right away and stepped back next to his dad, and that's when I noticed that he still had the bayonet with him, he was holding it in his right hand, and his dad told him to apologize, and he socked Prodán with all his might right in the pit of the stomach, and Prodán lurched forward and started heaving, black spit drooled from the edge of his mouth, and his dad again raised his hand, and Prodán stepped back and said, "I apologize," and you could tell he was about to faint, and that is when the bayonet dropped right out of his hand and stuck in the ground with its tip down by his feet, the blade was thick with blood, I saw, and Prodán's dad must have noticed too because he leaned down, pulled the bayonet out of the ground, wiped both sides on his shirtsleeve, and asked, "Where are those goddamn brats, those Frunzas?" Prodán pointed toward the woods and said they ran away, and after wiping the bayonet on his shirtsleeve some more, Prodán's dad looked back at his son and swore that if Prodán ever again laid his hands on those military keepsakes, he'd beat his son till he was bloody, he'd keep pounding away as long as Prodán was still moving. Prodán didn't say a thing back, he just nodded and looked out over his dad's shoulder and stared at the woods as his dad turned away and, I saw, broke into a grin.

10

Africa

■ ■ ■ ■ ■

B Y THEN almost a year had passed since they took Father away, and for more than four months we hadn't heard a thing about him at all, we didn't get any more letters or even those prewritten postcards from the camp letting us know that he was fine and proud of overachieving the benchmark every day, so we didn't know anything about him, and it did no good when I asked Mother why Father wasn't writing to us, she didn't even reply, but then on Saturday, when the mailbox turned up empty once again, her face turned all tense, and as we trudged up the stairwell she broke out in a sudden fit of coughing so violent that she had to grab the railing, and from the way her shoulders shook and how she leaned forward out of my view, I knew she wasn't really coughing but crying, that she was pretending to cough only because she didn't want me to notice the tears, because she didn't want to get me scared, and that is when I knew for sure what she was thinking, that Father had died down there by the Danube Canal, but I also knew that this wasn't true because if something had happened to Father I would have sensed it for sure, if at no other time, then in the morning on my way to school as I looked at the picture I'd taken out of his soldier's ID holder, because in looking at his image I always felt sure that Father was thinking of me by the Danube Canal, and also because when they took him away, he promised that one day he'd return and take me with him to the sea.

Even though I could tell that Mother was crying, I pretended not to notice, I even slapped her on the back a couple of times, as if I really believed that she was only coughing, and by the time we reached the fifth floor she wasn't sobbing anymore, no, she took out a handkerchief and wiped her face and said something had gone down her throat the wrong way but now she was okay, and I said, "All right, but be careful, because your eyes got really watery from all that coughing, plus your mascara smudged, so you should wipe your face," and she nodded and said, "Be a good boy now and go on into your room, do a bit of reading or look at your homework, go on now, don't you try weaseling out of it," not that I had the slightest intention of resisting, because there was a lead soldier in my pocket that I got from someone at school, and I wanted to see if it would really fit the armor I'd hammered out of the tin sheet I found in the garbage dump a week earlier, I really wanted them to be a good match, for I was the only one of the boys who had no genuine commander for the war game we played in the stairwell, Feri's commander had been cast from lead specially by his father, who even helped him paint it, and I had no one to help me. Mother didn't know a thing about this stairwell war game, when the wheat field behind our apartment block burned down on account of the real war game we had out there, she told me I couldn't play any violent games at all, which is why I went into my room without a word just like she said, and I even put my math notebook and my math textbook on my desk, so in case she opened the door she'd see that I was studying hard.

But the door stayed open a notch, just enough so I could hear Mother go into her room, come out again, and then open the door to the kitchen, the cupboard door now creaked just so, I figured she must have removed a glass, and sure enough, I heard Mother turn the faucet and let the water run so it would be nice and cold, she drank it down in no big hurry and finished by splashing what was left into the sink, and then she pulled a kitchen chair out from under the table and sat down, meanwhile I crouched carefully by the desk and, quiet as could be, I pulled out the bottom drawer and put it on the rug, because it was under that drawer where I kept things I didn't want Mother knowing about, the medal I got from Grandfather, my carbide-packed exploding tin can, my slingshot, my tomahawk, all my lead soldiers, my spent bullets that still really smelled of gunpowder, and last but not least, the armor, which I took out of the drawer in a hurry together with the rag it was wrapped in, and meanwhile not a sound came from the kitchen, which really made me wonder what Mother was up to, not that she ever came spying on me, but I didn't want her to discover this secret hiding place either, so I slid the drawer back in just as carefully as I'd pulled it out, and then I stood up, sat down by the desk, and put my color pencil and my ruler by the notebook to look like I was really doing my homework, and only then did I take the lead soldier out of my pocket and begin to unwrap the armor, but suddenly the kitchen chair gave a creak, which made me think that Mother must have stood up and would come in right away to see what I was up to, so I quickly slipped the lead soldier between my thighs, picked up the pencil, and began writing HOMEWORK at the top of the page in my notebook, and that's when I heard Mother burst out sobbing, I heard it for a moment only, she must have put a hand over her mouth because then everything went quiet again, but even through the silence it was like I could hear Mother crying, I gripped the pencil so tight my fingers hurt, and try as I did not to think about Mother, I saw her before me all the same, I saw her sitting there at the kitchen table leaning on an elbow and pressing both hands tight against her mouth as the tears streamed down her face, and I knew that shutting my eyes would do no good because I'd see her even then, and it wouldn't help going out there to the kitchen and telling her not to cry, that would only make her yell at me, and besides, at night she would cry again for sure, so the best thing would be if she didn't even realize I'd heard her, but I knew she wouldn't be able to stand it for long, she'd burst out sobbing again, and then she'd be angry with me for hearing her, even though I couldn't help it she'd bawl me out anyway, and so I figured I'd better put the lead soldiers back in the drawer or else I'd get into trouble for sure. But I couldn't help being really curious to know if the armor would fit this new soldier, and so I began peeling away the rag from around it, carefully, with my left hand only, and without even taking the soldier out from between my thighs, and with the pencil there in my right hand the whole time as if I was just doing my homework, I went on removing the oily rag, and then all of a sudden I heard Mother this time really burst out sobbing louder than ever before, which scared me so much that my hand jerked, pressing the pencil so hard against the paper that the tip broke, which is when I heard Mother shove the chair back, stand up, and start cursing. "Goddamn it," she said, "goddamn this whole goddamn life," and then there was this loud clatter, and I knew Mother had flung her glass to the floor, and then I did get really frightened because I knew it meant big trouble if Mother threw something on the floor, she had never broken anything even back before they took Father away, she had never so much as slammed a door, not even when she and Father had had their biggest fights, so anyway, all of a sudden Mother slammed the kitchen door so hard I could hear the ornamental plates rattle against the wall, and then she stepped into the hall and stopped by the little telephone stand, and I heard her take deep breaths before snatching up the receiver and starting to dial so fast that before the spring had a chance to pull back the dial, she was already wrenching the dial back the other way with her finger, which made the whole telephone click over and over again, and then everything got all quiet, Mother didn't let out even a sniffle, and I could almost hear the telephone ringing a bunch of times at the other end before someone must have finally answered, because Mother shouted hello into the receiver three times, "Hello, hello, hello," and then she said, "If you've picked up already then at least say something, what is this, not saying a word when I can hear you wheezing at the other end, so what's it going to be, say something already, don't you recognize the voice of your own daughter-in-law," and then Mother's voice got louder and louder and I could hear the telephone stand begin creaking as she nudged it with a knee, and then I knew for sure that she really was worried about Father because otherwise she would never have called my grandparents, no, they never ever said a word to her especially since Father had been taken away, and that's because they blamed Mother for the whole mess, saying that Father would never have signed that open letter of protest on his own, that he'd done it only because she'd goaded him into it, and then Mother got all quiet, even the telephone stand stopped creaking, and when she did speak again she did so quietly, but in that sharp, dry tone she always used when she was really mad. "All right, Comrade Secretary," she said, and she told him that she too had good reason to feel insulted and that he would do well to be less concerned about his own honor and more

135

about his son's life, and as soon as she said this Mother hushed up, and for a moment everything got completely quiet again, and then I finally opened up the suit of armor and tried slipping it onto the lead soldier, which was an unpainted Swiss guardsman without even a halberd, but the armor was too big, there was just no way to clasp it on, and that is when Mother spoke again, yes, she said that's why she called, what did my grandfather think she called for, what the hell else could they still talk about, of course it was about that, and meanwhile I was examining the lead soldier, which Feri sold to me because its upper part was flattened on account of botched casting, but I'd figured that wouldn't be noticeable under the armor, and so it seemed like a good buy except now I knew that it would be of no use to me either. And meanwhile the telephone stand began to creak again, Mother must have leaned against it, and she now told my grandfather not to go lying to her, she knew full well he still had contacts, he'd been a Party secretary for long enough so more than a few folks owed him a couple favors, come on, she said, he could at least tell her the name of someone who could help, and then for a while she didn't say a thing, but all at once she took a deep breath, gulping down air like water, and she spoke really loud into the phone, she told my grandfather that she wasn't about to wait, was that understood, she said, she wasn't about to wait, let it be now or never, was that understood, now or never, and by the time Mother said all this she was shouting, and I knew she was about to slam down the phone, and sure enough, at that very moment she did hurl it down so hard that the phone gave a loud clang before everything turned quiet, and then she yelled, "Enough is enough, I don't give a damn, the time has come for the old prick to do something for his son already," and then I heard her start off for my room only to stop after two steps, and quickly I covered the soldier and the armor with my math book, Mother now flung something soft to the floor, at first I couldn't figure out what it was, but then I heard her pulling the zipper down on her skirt and giving a curse under her breath, she must have tried sliding off her skirt so fast that it got caught on her foot, and by now I knew it was her blouse she'd thrown on the floor, and then I heard Mother hopping toward my room, on one leg, it seemed, and she was shouting for me to go help, her pantyhose was about to rip, and when I opened the door I saw Mother standing there in her bra, she really was on one leg, her skirt and pantyhose were pulled halfway down the leg she was holding in the air, and so I went over, and Mother told me to hold her side to keep her from falling, and then I stood right up beside her and put an arm around her waist, her face was streaked with tears, I saw, and then Mother bent down her head and began carefully pulling down her pantyhose, and while holding her I could feel her heart beating really fast. I thought of my grandfather and wanted to know what he'd said to Mother, but I didn't want to ask, and then Mother stepped out of her skirt and pantyhose with her other leg too, and I let her go, and there she stood beside me in nothing but her panties and bra, the only other time I'd seen her like that was when we went to the beach, but right now I didn't want to look all over her as she stood there like that except I didn't have a choice, Mother turned away and picked up her skirt and wiped her face with it, and then she told me to go to my room and put on my Sunday best like a good boy because we were going somewhere, and I was all ready to say I wasn't about to wear my disgusting knit vest, but then Mother lowered her skirt from her face and gave me this stare that kept my mouth shut, so I turned around and went to the closet to fetch my Sunday best, and I didn't even ask her where we were going.

Mother got on her smartest red suit coat and matching skirt together with a pair of high-heeled shoes I'd never seen on her before, and as we headed down the stairs she stumbled and had to grab hold of the railing right when I was about to ask if we were going somewhere to sort things out so Father would be allowed to come home or only because Mother wanted to find out exactly what happened to him, but I hadn't even opened my mouth to speak when Mother told me to keep quiet, that she needed a little bit of silence to gather her thoughts, so I kept my mouth shut and didn't even try figuring out where we were headed, instead I counted steps once we were outside, when we reached a corner I always bet myself how many steps it would be to the next corner, but since we kept walking in different directions, and always turned before I wanted to, it was pretty hard guessing in advance, and by the time we arrived at that brand-new neighborhood of high-rise apartment blocks at the edge of town, I wasn't really guessing anymore, no, the streets looked so much the same that I couldn't even tell one from the other.

We went into several apartment blocks, and by the stairwell just inside each entrance, Mother would scan the names on the adjoining metal mailboxes lining the wall, but every time we came back out I could tell she was more and more anxious, that we were lost for sure, either that or else we couldn't find the right building, but I didn't say a thing, I knew I couldn't help anyway, and then when we entered what was at least the fourth stairwell Mother must have found what she was looking for because she stopped in front of this huge mailbox, looked at the name, nodded, took her pocket mirror and lipstick out of her purse, and right there at the foot of the stairwell she put on her lipstick, and after tucking away the lipstick and the mirror she adjusted my shirt, my tie, and my vest, and she licked her palm and used it to pat down my hair, and then she said that we were about to go up to the fifth floor to see Comrade Ambassador and I should behave, I should speak only when asked to speak, and I should reply politely, and I shouldn't be scared because there wouldn't be any trouble, I'd see. I nodded and said, "All right, I'll do my best to behave," and on reaching the second floor I asked her if it was true that we'd come to help Father, but Mother replied that no, she was here because she was in a good mood, and she bit her lips and told me not to say a word.

Up on the fifth floor I was in for a real surprise, which is that only one door opened from the stairwell, not four, like on the other floors, plus the concrete floor was covered with a large rag rug, it was just like the hall inside an apartment, not a landing, but Mother didn't look surprised at all, she went straight to the door, looked at the brass nameplate, and pressed the doorbell hard, and from the way she took my hand and squeezed it tight I thought she wanted to say something, but at that moment the door swung open.

Standing on the threshold was a tall gray-haired man in a light brown suit that made his face seem even paler than it was, and as soon as Mother saw him she spoke, she was sorry to be disturbing Comrade Ambassador, she said, but she didn't know who else to turn to, and she asked for only a couple minutes of his precious time. The ambassador passed his cold gray eyes over Mother before finally breaking into a grin, and only then did he speak. "Well, well, my dear," he said, "you are lovelier than ever, you've become at least ten years younger since I saw you last," and as he spoke I noticed that lots of his front teeth were gold, and then he looked at me and even though he kept smiling, his eyes glistened more harshly as he now called out, "And you, my boy, who might you be?" I didn't say a thing, but Mother squeezed my hand and told me to be a good boy and tell Comrade Ambassador my name, as if I was a five-year-old kid, and then I said my name, and Comrade Ambassador nodded and said, "Splendid, splendid, so your name is the same as your grandfather's, is it, and you look like him too, you sure do, a whole lot more than you look like your father," and although I didn't say a word, I thought, "Motherfucking hell I do, Comrade Ambassador, I do too look like my father and not like my grandfather," and then the ambassador looked again at Mother and asked what he could thank for her unexpected visit, and Mother adjusted the brooch on her suit coat and said that maybe the stairwell wasn't the place to discuss this, and the ambassador nodded and begged her pardon and said he didn't understand how he could possibly have been so impolite, naturally it would be best if we stepped inside, and then Mother told me to wipe my feet, and then we went in and the ambassador shut the door behind us. "Step right in," he said, "straight ahead," and I heard the dead bolt behind us click twice as he turned it, and he said, "Please, please, do go on in," and then we went into the living room, and I was surprised to see that the room was exactly like some museum, with animal trophies of different shapes and sizes all over the walls, the mounted heads of antelopes, buffaloes, black bears, leopards, and jackals, in one corner there was a great big hippopotamus with a gaping mouth, and opposite the entrance, on the middle of the wall above the fireplace, was a huge, ferocious-looking lion with its mane standing on end, and towering above the room right next to the lion were two big rhino horns on a black wooden board, and then there were a bunch of colorful shields and spears and yellowed bone swords that filled out the space between the trophies, which is not to mention a huge photograph, in a wide golden frame, of a black man with glasses, only his head and his shoulders were visible, he wore a military uniform trimmed with gold braid and he had a little leopard-skin cap on his head, and even though he looked pretty good, I couldn't help but think that his head was all sweaty under the leopard-skin cap in that awful heat, but anyway, as I turned around to look some more, I heard Mother say, "Comrade Ambassador, this is remarkable, both the Folklore Museum and the Natural History Museum would have reason to envy this extraordinary collection," and the ambassador broke into another smile and said, "Oh come now, this is just a humble little exhibit, four apartments had to be made into one to fit it all, and even so, there was room only for a fraction of the entire collection, but of course," he added, "this is something too," and then he gestured toward the leather armchairs around the little glass table in the middle of the room. "Please do sit down," he said, and once we'd taken our seats, he asked if he could get us something, and Mother replied, "Oh please don't bother," but the ambassador had already left the room, and a minute later he returned carrying a silver tray with some crystal shot glasses and a four-sided bottle on top, and the ambassador placed the tray on the table, sat down, and then poured a glass for Mother and one for himself, and he explained that this was delicious home-made cherry liqueur, and without clinking glasses he downed his drink right away, and only afterward did he say, "To your health," and then Mother drank her own glass of liqueur, and the ambassador immediately refilled both her glass and his own, and again he gulped down what was in his glass, but this time instead of refilling he sat back in his armchair and just stared at us without a word, and I looked at Mother, and from the way she was holding her shot glass with both hands I could tell she was really nervous, and it was so awfully quiet that I just had to say something, I looked at the ambassador and asked, "So where were you an ambassador, Comrade Ambassador?" and he nodded toward the wall, toward the trophies, the shields and the spears and the bone swords. "Why," he said, "in Africa," and I didn't respond, I only looked down and saw that he wasn't kidding, even the carpet was made of a whole bunch of zebra skins all sewn together, and then I looked up again at the ambassador and asked, "But Comrade Ambassador, where in Africa?" to which the ambassador said, "Everywhere, but mostly in the heart of Africa, right in the middle of the darkest, blackest Africa, so what do you say, boy, which country might that have been?" and I said right away, "Zaire," and the ambassador smiled and nodded. "Very well done," he said, "I'm quite pleased with you, for you evidently know your geography well, you deserve a bit of cherry liqueur too, you certainly do, you're already a big boy after all," and he lifted the third crystal shot glass, filled it with the red liqueur, and pressed the tiny glass into my hand and said, "Go ahead, boy, drink up, to your health," and I took the glass and looked up to see Mother nod, and so I took a well-mannered sip, and even though the liqueur was terribly sweet, it still had a bite to it, and it warmed my throat all the way down, the ambassador now poured a bit more for himself and again gulped it right down, and then he put his glass back on the tray, and he fixed his eyes on Mother and asked, "How's your husband, anyway?" and then Mother swallowed her glassful of liqueur, crossed her legs, and said that in fact that's just why she was here, that was exactly what she herself hoped to find out, considering that we hadn't had any news of him for four months already, she was really worried by now, and with his exceptional contacts, surely Comrade Ambassador could sort things out in no time, so we'd know what had become of him.

The ambassador nodded, downed his fourth glass of cherry liqueur, and then he looked again at Mother and asked, "Now what makes you think such a thing?" and Mother told Comrade Ambassador not to be so humble, she knew full well just how important his standing still was, what with his past and his achievements, so this would really be nothing much for him, why, he could sort out much more serious matters if he wanted, and now the ambassador nodded again and said yes, his opportunities were indeed fairly broad, after all, he really could clear up many problems if he wanted to, but it would be best to discuss the details in private, wouldn't it, and he looked at me and said, "Now be a good boy and go to the other room, you'll find a lot of neat stuff in there, including all sorts of games." But then he added that maybe it would be best if he were to take me there himself, the apartment was pretty big after all, and he wouldn't want me getting lost the way he got lost in the jungle back then. Mother now stood up halfway and told Comrade Ambassador not to go troubling himself, this really wasn't at all necessary, I was a smart, big boy, I wouldn't be a nuisance, but by then the ambassador had already sprung out of his chair and was saying that he knew children like the back of his hand, yes, he knew there was nothing more boring to them, nothing they couldn't stand more, than having to listen to adults talk things over, so he really couldn't expect me to endure this when he knew full well that boys my age would rather spend all day playing football or chasing girls, and then he stepped over to me, dug his fingers into my shoulders, and wrested me to my feet and said, "Let's be off, then," and Mother didn't even look at me but just stared down at those crystal shot glasses, so I knew it would be best if I did as I was told, which is why I let the ambassador shove me into the hallway. Before stepping out the door he turned back, looked at Mother, and asked her to excuse him for a few moments, he'd be right back, and he waved a hand toward the bottle and said it would be best if she had herself a bit more of that delicious cherry liqueur in the meantime.

Once he too had left the living room, the ambassador dug his fingers back into my shoulders and shoved me at a good clip down the hallway and then through a smaller room and out to another hallway, and everywhere the walls were full of bone carvings, animal skins, trophies, and stuffed birds, we passed through at least two more rooms and I was just about to ask, "Comrade Ambassador, could it be that you really have three separate toilets, bathrooms, and kitchens?" but then he opened a door and shoved me into a third hallway where Persian rugs hung one beside another all along one wall, and the other wall was covered with pictures, and as we passed through there I noticed that every single one of the photos was of the ambassador with a whole lot of black women and little black kids standing all around him, and I was so surprised that I turned my head and just stared at the pictures, and the ambassador must have noticed, because he said indeed, it wasn't by chance that he claimed to know children, he'd have me know that every one of those kids there on the wall was his, and I wanted to ask him why, if those children were his, they were so black, but then we reached another door, which the ambassador opened and pushed me through but without following me in this time, and while standing there in the doorway he told me to be a good boy and wait there for my mother, I shouldn't touch anything, he said, and above all I'd better not try to steal anything because I'd be sorry if I did, and he said again how well he knew children, he knew they were all nothing but shameless little thieves you couldn't trust for a second, so I'd better be careful because there, where these objects were from, the custom was to poke thieves' eyes out. All I did was nod before the ambassador slammed the door behind him, and as he went down the hall I could hear him still mumbling away about how he knew children inside and out, about how he knew the rascally, thieving sort, and then another door closed behind him and suddenly everything turned silent, I couldn't even hear his steps anymore, and a cold shiver ran down my spine, I sensed that someone was watching me.

At first I was so scared I didn't even dare to move, but then I figured that this could only be on account of the trophies, so I finally did turn around, which just made things worse though, because I now saw that one of the walls, from the ceiling almost all the way to the floor, was covered with skulls and human heads nailed to wooden boards, but when I went closer I realized that these weren't really human heads after all, but chimpanzee, gibbon, and gorilla heads, and that not even the skulls were entirely authentic, that each of them had only one or two real bones in it and the rest was filled out by plaster of Paris, and each one had a little drawing next to it that showed how it would have looked as the real head of a monkey or other ape or prehistoric human, and every one had its Latin name next to it, but I didn't read the words, no, that chill down my spine wouldn't go away, I still felt like I was being watched, and then I turned back around and saw that there really was someone there, sitting in the opposite corner of the room at a little table with a chessboard on top, a chessboard with the pieces all laid out, and that this someone was, in fact, staring right at me.

A thin old black man sat there at the far side of the table, watching what I was up to, and even though I was a little scared at first, in no time I said, "How do you do," not that he said anything back, he just waved a hand for me to go closer, and so I did, and still he didn't say a thing, he only pointed at the chessboard. "Thank you," I said, "but I don't like to play chess," and again he gestured for me to go closer, and he pointed at the chessboard one more time, so I did then sit down in the chair across from him at the table, the chair creaked as I did so, and in that instant the black man reached out a hand and took the pawn in front of his white king and pushed it two squares ahead, and then he also placed the pawn in front of his queen, but by one square only, and I felt like saying that I should have the white pieces and he the black ones, he was the black man after all, but then I didn't say it, instead I moved with both of my knights so they ended up almost next to each other, with just two empty spaces be-tween them, an opening move my grandfather taught me so one day I might use it to my advantage, and as soon as I let go of the second knight, the black man stepped his bishop forward on the queen's side, and as he moved his hand I heard something creak in him. I stood up to get a better look at the man, which is when I noticed that it wasn't a living person I was playing chess with but a robot, an automaton, yes, in math class we learned that even as far back as the Middle Ages there were chess-playing automatons, but I never believed it, besides, this one here before me was just like a real person, a very thin, very old black man who even looked up as I stood and then returned his eyes to the chessboard as I got really close to him, looking him over to see how he was made, what was directing his movements, and where his power supply was, and then I even touched his hand to figure out if he was carved of wood, but he wasn't, he was made of real skin, and his hand felt just like a human hand except it was much colder, and as I touched it some more I could feel bones and tendons twitching under the skin, and again I heard that hushed creaking, his joints must have grated as he pulled his hand away and picked up another one of his pieces, a knight, and that's when I noticed for the first time how really special even the chess pieces were, the black ones were carved of ebony and the white ones of ivory, and each one depicted some monster, the white pieces were all skeletons and the black pieces were human-headed demons with animal bodies, and every one held a spear or a sword or a hatchet or a saw-toothed knife in its paw, and the officers wore necklaces and belts of skulls and bones and human ears and human hands, everything was carved to the finest detail, and the face of the white king looked just like the ambassador, and it looked pretty scary.

But I still couldn't tell what made the chess-playing gentleman move, no, even though I looked all over his back, nowhere could I see where any sort of cable or drive belt might have entered his body, which was dressed in a tattered military uniform except that he was barefoot, and his feet were made like his hands, and he looked very thin and very old, and then it occurred to me that maybe he was moving on his own, that maybe he wasn't an automaton but really was alive, or if not, that he was moving on account of some African witchcraft, and an icy fear came over me and I couldn't even move, but then I took a good look at his thick reed chair and I realized that he got electricity through the legs of that chair, that's what made him move, and when I then gave the chair a careful little kick and it didn't budge, I knew I was right. And then I thought there must be a quiet little electric motor in his belly that was making his joints move through some network of connections, through hydraulics and control cables, such things were possible these days after all, and so I sat back in my chair and made another move, just as a test I put him in check with one of my knights, but of course he noticed right away and captured my knight, with a precise, creaking movement he lifted it up and placed it next to the board, and one after another he kept capturing my pieces no matter what move I made, responding right away every time, not thinking even for a second, and when I offered him my bishop so I could nab his queen, he didn't take the bait, it was like he knew exactly what I was up to, and something must have heated up inside him as his hand creaked along because he began to smell like rancid butter, and his movements seemed to speed up as he kept cornering me and taking more of my pieces, he even held his head a bit differently as if it was all he could do not to laugh, and then, when he captured my second bishop and put me in check, I knew it was all over, that no matter what my next move was, I would be in checkmate in no time, and I looked at the automaton, at that old black man's face, at his dusty gray parched skin, and I knew I wasn't about to let him checkmate me if I could help it, so all at once I snatched the white king off the board, and right away the automaton started reaching out after my hand, but with a slow, squeaking motion much slower than mine, and the automaton let out a loud murmur and looked at me and his eyes seemed to glisten with rage, but for a split second only, and then with a wild, creaky swing of his arm he swept the chess pieces off the table, they went tumbling all over the floor, and then he flung back his head and opened his mouth wide and burst out laughing, and smoke started pouring from his mouth and nose, and I stood up so fast that my chair toppled over, but the white king stayed in my hand, the automaton was still cackling so loud that even the walls and the floor were shaking, and that is when I realized that it wasn't the automaton that was laughing, it was Mother.

Yes, I could now hear clear as day that it was her, Mother was laughing really loud and shouting too, even through all those walls and doors I could hear her saying, "Bravo, Comrade Ambassador, splendid, bravo, splendid, magnificent," and she told him not to be scared, to go ahead and hit her one more time, to go ahead and hit her with all his might, to go ahead and hit her if he thought that by hitting a woman he was more of a man, and then he could go on hitting her until morning, yes indeed, he could go right ahead and feel free to hit her, and even as she shouted she was laughing the whole time, so loudly that, I knew, her tears were flowing too, and by then I'd already opened the door and was running toward Mother's laughter, from one room to the next, down the hallways and through room after room, every room was teeming with objects, with crystal vases, glass fish, porcelain soldiers, shot glasses, and wineglasses that tinkled against each other from Mother's laughter, even the framed maps and photographs and the ivory carvings swayed on the walls, and dried tropical fish, shiny with varnish, quivered on their copper wires in an empty aquarium just as if they were swimming, which is not to mention the copper bracelets and anklets strung onto leather belts above the doors, yes, they were moving too, along with some bottles up on shelves, bottles filled with a golden liquid and with official-looking seals on them, and every last chandelier was also swinging to and fro, everything was shaking just like in an earthquake, and I was so afraid the trophies would come tumbling off the walls and bury me under them that I just kept running, opening one door after another, heading from one room to the next, and just as I was beginning to think that I would never find Mother, I flung open a door and there I was, back in the living room, and there was Mother, standing on one leg next to one of the leather armchairs, laughing hysterically, the little table was toppled over and the cherry liqueur had spilled all over the zebra skins, oozing among the crystal shot glasses and slivers of glass scattered on the floor, and one of the antelope heads had fallen off the wall, and even that big lion's head had half come off, the ambassador was standing underneath it, clutching it with one hand to keep it from plopping into the puddle of cherry liqueur while he was trying to put his shirt back on using his other hand, and when he saw me he shouted, "So then, finally you're here, it's high time you cleared out of here once and for all, and you'd better take along your whore of a mother with you," and he said he didn't even know why he'd let us into the apartment in the first place when he might have recognized our sort, not even my grandfather was ever worth a piece of flying shit, and it would be best if I just forgot that my father ever existed, never in this stinking life would we ever see him again because he for one could guarantee that my father would rot away right where he was, at the Danube Canal, and my father could thank his lucky stars if he didn't wind up in a reeducation camp, no, we would never see him again. And I felt my heart in my throat, but Mother just went on laughing, and suddenly I couldn't help but crack up too, because this really was hilarious, how the ambassador was standing there in his undershirt beneath that huge open-mouthed lion's head, clutching the trophy's face with one hand and prancing about as he tried pressing it back onto the wall while furiously attempting to stick his other arm back in his sleeve, so it really was impossible not to laugh, and now Mother also looked at me, and I saw that her nose was bleeding and her mascara had run. "Let's get going," she said through her laughter, I put a hand on her shoulder and we left the room, the ambassador was of course still ranting as he stood there under the lion's head, we could hear him even as I opened the dead bolt on the front door to let Mother out ahead of me, but when the door finally slammed shut behind us, we could no longer hear a thing he was shouting, but Mother was still laughing as she told me to give her a hand because one of her heels had broken off, so I let her put an arm around me, and that is how we went back down those four flights of stairs. On reaching the bottom Mother stopped, adjusted her stockings with one hand, and pressed a handkerchief to her face with her other hand even as she continued shaking with laughter, and right then I reached into my pants pocket and squeezed that white king hard. The cold ivory felt smooth in my hand. No one would defeat me in the war game ever again, I knew, because compared with this commander of mine even the most beautifully painted lead soldier was nothing but a cheap little puff of pussy smoke.

11

Playing Search

■■■■■

M OTHER TALKED everything over with me most of
the time, often she told me why things were the way
they were, and when she did that, she answered my
questions too, or when she didn't, then I knew she thought it
best that we didn't talk about it, because what I didn't know,
I couldn't tell anyone else even by accident, and I had to admit she was right about that because I knew there really were
things it was dangerous to even mention, for example, exactly
what happened during the civil war or how much so-and-so
could get meat or coffee for, or how much it took to pay off
so-and-so, or why the Party General Secretary, who was also
commander of the armed forces, was a treasonous brute, or
which of the people we knew had been taken away, or who
had their homes searched and why. When I asked her about
things like that, Mother either said only that this was serious business, let's not talk about it, or else that I should ask
Father instead when he finally got home. But lots of times
she didn't even have to say this much, no, from the way she

looked at me I could tell it would be best if I didn't ask questions to begin with.

That's just how it was when Mother came home one Thursday and asked me if I had any money saved up, and how much. I could tell right away from her voice that she wasn't kidding around, and so I told her the truth, that I had two tens, but I didn't tell her where I got them from because I knew she wouldn't have been happy to find out that I got one of them from my grandfather and that I won the other at cards, because I wasn't supposed to play cards or accept money from my grandfather, but even Mother must have figured it was best not to go asking where I had such a load of money from because she didn't say a thing, no, she just went into the living room and straight to Father's picture, which she took off the wall, there was an envelope stuck to the back of the picture with electric tape, Mother opened it and took out a bunch of bills and licked her index finger and counted the money right away, and then I heard her saying softly, "Five hundred twenty-five plus twenty is five hundred forty-five, so we still have to scrounge up one thousand four hundred fifty-five to make two thousand," and she told me to go look around my room to see what I could do without, and meanwhile she'd pick out some of her clothes and scrape together everything she thought we might get a good price for and didn't really need, and I shouldn't make any plans for Sunday morning, we were going to the flea market because we needed the money by Monday.

I just nodded and went into my room, where I opened the closet and pulled out the drawers of my desk and looked over every square inch of my bookshelf and walls, at the posters and bird feathers and bird scalps and weapons above my bed, but I didn't see anything I would have wanted to sell, so I sat down on my bed and leaned back and tried going through a mental list of everything I had, my lead soldiers, my matchbox car collection, my gum wrappers, my tennis racket, my badminton racket, and my Ping-Pong racket and balls, the little clay figurines I made a while back at the Young Pioneers center; my cartoon character emblems, which I cut from plywood with a jigsaw and painted myself; my French, German, American, and Yugoslavian comic books, which I got from Father's coworkers; my hunting knife, my tomahawk, my slingshot, my bow and arrows, my toy pistols; my three old shotgun shells, which still smelled of gunpowder; my three miniature soccer teams, all of whose players were buttons; my hand-carved chessboard, which also had backgammon; all my posters, one by one; my pocket calendar with pictures of actresses, which I kept under the bottom drawer; and my thirty-six-color set of felt-tip markers, of which only the turquoise still wrote. Anyway, I just sat there looking at one thing after another and trying to imagine what it would be like if each one wasn't there, whether I'd go looking for it or want to play with it anymore. For example, I hadn't even taken those matchbox cars out of the desk drawer in at least a year, and I hadn't played badminton in a long time either, and I knew most of the comic books by heart and I hardly ever looked at them anymore, but no matter how I tried, I just couldn't imagine what it would feel like to open the matchbox drawer and see that it was all empty or to look at the shelf and not see a single comic book at all.

Meanwhile I could hear Mother in the living room opening closets and pulling drawers open, flinging out her clothes and other things, and I imagined her taking her old outfits off their hangers in the closet one after another and putting each one on the couch, so I leaned up against the wall and just sat there on my bed with my hands around my knees, listening to the rustling of clothes in the living room, but then Mother left the room, and seconds later I heard the pantry door creak open and Mother let out a big moan, I knew she was taking the suitcase off the top shelf of the pantry, and then the wheels of the suitcase kept hitting the kitchen's tile floor as Mother carried it into the room, and that's when it occurred to me that she wasn't only going through her own clothes, but maybe she was also looking over Father's shirts, ties, shoes, belts, and suits.

Before then, we never touched Father's things, we didn't even open his closet or his desk drawers so if he came home he'd find everything just the way he left it the day they came and took him away, and ever since then I stood in front of Father's closet lots of times and looked into the shiny polish of its door as if it was a mirror, and I thought of the smell the closet must have had when Father opened it to take out some hidden piece of chocolate or chewing gum, and I tried imagining that Father was standing there behind me and that the only reason I couldn't see him was because the polish was too shiny, and as I sat there on my bed listening to Mother pack that suitcase, I again tried thinking through my things one after another because I knew I'd have to pick out something anyway, but then I started remembering when I got each one or where I got it from, plus what I'd done with it or wanted to do with it, and I knew this just wouldn't work, that I wouldn't be able to pick out anything this way either, and then I clearly heard Mother opening Father's closet door and giving a big sigh, and I heard the rustling of Father's suits as Mother threw them one after another onto the couch, and then I stood up and stopped in the middle of my room and snooped slowly around like I did whenever I played search-the-premises or pretended I was a burglar, as if it wasn't even my own room but some stranger's, as if I didn't know what anything was and where it was from and what it was for, as if I was simply looking for something, and that everything else was just in the way, and then suddenly I heard Mother sniffling softly out in the living room, so I knew for sure that she was packing Father's clothes, and then I leaned down and pulled an empty cardboard box out from under my bed, a box I wanted to cut up into a suit of armor for the next time my friends and I had ourselves a little costume party, and I went over to my shelf and began taking things off it one after another, and without picking and choosing at all I just threw all my comic books, model airplanes, and hand-painted lead soldiers into the box, and I didn't stop even when my old stamp album ended up in my hands, no, I placed even that right in the box, and then my slingshot and my blowgun too, and my Indian books and hunting books, one after another, and I went over to my desk and pulled out the matchbox drawer and poured all my cars into the box, but then one of the cars, the red Ford with the doors you could open, accidentally fell on the floor, so I leaned down and picked it up before putting it in the box by the other cars, and then I set the drawer on the floor and I stood up on my bed and tried taking my posters off the wall, but I couldn't do that as fast, no, I was worried they'd rip, I'd glued them to the wall because I didn't have thumbtacks and I was especially worried about those double-page soccer team posters I'd gotten from an illustrated magazine and about my movie posters with Indians on them, and about the picture of that champion goalie with his signature specially printed on it, so anyway, I had to be really careful taking those posters down so that even if the paint peeled off the wall at least the pictures themselves wouldn't rip, and I did it by leaning up against the wall and squeezing my palm under the middle of each poster and then working them off like that, one by one, and then I put them all on my bed, I laid the posters on top of one another and rolled them up together and set the whole bundle in the corner of the cardboard box, and then I went over to my desk and from the shelf above it I removed my badminton rackets and my genuine rubber-faced Vietnamese Ping-Pong paddle and my yellow competition-grade

Ping-Pong balls, all four of them, and I put all of that into the box too, and then I opened the closet and took out my button-soccer box containing not only my three champion teams but also the goals I'd made from copper wire and pantyhose, to look like real netting, yes, I threw my whole button-soccer collection into the cardboard box, and as I did so I heard the buttons scatter, meaning the teams had just gotten all mixed up, but what did I care, and next I went to the closet and removed my gun belt with its fake-leather holsters containing my two plastic pistols that fired caps, and then I took out my cowboy hat, which I'd made by sewing bits of elk skin on a straw hat, and as I stood there holding the hat by the sliding copper ring of its chin strap, it occurred to me that one of the pistols must still be loaded with that red phosphorus powder I'd scratched off match heads and filled the old caps with, and I was just about to draw one of the pistols from the holster when I heard Mother out in the living room slamming down the top of the suitcase, so instead I just went ahead and threw the gun belt into the box and tossed the cowboy hat on top, but the box was so full already that the hat almost fell out, its chin strap got caught on the rolled-up posters and the hat just hung there, and then I heard the suitcase snap open out in the living room, its lock was really bad, it took two people to close it, one person had to press it shut while the other person locked it with the key. I heard Mother slamming down the top of the suitcase over and over again, and I heard her gasping for air while trying all by herself to click the lock shut, and I knew she wouldn't call me over to help, but I also knew I'd go out there and help her all the same.

12

Gold!

. . . . .

BEFORE THEN, we used to think the old clay pit was closed because its wall collapsed in the big earthquake, revealing a bunch of priceless prehistoric reliefs, but ever since Zsolt showed us a gold nugget one time, everyone knew that wasn't really why you couldn't go there, that it was actually because the quarry walls were full of gold, yes, all you had to do was swing a hammer on the slate where the veins of ore ran, and the nuggets would come flying right out of the wall. Zsolt told us he stole the gold nugget out of his dad's desk drawer, from beside his railway worker's ID and worker's medals, and he even let us take it into our hands, it was damn heavy, it was real gold, no doubt about it. Often we wanted to go to the clay pit and give it a try to see if we could really get ourselves some gold, but as long as old Mr. Vászile guarded the site with his two German shepherds it didn't work out, because he was there day and night, he lived in an old trailer and never let anyone into the clay pit or even onto the property around it, and he never kept his dogs chained, one time when Zsolt climbed over the fence on a dare, one of the dogs bit his ankle so bad that afterward Zsolt had to get thirty shots in his belly, so when we got the news that Mr. Vászile had hanged himself, none of us were sorry at all, and indeed we were glad to hear that he first shot both of the dogs. Zsolt said right away that we should take advantage of the opportunity and go get ourselves some gold before a new guard got appointed, yes, it would be best if we headed off right away, so we should go home and get hammers, besides, he was itching to see those prehistoric reliefs for himself.

Because the quarry was far away, we went by bicycle. I sat behind Zsolt, on the rack, and on the other bike Jancsi rode in front of Csabi. The fence was pretty high and had barbed wire up top, but at least there wasn't any barbed wire above the locked gate, and Jancsi figured out that if we leaned one bike against the gate, then from the seat it wouldn't be hard to climb up to the top, and we really did get up there pretty easy, and only when all four of us were inside did Zsolt say we were complete idiots not to have pounded off the lock with a hammer because then we could have at least brought in the bicycles too, but Jancsi just waved a hand and said it didn't matter, the important thing was that we got inside and didn't have to worry about those lousy dogs.

As for the prehistoric reliefs, I thought they would be a lot more exciting, sure, they looked nice and big, high up there on the quarry wall around twelve feet from the ground, I couldn't really imagine how the folks who made them could have climbed so high, but they sure seemed pretty worn, you could hardly tell what they were supposed to show, I could make out some sort of houses and animals and a bunch of human figures, a couple of the people were shooting with bows and arrows, and some were hunting for wild boar and for bears from a horse-drawn cart using a spear, plus there was a gigantic person lying on the ground, you couldn't tell if it was a man or a woman, and practically all that was left of the face was the eyes, the rest had been washed away by the snow and the rain, and even Jancsi said he didn't understand what was so priceless about these reliefs when you could hardly see a thing on them, but then Zsolt said he'd heard that they weren't prehistoric at all, no, the miners had made them out of boredom but then half plastered them over because they turned out so badly, and there really wasn't much to see on them at all.

Mr. Vászile's shack was there at the foot of the quarry wall under the prehistoric reliefs and around ten yards from the lake, it was a trailer with wheels, like the sort construction workers live in, and when we passed by it Zsolt said we should go in and see what the old man left behind, but Csabi then made the sign of the cross and said, "God forbid we should go in there because that would stir up Mr. Vászile's ghost, and the clay pit is haunted to begin with," but Zsolt said that was just a superstition, that he didn't believe in ghosts at all, though he himself had heard the quarry lake was full of bones, but he didn't believe even that, people said things like that only because they liked scaring each other, if the water cleared up enough, maybe he'd dive in and see for himself, and as for Mr. Vászile, he couldn't have a ghost because ghosts didn't exist at all. And when Zsolt said that, he pulled his hammer from his belt and took a couple of good whacks at the side of the trailer and yelled for Mr. Vászile's ghost to come forward if it dared.

At first nothing happened, but then all of a sudden something moved inside, we could hear snarling and scratching plus some groans, the whole trailer moved just a little, and I got so scared that my hammer almost fell right out of my hands, even Zsolt turned stone white, I saw, and I knew we should run away, but my stomach knotted up so much that I couldn't move at all, and the others didn't budge either, no, all four of us just stood there next to the trailer, and then I saw this white skeleton hand reach out from underneath, from between the trailer's big wheels, and then Csabi cried out, "God help us, now we're done for," and the skeleton hand was groping around, I wanted to cry out too, but I couldn't, not even a peep left my throat, and then another hand reached out beside the skeleton hand, but this one was a real person's hand, and by then I saw that even the skeleton hand wasn't really a skeleton hand but just the end of a crutch, and then the whole crutch came flying out from between the wheels followed by another crutch, and then we could hear all this swearing and snarling and panting, and we saw this one-legged man struggling to crawl out from under the trailer, one leg of his military trousers was tied in a knot up where his leg was almost completely gone, and he had long matted hair and a big black beard, and when he finally managed to pull himself out from under the trailer, he grabbed one of the crutches and sat up on his knees so he was leaning against the crutch with his good leg, and then he reached back into the trailer and pulled out a huge green backpack by its strap and took out a little corked bottle and stuck one of the crutches under his arm and with a groan he stood up straight, and that's when we saw that he was really thin and really tall, at least a head taller than even the trailer, and using his teeth he then pulled the cork out of the bottle, and he spit the cork on top of the trailer and took a big swig, and only then did he finally get around to asking who we were and what the motherfucking hell we were doing inside the fence.

By then Zsolt's face was back to its usual color, he straightened himself out right away, saluted, and said, "I hereby report to Comrade Corporal that we're looking for Comrade Vászile," and he explained that we came from School No. 13 to do community service work, that our shop teacher sent us to hammer some tin plates, and Zsolt even showed his hammer, and I saw that the one-legged man really did have a corporal's epaulet on the shoulder of his fatigue jacket, but he had only one of them, only the threads showed on the other shoulder.

At first the corporal didn't say a thing, he just looked us over, loosened the crutch under his arm, and took another swig from the bottle, and then he asked if we'd really come to see Mr. Vászile, we should tell him honestly, he said, because as far as he knew, his poor father had had no friends and no one was mourning him, why, he'd even heard that everyone was happy about his dying, folks hadn't really liked his father much, God forgive them, not even now that his father was dead and gone did they have any good words to say about him, they were talking up all this nonsense about how he threw his life away, saying he hanged himself, yes, they were out to besmirch his father's memory with lies like that, and then here we were looking for the poor old fellow with such love, why, maybe we hadn't even heard the news, and then Zsolt said, "No, when did it happen?" and the one-legged man replied that not even three days had passed, and he'd have us know it wasn't suicide, and then we all gave him our sincere sympathies and said we were really sorry and that we didn't want to bother him anymore, and I was already turning back toward the gate when the corporal told us to wait, not to hurry, because he wanted to ask us one or two things and that we shouldn't offend him by leaving him high and dry to go on mourning all alone, so all four of us then turned back, and the corporal asked how long we'd known his father, and Zsolt answered, "A pretty long time, almost three years," and the corporal nodded and took another swig, and he said he was asking us to answer honestly and not to besmirch his father's memory by being all prim and polite, we should tell him just what sort of person his father was, what we knew him to be like, and at first Zsolt didn't say a thing, he just stared at the ground, but then he finally did look back up at the corporal and say, "He was a good man, he was, strict and hot-tempered, but a really decent, really straight-shooting fellow." As Zsolt was saying this, I noticed him waving one of his hands behind his back, so then I spoke too, "That's right," I said, "Mr. Vászile was a good man," and then Jancsi and Csabi said the same thing, and they also said, "May God rest his soul."

The corporal nodded and told us we were good boys. "God bless you," he said, and then he reached out his bottle to Zsolt and told him to drink up in memory of his father, and Zsolt took the bottle and drank, and the corporal took out a handkerchief and blew his nose really loud, and when Zsolt wanted to give back the bottle, the corporal told him through his handkerchief to pass it along to the others, they also deserved it, he said, they loved his father too, so Jancsi and Csabi then also took swigs, and then they handed the bottle to me, and I too had a gulp, it was plum spirits with a real bite, it was so strong I had to cough, and as I lowered the bottle I saw the trailer door open up and three really huge sheepdogs saunter out one after another, each one was at least as big as a Saint Bernard, and their heads were as big and round as a bear's, they stopped right in front of us and they didn't bark and they didn't growl, they just stood there looking at us, but even that was enough for me to feel my body get all cold and heavy right away, and I could tell that the others were at least as scared as I was. But then the corporal clicked his tongue, and the dogs all sat at once, and the corporal said he was sorry, he didn't want to scare us, the dogs had come out at the sound of coughing because these dogs, they were real man-killing machines, but we shouldn't be scared, they wouldn't bother us, the only thing we had to be careful about was to avoid running, because then the dogs would catch us for sure because it's coded into their genes that a running person has to be wrestled to the ground and mauled, so we shouldn't even think of running from them, no, we should move nice and slowly instead, and we shouldn't look directly in their eyes, and as long as we didn't do any of that we wouldn't suffer any harm, and then he took the bottle from my hand, drank down the rest of the plum spirits, and flung the bottle into the quarry lake, and he gave a big sigh and said the only thing he was ashamed about was that he arrived late, that he couldn't be there at his father's burial, he left as soon as he got word, he did, but they buried the poor old fellow really quick, it's just awful that he couldn't say a proper goodbye, and now he'd been here for half a day already, but he hadn't yet gotten up the courage to go inside his old man's shack, no, he'd sent the dogs not long ago so they could look around a little, that's all, because he could remember this trailer from when he was a kid, and he was pretty scared of memories, though we had to believe him that he wasn't a coward, he didn't even know why he was telling us all this, we were kids, we wouldn't understand anyway, but he had to tell someone all the same, and for some reason he felt he could trust us. And so he'd ask us for a big favor, we had the time as long as we came here to work anyway, so we should be so good as to help him take stock of his father's estate, he was afraid that he wouldn't have the strength to do this alone, of course sorting through things while on crutches wasn't easy to begin with, and as he said this he waved one of his crutches toward us, which made the dogs growl, and then Zsolt said that this was only natural, it was the least we could do. The corporal nodded and again blew his nose and said he really appreciated it, he saw right at the start that he could count on us, and then he pointed to the picnic chair, the folded-up metal picnic table, and the great big sun umbrella leaning against the side of the trailer, and he said we should begin by setting up the sunshade and putting the chair and the table underneath, because he wanted to just sit around here a bit like his father used to do, and then we could start emptying out the trailer so he could take stock of what his father left behind.

Sticking the umbrella into the loamy earth was pretty hard, and then once we did and tried opening it, it closed up three whole times, the dowel didn't want to catch no matter what, and that made one of the dogs sit up and let out these belly-deep barks, but as soon as the corporal pointed one of his crutches at the dog and snapped, "Quiet, Kloska," the dog shut right up and cowered back. Meanwhile we finally managed to open the umbrella, and we put the picnic chair underneath and then set up the picnic table too, and then the one-legged corporal hobbled over and struggled to sit down in the chair, and he laid his two crutches down on the table in front of him, leaned back, wiped his face, and said he now felt ready, so it would be best if two of us climbed into the trailer and started handing out everything bit by bit, anything that could be moved, and the other two of us should put it all in a nice neat pile, and then he'd go on over and look to see what we found, so far he'd only had courage enough to peek in the door, but he saw so many familiar objects that he got really scared, so it would be best if we got started right away because we'd have a whole lot to bring out. Zsolt headed straight toward the trailer and he called for me to go along too, not that I really wanted to, but I wasn't in the mood to resist either, and as we stepped toward the trailer the dogs perked their ears and started growling again, and only then did I notice that each of them had one ear cut off, the corporal shouted at them to sit still, telling them they didn't need to guard against us, we were his father's friends, so the dogs just stared but didn't stir, and I thought I was lucky after all that Zsolt had chosen me, and not Jancsi or Csabi, because at least inside we wouldn't have to worry about the dogs.

As soon as I stepped up on those bricks stacked vertically

by the door, I remembered what Csabi had said about ghosts, and I felt like the strength was about to drain from my legs so I'd crumple up like a rag, but then I looked at the dogs and I grabbed the doorjamb, and Zsolt gave a big sigh before opening the door, and I took a deep breath of the fresh air outside, I was still really scared, but I got up the guts to step inside so fast that Zsolt and I stepped in together. Never had I been in a place like that before, a place where someone had died, both of my arms were covered with goose bumps, but I was a little curious to see what it would be like. On the inside the trailer seemed at least twice as big as on the outside, and the air was really damp and had a mildewy odor, at first I could hardly see a thing because light entered only through the door and I was blocking it completely, but once Zsolt tore off the tarp hanging over the window we could see pretty well, the trailer really was one big mess, there was a phonograph on a stool in the middle, a real antique phonograph with a horn, the floor around it was strewn with crumpled newspapers and old tin cans and empty beer bottles, I tripped on one of the bottles and almost fell, but then I grabbed hold of a winter coat on a hanger, at least fifteen other winter coats were hanging there next to it, and there was a heap of coats even on the floor underneath, and as I kicked at them, the coats gave off a gluey stink so strong I almost had to puke, and I called over to Zsolt to say he sure got us into a nice little fix, but he told me to keep my trap shut because if I had a better idea, why hadn't I said so, and anyway, maybe Mr. Vászile even dug up a little gold for himself and we might just find it, or if not, then not, but we could at least thank our lucky stars we got off so easy, and then he turned all quiet and threw the tarp out the door and grabbed the phonograph off the stool and handed that out too, so I picked up about three coats and tock them over to the door and tossed them all out at once, and since that made the stink go away a little, I started throwing the other clothes out the door also, one armful after another, there was a tower of suitcases in one corner, at least eight of them, and crammed in next to them were a bunch of plastic bags, buckets, and folded blankets, Zsolt started handing out the suitcases, after the third one he hunched over and just about puked, and then he took off his T-shirt and tied it in front of his nose, so I took mine off and did the same thing, and starting then both of us worked like that, but even so, that musty odor was intense. At first I was careful about what I picked up, I checked whether it was a pile of books tied up with belts or a bunch of tin cans tied together with string, but then I ended up handing out everything to Csabi without picking and choosing at all, I stopped only when I tried lifting a big green five-gallon gasoline can that wouldn't budge, so I called Zsolt over to help, and the two of us lugged it over to the door, but then Zsolt said we should leave it for last as long as it was so damn heavy, so anyway, by then the trailer was almost completely empty, all that was left was a plank bed on top of a bunch of bricks by one of the walls, Zsolt gathered the dirty bed sheets and the blanket along with one of the planks and took them to the door, and I went to get the other plank, and that's when I noticed a newspaper page glued to the ceiling above the bed, which meant that whenever Mr. Vászile had laid down on his back in bed, this is exactly what he must have seen, I reached up and ripped it off the ceiling so I could read it, it was an article about the clay pit, about what amazing finds those prehistoric reliefs up there on the quarry wall were, about how they carry a historical message and are works of art of priceless value, and half the newspaper page was a picture of that ancient giant lying on the ground that we'd seen earlier on the quarry wall, and written diagonally across the picture in big letters and purple indelible ink was the word ENOUGH! and I'd already half crumpled the page to toss it on the ground with the other newspaper pages when I stuffed it into my pocket instead.

Finally we threw the last plank from the bed out the door, and then we grabbed hold of the gasoline can and struggled past all the stuff outside the door to climb out of the trailer, Mr. Vászile's son was still sitting in the picnic chair, he was scratching the neck of one of the dogs, and Jancsi and Csabi were flinging clothes into one big pile. When the corporal saw us with that gasoline can, he shouted to us right away to take it over to him, and that's when I noticed that he had another bottle of plum spirits in his hand, it was still almost full, and when we put the gasoline can down in front of him, he wedged the bottle of spirits between his thighs, undid the clasp lock on the can, took a sniff, and took the can in his hands, and then he let out a big groan, raised the can above his head, and dribbled a little of its contents into his mouth, but he spit it out right away and flung the can to the ground, at least a cupful splashed out, and he started shouting on and on about this fucking world, about life being so unjust, and about how his poor old man had had to scrape by on hospital-issue disinfecting alcohol, which was almost undrinkable even when you filtered out the blue dye they mixed in to keep folks from drinking it, and the whole time his father had been drinking this shit, he, his son, had been guzzling topnotch plum spirits by the bottle, why, even now his knapsack was full of the stuff, but from now on, he said, things would be different, and he stood up and lifted the bottle of plum spirits and turned it upside-down and splashed it out on the ground, flailing his arm so wildly while doing so that he almost fell over twice, and when the bottle was empty he flung it into the lake, and then he hobbled over to the small heap of odds and ends, poked at it with a crutch, pried out a pickle jar from among all the clothes, picked it up, and threw it over to

Jancsi, telling him to go wash it out, and Jancsi hadn't even gone two steps when the corporal also threw over a bucket and told him to clean that too and fill it with water, and then he picked up one of the plastic bags and said yes, he knew there would be charcoal here that his poor father had used to filter that nasty blue stuff out of the disinfecting alcohol, and he shook a little charcoal out of the bag to the ground, stomped a piece to bits, and said, "At least it's nice and powdery," and then he went back to rummaging about the pile, picking up one piece of clothing after another and turning it about in his hands before tossing it back on the pile, and at the same time he went on and on about his poor old man, about how he'd loved objects, about how he'd collected so many things, yes, said the corporal, his dad had been so thrifty that now he, his son, didn't have the heart to throw out a thing, he sure had argued a lot with his dad about this, God forgive him for always telling him that all this horseshit is unnecessary, but for his part he never could understand why folks need so much junk when all you really need to make you happy fits in a knapsack, it's not like we can take anything with us to the grave anyway, at most only what we drink, but his old man was the sort who saw potential in every object, in his dad's eyes every single cheap, shabby piece of clothing might as well have been new, and not even now could he quite forgive his poor old man for this, and all at once the corporal fell silent and blew his nose again before leaning down, picking up a big canvas bag, opening it, reaching inside, and cupping out a little flour and giving it a lick, and then he scattered the flour on the ground and said his poor dear father had to live for years on nothing but grits, and all the while he, his son, was able to stuff himself silly with bacon and ewe curd on the plate next to his own grits. "Life is so unfair," said the corporal, but now we would hold the old man's funeral feast just like he would have done, with nothing but grits and filtered disinfecting alcohol. "As long as we couldn't be there at his funeral," he said, "then at least there should be this much, yes, in our own way we'll pay our last respects," and he said he'd now show us how they cook real grits in the hills, one of us should go behind the trailer to get some wood while the rest of us opened up the bags and the suitcases so he could finally sort through the whole kit and caboodle, so anyway, we then started scattering the clothes and scraps of cloth from the bags onto the ground and we opened the suitcases one after another, there were clothes in them too, but sorted by type, one suitcase had only shirts, another just had rolled-up socks and underwear, a third had stylish women's shoes, at least fifteen pairs, including some with really high heels, and another suitcase was full of ties and folded pants, only two suitcases had no clothes in them, one had the records that went with the phonograph, and another had a big leather-bound book in a bunch of crumpled old bank notes, and it said on the book, in gold lettering, AN ENCYCLOPEDIA OF THE HISTORY OF THE WORLD FROM THE BEGINNING OF CREATION TO THE FINAL DAYS, and when the corporal saw that, he threw aside the mud-stained winter coat whose pockets he'd been going through, he picked up the book and paged through it and told us that this had been his father's favorite book, when the corporal was a kid his father had told him lots of stories from it because history was everything to his father, but it did no good his father telling him all that stuff, he never could bring himself to love history, at most only the parts about kings. Sure, even his father had liked talking most about the rulers of bygone ages and about kings' funerals, about how the Vikings were sent on their final journey in burning boats, about the tombs the Egyptians and the Aztecs built for themselves and the priceless treasures buried inside them, and about how many servants they took with them in death so they'd have folks to serve them in the world beyond, and when he was little, for a long time he believed that his father was a king of sorts, who'd had to give up his rule in the interest of the people.

Meanwhile Jancsi got back with the water, and Csabi brought three big pieces of firewood. The corporal pulled a sooty stew pot out from under the trailer, poured around two quarts of water into it from the bucket, and splashed the rest on the ground, and then he turned the bucket upside-down, took a pocketknife from his pocket, pulled out its biggest blade, and jabbed the bottom of the bucket three times in a row. Next he filled the bucket with charcoal, set it right over the mouth of the pickle jar, and poured the blue disinfecting alcohol into the bucket up to the brim, and then little by little the filtered alcohol started dripping into the pickle jar underneath, it was black, like diluted liquid mud. The corporal wiped his hands, looked at us, kicked Mr. Vászile's old tin washtub our way, and said he'd ask us for one more favor, he wanted everyone to find themselves a rag and then to rub down the trailer on the outside a bit, not a whole lot, just enough so its original color would show, and in the meantime he'd set a fire under the grits and then we'd hold ourselves that funeral feast, a proper one at that.

The water in the quarry lake was gray and murky and its smell was pretty strange, I remembered what Zsolt had said about bones being at the bottom, so when I dipped in the washtub and it sucked in water really loud, I yanked it out almost right away, the water swirled around inside like a little eddy, but then I splashed it out on shore, and the second time I dipped the washtub more carefully, filled it up, and took it back up to the others. Csabi pressed a wrinkled necktie in my hand and I wet it, and then we all got down to rubbing the side of the trailer with crumpled rags, and Zsolt whispered over to me that we were lucky it wasn't the inside of the trailer we had to rub down, and I whispered back that I was worried that that would be next, because if it was up to those lousy dogs, we'd be here till night, but Jancsi whispered that then we could at least find the gold, and I said I thought I knew where it was, and I told the others what I found while cleaning, and Csabi said it was now for sure the gold had to be there in the quarry wall under the prehistoric reliefs, we just needed to get there somehow, yes, as long as we had to work our tails off like this, we should at least get something out of it. But Zsolt didn't say anything to that, he just threw his rag into the washtub, sighed, took out the rag, rung it out, and went on rubbing the side of the trailer.

The whole time we worked, the corporal stayed right there in that picnic chair and paged through the thick history book, but all of a sudden he stood up, flung the book to the ground, splashed a good quart of the disinfecting alcohol onto it from the decanter, and threw a lit match on top. The alcohol burst into flames with a bluish light, and as the book's paper began to burn, the pages opened as if someone wanted to read them, and the corporal didn't even wait for the fire to die down, no, instead he packed on some charcoal from the bag right away, and then, without putting anything underneath, he put the stew pot on the charcoal, pulled up the picnic chair, sat down, waited just until the water started boiling, and began sprinkling flour into the pot and stirring the grits with a branch, and while washing the trailer I saw the dogs get up by turns and sidle over to the pot, and every time that happened the corporal would swish his stirring stick at the dog, but not a single dog even looked at him, each one just avoided being hit and slowly made its way around the corporal's chair, and nice and slowly it then went back to its place next to the other two dogs, and before long, another dog got up and circled around the corporal, and so on, just like that.

The trailer was still practically as gray as at first, even though we'd scratched a whole lot of grime off it, and by now even the water in the washtub was like liquid mud, we didn't even stick the rags into it anymore, no, I noticed that the others were also mostly just watching the corporal stir the grits. Suddenly he took the stew pot off the fire and threw the stirring stick over to the dogs before standing up and calling us over, and now he stepped to the bucket and put the stew pot on the ground next to the pickle jar, picked up the jar, took such a long swig from the now mostly grayish disinfecting alcohol that he stopped only when we got there, and that's when I noticed six little mason jars put out beside one another on the picnic table, the corporal poured the alcohol into them from high above, and since the mouth of the pickle jar was pretty wide, a lot of the liquor spilled out onto the table beside the little jars, but finally every one of them was filled to the brim, and the corporal handed each one of us a jar and he too picked one up, and he took a match and lit the disinfecting alcohol in the last jar, and then he told us to drink up, to the last drop, in memory of his father.

I didn't really want to drink, my throat was still full of the taste of the plum spirits, but as I watched that flickering blue flame I picked up the mason jar all the same and sipped the disinfecting alcohol, it tasted like liquid smoke, at first it scratched its way down my throat and then it started to burn, which made me have to cough, and the others coughed too, only the corporal drank it all down no problem, and then he put his jar on the table and said his father really loved his liquor, that that's what took him to the grave, this year he would have been seventy-six, if it hadn't been for his drinking he would have reached a hundred for sure, but at least this way his life had been a little easier because liquor makes life a bit easier, he said, not that we know this yet, no, we're kids, but we'll learn it yet, we would indeed, a while back he didn't understand it either, why, he'd even argued with his father over drink, but since then life had taught him this, it sure as hell had, and as the corporal said that he wiped a hand on his pants where the stump of his cut-off leg was, and then he refilled his mason jar and waved a hand for us to hold out our own jars, and after refilling everyone's he picked up the stew pot, poured the grits right onto the table, cupped out a big clump with his bare hands, and said with a full mouth, "Dig in, everyone, let's honor Dad's memory." After also cupping out a handful of grits, Zsolt said, "May the earth be light upon Mr. Vászile," and after chewing up the grits in his mouth he sprinkled out a bit of the filtered disinfecting alcohol from his mason jar and took a swig, and then the rest of us also scooped out some grits, which in places was black with soot, and I could feel it crackling under my teeth as I chewed, not that it was bad. Besides, it took away the bitter smoky taste of the filtered alcohol, and the others also ate, and after taking another big handful the corporal raised his mason jar and gulped down all the alcohol inside and flung the jar against the wall of the trailer so hard that it shattered, and then he called out, "All right, we've cried enough, so let's have a good time already, no more looking back, only forward," and then he pulled a record from the heap and set it on the phonograph and told us that this was his father's favorite tune, he'd have us know that there was no one in the world who could sing like this, and he called over to Jancsi to sit down by the stool and make sure the music didn't let up, and then he set the needle down on the record, this was the first time I ever heard music coming from an old phonograph, the horn made the music really loud, sure, it crackled and scraped a whole lot, but I could clearly hear the wooden flute, the violin, and the accordion, and the harsh, raspy voice of an older woman singer. The song was about some forest, about how this forest is full of shadows, shadows and darkness so thick that they smother goodness and love, I don't really remember the lyrics, all I remember is how that old lady singer made her voice quiver, like when dry branches brush up against each other in the wind, even the dogs raised their heads and began whimpering, softer or louder depending on the music, and then all at once the corporal began to dance, right there among all those scattered clothes, shoes, and odds and ends, plus he sang, but it wasn't real singing, it was more like the deep, throaty rattle crows make, and come to think of it, he really did look like a big gray crow as he jumped about raising a crutch into the air, but somehow he didn't seem ridiculous, and as I watched him the liquor got moving in me too, and not only in me but also in Zsolt and in Csabi, plus in Jancsi there by the stool, yes, all at the same time our legs began moving and our arms spread out, and before we knew it we too were dancing right there among all that junk, at first I was careful not to step on any clothes or glass jars or books or whatever, but then I accidentally kicked a gutted radio and heard something crack, and Zsolt jumped right on a straw hat, and then the music got even louder, by now the liquor was moving my arms and legs like wild, I didn't even know what I was kicking out of the way or what was cracking apart under my boots, a plastic ice cream cup or an old model airplane or a pair of sunglasses, and the others weren't paying any attention either, Jancsi kicked a book dead on, and as it flew up into the air it opened completely and all the pages tore right out of the spine, not that I saw it fall, no, the music was spinning me round and round, and the corporal now squatted down on that one leg of his before suddenly kicking himself up into the air while leaning on his crutches, objects swirled all around him like a whirlwind, ties and record jackets and pictures and sheets of paper and bank notes and handkerchiefs and stockings, and meanwhile we also kept jumping about, the loud crackle of the phonograph needle scratched away in my chest and the blaring of the accordion buzzed in my head, and then all at once the corporal flung away his crutches and picked up the gasoline can and hugged it like it was a woman and whirled his way toward the trailer on that one leg of his, almost falling at one point, but then he kept spinning upright to the rhythm of the music as he proceeded to unclasp the gasoline can and splash the disinfecting alcohol all over the trailer, the smell wafted our way along with the scent of the earth, it was really strong, and finally the gasoline can emptied out and the corporal flung it aside so hard that he flopped on his back, and at that instant the phonograph record stopped and everything got really, really quiet, Jancsi didn't put the record back on, so we stopped too. I was dizzy as could be, everything around me was spinning as if I was still dancing, the ground kept sinking and swelling under my feet so much that I could hardly keep standing, and the others were also lurching about, hunching forward and leaning back like they too were still dancing, the disinfecting alcohol let off a thick steam that looked like pale gray smoke, but I could make out the corporal lying there on his back and taking a pack of matches from his pocket, and the moment he finally managed to light one match the whole pack flared up in his hand and he flung it at the trailer, shouting on and on about how the world should be set on fire, the whole fucking world, so every last bit of it would burn to a crisp, and the flames ran along the side of the trailer, at first following the lines left by the disinfecting alcohol the corporal had just splashed there, but in no time the paint and the wood burst into crackling big yellow flames, and although the corporal was still there lying on the ground, he managed to reach out and try like hell to pull the wedge out from under the wheel of the burning trailer, and finally it worked, the trailer began shaking violently and rolled slowly down toward the lake, and try as he did to stagger to his feet, the corporal had nothing to grab hold of, so he flopped back down on the ground and turned on his side and watched the trailer roll ablaze into the water, the flames fizzled along the bottom as it entered, but the trailer didn't sink, no, the top half was still in flames as the whole thing floated out toward the middle of the lake before coming to a standstill without sinking any more, as if it had run aground, all it did was give off flames that glistened red against the gray water as if the whole middle of the lake was on fire, and the corporal just lay there motionless on the ground, his head leaning against his arm as he watched the fire.

While gazing at those flames I imagined that maybe they were lighting up the whole lake, meaning that if I went down next to the water and looked in, I'd be able to see what's on the bottom, and I was just about to do so when Zsolt said it would be best if we got going because the corporal would wake up in no time and think up some other festivity in memory of his father, and I looked at the corporal lying there on the ground with his arms spread out and his mouth open wide and snoring away, and I said I agreed that we really should leave because we'd pass out in no time too, but then Jancsi said that as long as we'd held out so far we should definitely see if there really was gold in the quarry wall, besides, the dogs wouldn't let us leave the property anyway, the corporal said they were man-killers, and then Zsolt nodded and said Jancsi was right, we really should do something about those dogs, and I said I knew just what we should do. I went over to the picnic table and swept all the leftover grits to the ground and poured on top the remaining disinfecting alcohol from the pickle jar, at least two quarts, and when I then threw the empty jar on the ground, the dogs looked up at the noise and I called out, "Come, come, get the yummy mush," and sure enough, they came right over and dug their snouts into the liquor-soaked grits.

Even though I was still pretty dizzy, I went along with the other guys to the quarry wall and the dogs didn't come after us, we went straight to below the worn prehistoric reliefs and stopped next to the wall, which looked scaly from close up, like dragon skin, as if that was also part of the reliefs, at first I didn't even want to touch the wall, but then I swung my hammer after all, as the others also started pounding, the wall was so crumbly that we hardly had to drive the hammers in before fist-sized clumps of clay came tearing out, and although the earth had this greasy sparkle to it that made me queasy, I took one swing of the hammer after another all the same, and suddenly I heard a hollow clang, and then I looked straight ahead and saw a flat, glistening metal nugget drop out from under the head of the hammer, and I leaned down and picked it up. It was just like the nugget Zsolt had shown us, and I stood up fast and again swung the hammer into the quarry wall, and by now glistening gold nuggets were popping out one after another from under the blows of the others' hammers too, two or three at a time, more with each blow, a whole lot of nuggets were sparkling by our feet, and after a while we hardly even needed to hammer anymore, the nuggets showered from the wall practically on their own. We threw the hammers down and Jancsi said he wouldn't have thought so, but he now saw that it was true, there really was gold here, and he crouched and began stuffing his pockets, and then the rest of us also began filling our pockets with those nuggets exactly the way they were, full of dirt, and just when I was about to say "Enough, let's go already because there'll be trouble," all of a sudden we heard the corporal yelling, "What the motherfucking hell are you kids up to?" He was standing right behind us, leaning on his crutches, and we all turned and stood up straight, and he asked again what we were up to, and as he spoke, the stench of booze was so intense that I felt sick to my stomach and couldn't get a word out, but Zsolt replied, "Can't you see we're mining gold? We know full well that this was why your dad had guarded the clay pit like he did, it wasn't because of those shoddy prehistoric reliefs." But the corporal shook his head and said, "There's no kind of gold here at all, damn it," and Zsolt then held out his gold-heaped hands to the corporal and asked, "Well then, what's this?" but the corporal just shook his head and said we were plain crazy, how could we even have thought we'd find gold in a clay pit, couldn't we see that these were just spent machine-gun bullets? He raised a crutch into the air and swung it down on Zsolt's cupped hands so hard that all the metal nuggets went flying, and he yelled at us to get out, to scram as fast as our legs would take us because if he saw us inside those gates one more time he'd knock our brains out and pour gasoline all over our corpses and set us on fire and throw us into the lake, he would, there'd be nothing left of us except a bunch of charred bones, and maybe not even that, so we'd better run and keep running, and not look back.

13

Chestnut Roll

.....

I WAS DOING my homework and Mother was correcting papers, ever since not being allowed to teach she spent a lot more time doing this, the ladies she used to work with would give her papers in secret, papers to correct, because they knew there was no way we could make ends meet from the money Mother got for cleaning, so that's how they wanted to help her out.

Anyway, I really wanted to finish my homework already, and that's because I couldn't wait to get some of that chestnut roll Mother made specially for me for my birthday, she had a really tough time getting the cream and the chestnuts for it, but then we made the chestnut purée together by cutting the boiled chestnuts in half and scraping the meat out using small spoons, yes, chestnut roll was my favorite dessert, the last time we had one was back when Father was still at home, before they took him away to the Danube Canal, chestnut roll was also his favorite dessert, and this was the first time since then that we managed to get chestnuts at all, and I knew that as soon as I finished my homework we'd take that chestnut roll out of the fridge and put the candles on it and celebrate my birthday together, so I really wanted to be done with my homework already, and then all of a sudden the doorbell rang.

Mother winced, of course, because ever since the time our flat was searched she got scared whenever the bell rang, and it's not like we were expecting anyone either, and no one ever really visited us, even the neighbors dropped by more at night to ask for something or bring something, but just about never did anyone ever come by like this in the afternoon, so it's no wonder I now saw Mother turn pale. I told her to wait, I'd go see who it was, and if I didn't recognize the people I wouldn't let them in, I went out to the hall and looked out through the peephole but didn't see anyone, the stairwell was empty, so I figured it must only be the guys fooling around even though I told them not to do that sort of thing with our doorbell, and I was just about to go in and tell Mother there was no one there when the bell rang one more time, and I looked out again, and again I didn't see anything, so I reached to open the door, but only because I wanted to see if anyone had taped the doorbell down, and then the door swung open.

Standing there right in front of me was this kid, he couldn't have been more than six years old, which was why I hadn't seen him before, he must have just barely reached the bell, and he was in school clothes, except that his school jacket was at least six sizes too big for him, it reached down almost to his knees and its sleeves were cut off around where the elbows originally were, and this kid was loaded with clothes hangers and wooden knives and wooden spoons, he had at least a hundred hangers on him and rolling pins too, and a whole string of clothespins was tied around his waist, a whole lot of them, at least five hundred, I swear. Anyway, as soon as he saw me he asked if my mom was home, but I told him to get lost, we weren't buying anything, but he said that he didn't ask if I wanted to buy something but if my mom was home, and I told him to beat it because if he didn't, I'd kick him right down the stairs, but first I'd stuff at least a couple of those hangers down his throat, but not even that seemed to scare him, no, he just pressed the doorbell again and then Mother called out from the inside room, "Who is it?" and I shouted back, "No one," but then that little shrimp took to shouting that he had dirt-cheap hangers and that the good lady of the house really should come take a look because she'd never seen such high-quality wood in her life, and then I gave the kid a shove, but he didn't fall over, he just stepped back and grabbed the railing, and I said, "Scram, hit the road," but by then Mother was there, she looked at me and her lips stiffened as she said, "Go straight to your room," but of course I didn't go all the way, I went only as far as the back hallway and watched from there to see what would happen.

Mother asked the little runt what his name was and how old he was, and he said, "Máriusz, six and a half," and then she was already asking him how many brothers and sisters he had, and the kid said seven, and Mother said, "All right," and she told him to come on in and not to stand out there in the cold even though it wasn't cold in the stairwell at all, and then this Máriusz wiped his feet and meanwhile all that wood rattled on him so loud it was like he wasn't even alone, and he came into the entranceway and stopped and took the whole kit and caboodle off his shoulders, it was all fixed to a harnesslike strap, he set it all down on the rug and began telling Mother about how his father splits the wood and dries it in their attic, and how he and his brothers and sisters carve the hangers and the clothespins, and how it's almost impossible these days to find such first-class craftsmanship. He spoke just like an adult, he did, without stopping once, sometimes taking out a hanger and sometimes a clothespin and holding it up for Mother to see, like he really was proud of them, and my mother didn't say a thing, no, she just looked on, and when the kid finally shut his trap, all she asked him was who had taught him to talk so cleverly, and the kid looked at her and said his father had, and then Mother asked him if his other brothers and sisters did the same thing, and Mári-usz said yes, they were going around to the other apartment blocks around here and that they'd be staying in our town for a week before moving on, and that they'd be getting home only for Christmas, after traipsing over half the country. And then Mother asked him if he didn't even go to school, and Máriusz said no, he didn't, and his brothers and sisters didn't either, and then Mother asked if that meant he couldn't read either, and Máriusz smiled and shook his head, but he said right away that he sure could count, though, and especially add, and when the time came to figure the price of the hang-ers, then she, the good lady of the house, would see for her-self that he'd tell her the right price in no time, and then he asked her right away how many hangers she wanted to buy and how many clothespins, and he would have started tell-ing her all over again what good-quality wood they used, but then all of a sudden my mother asked Máriusz if he was hun-gry, and of course he said, "You bet," and then Mother took him by the shoulder and told him to come out with her to the kitchen, and then I got really scared because I thought right away about the chestnut roll, about what would happen now.

Not wanting Mother to yell at me, I was really careful sneaking out to the kitchen, and by the time I got there Mári-usz had already eaten half a thick slice of bread spread with lard, and then Mother got a mug and took the milk bottle from the fridge and filled the mug for him, and the kid took the mug right away in both his hands and drank the milk with really loud slurps, and then he put down the mug and wiped his mouth with the sleeve of his jacket, and when Mother re-opened the fridge to put the milk bottle back in, that's right when Máriusz looked straight at the chestnut roll there on the shelf inside, and he even pointed at it with one of his hands and asked, "What's that?" but then I couldn't stand it anymore, I just had to say something, so I said, "It's nothing, don't go bothering about it," but as soon as I said that I knew right away I shouldn't have because Mother looked at me and smiled that stern, cold smile of hers, and she said, "Son, it looks like you have a guest, now that's a real celebration for you," and then she opened the fridge back up and took out the chestnut roll and put it out on the table, and she told me to go get two plates and two small spoons.

Her voice was so firm I didn't dare raise a fuss, instead I only went to get the plates and the spoons and I put one of each in front of the kid and one in front of my place and then I sat down, and Mother stuck a candle in the top of the chestnut roll, where the number twelve was written in chocolate, and she lit the candle and said, "There really should be twelve of them, but now one will have to do," and then I blew out the candle and made a wish, I wished my father would finally come home or that we'd at least get some news about him, and then Mother cut the chestnut roll, and she gave the first slice to Máriusz and the second one to me, and Máriusz dug in right away without saying a thing to me first, so just for that I didn't wish him a good appetite either, and I took the spoon into my hand, but I didn't start eating yet, instead I looked at that slice of chestnut roll there on my plate for a little bit, at the white whipped cream in the middle of the chestnut purée, and I think I thought of Father, and then I ate a spoonful, and it was just as delicious as I remembered, if not even more so, it was sweet and soft, and only when I then took the second spoonful into my mouth did I look at Máriusz's plate and see that he was already on his last mouthful, and then he looked up at Mother and said he'd never eaten anything as good in his whole life, never ever, and he asked if he could have one more slice, and I really felt like saying, "Hell no, you can't," and telling Mother that it was a waste letting him stuff even that first one into his trap, but she was already cutting him another slice, and then I too started eating faster, I didn't slow down to savor the sugary chestnut purée anymore, instead I just kept stuffing one spoonful after another into my mouth, but all the while I was looking at Máriusz, he was spooning the stuff as fast as it would fit in him, he cut such big bites out of the slices that he had to hold each heap with his thumb to keep it from falling off his spoon, and his chin was smeared with whipped cream and chestnut purée, and when he finished it he looked again at Mother, and Mother cut him one more slice, and meanwhile I got my second slice, and hardly any of the chestnut roll was left anymore on the china plate, the only part left was where the numbers were, and Máriusz was still eating just as fast as at first, he was leaning really far over his plate, and he had the elbow of his free arm on the table, half covering the plate, but Mother didn't tell him to sit properly, though she would definitely have told me, and when that third slice of his disappeared too, Máriusz then poked his spoon at the china plate and said she should go ahead and give him that last little bit, "Let's not let it go to waste," he said, and I could tell Mother wasn't happy about taking up the knife again, but then she cut that last piece in two all the same, and she gave one half to him and the other half to me, and when it came time for me to begin eating my half, all of a sudden I felt I couldn't eat any more, but by then Máriusz had long finished his half, and I saw that his eyes were on my plate, so just for that I ate one more spoonful, I couldn't even taste the chestnut purée anymore, only the sweet flavor of rum, but I kept eating it anyway even though I could hardly swallow it anymore, Máriusz was staring so hard that I did swallow it after all, and I even spooned out every last bit of whipped cream from my plate and licked it off my spoon, and when I finally put down my spoon, my belly felt all queasy, but I forced out a smile all the same, and then Máriusz looked at me and said, "Happy birthday and many returns," and he looked at Mother and thanked her for serving him so well, and he said that now she should tell him if she'd buy any hangers or not because he had to get going, he'd hardly sold a thing yet all day, and then Mother said all right, she'd buy five hangers and ten clothespins but only if Máriusz gave them at a low price, and then they started haggling, Mother loved haggling, and I thought that maybe she'd done the whole thing just so she could haggle, ever since we'd had to sell some of Father's clothes we had enough empty hangers, after all.

By then my belly was really churning, and I felt like the whole chestnut roll was about to come right up at any moment along with the boiled potatoes I'd had for lunch, so I stood up and went out to the bathroom and clenched my teeth, I wasn't about to puke if could help it, so I stopped by the faucet and let the cold water run and then I splashed some of it on the back of my neck because I learned in school that doing that stops nausea. I even drank a little water out of my hands, and luckily that took care of my queasiness in no time, and when I went back into the kitchen, Mother was already done haggling and Máriusz was just putting the harness full of hangers back on his shoulders, and when he saw me he said that as long as it was my birthday, why then, I had a gift coming to me, and he took a wooden knife off one of the strings tied to the harness and put it in my hand, and he told me to use it in good health, but all I did was nod, I didn't want to thank him, plus I was afraid of getting queasy all over again, and then I opened the door for him to go and closed it after him too.

We could hear him clattering up a storm as he went down

the stairs, and Mother looked at me and said I should be glad I didn't know what being hungry meant, and then she went back to the living room and those papers, and I hurried into my room and stood up on my bed and opened the window and just caught sight of Máriusz as he turned out onto the sidewalk from the path to our building, and I gripped that wooden knife tight and took a deep breath, but then I didn't try throwing it at his head after all, because I knew I wouldn't hit him, that he was already too far away.

14

Plenty

.....

THE ONLY REASON I headed off toward the grocery store was because I found this huge wheel nut and two big bolts on the dirt road leading to the construction site, and I wanted to stuff the nut with match heads because I remembered Zsolt saying that if you then screw on the bolts from both ends and tie a shredded plastic bag to one of the bolts, like feathers on an arrow, and then toss the thing out the fifth-floor window, those gigantic tractor-wheel nuts explode like the devil and blow a hole even in the pavement, and so I wanted to buy some matches, at least four or five bundles with a dozen packs in each, but the pastry shop where I used to buy them wouldn't sell me anything ever since Szabi and I put a smoke bomb under the glass display case and they had to throw out all the pastries because every one of them smelled like burnt plastic, thanks to the tractor-tire shavings and shredded Ping-Pong balls we mixed into the bomb, and because of that I had to go to the grocery store when I wanted to buy matches, but at least there I could buy as many as I wanted at one time, and that's because I knew one of the stock ladies, Miss Ani was her name, but everyone called her Fat Ani because she was as big as a pig, like a house even, not that I ever called her that, no, she was Mother's friend, one time she even stayed with us for two days when her alcoholic husband chased her out onto the street, and ever since then she'd been really grateful to Mother, and whenever I asked, she always brought me unopened bundles of matches and acetone for smoke bombs, sometimes as many as four or five bottles a time, and she never even asked what I needed the stuff for, no, all she asked was if my mother was doing okay, so it really was worth it walking all the way to the grocery store, even though it was pretty far.

When I reached Harvest Street, all of a sudden someone ran by me, and then another person and another one, and each one turned onto Ant Street where the grocery store was, and I thought right away that I should hurry up, that they must be heading to the store because they heard that something or other was in stock and being sold, but then I thought right away that that was dumb, what could they be selling that was all that special, and besides, I wasn't really in the mood to stand in line for margarine, flour, or eggs, but then someone else ran by me too, and I couldn't resist, so I called after him to ask if he knew what was being given out, but he didn't even stop, he only called back while still running, "Nothing," he said, except by then I'd picked up my pace all the same, but I really started running only when I noticed Mr. Szövérfi walking toward me with a jam-packed plastic bag in his hand, and I saw he was eating a banana.

Sure, I'd had bananas a couple of times, but I never ever saw anyone eating one in public before, my parents always got them under the table somehow or other, and most times they were still green and we had to wait a long time until they got ripe, one time I tried eating one green, sliced up with sugar on top, but it wasn't very good like that, and Father really bawled me out when he noticed. For three years already I hadn't eaten any sort of tropical fruit, and so I ran toward Ant Street as fast as my legs would take me. I could hear the shouting from far away, and as soon as I turned the corner I saw the line, it reached all the way to the middle of the road, yes, it must have been around fifty yards long and four or five people wide toward the end, but it narrowed by the store entrance because only two people at a time fit through the door, and at the front of the line an ironworker was shaking a red-faced man in a trench coat by the collar and shouting what did he think this was, did he think they'd just let him cut in line, they knew his shifty sort inside and out, well, this time he wasn't going to worm his way in among all these decent folk standing here in line. The man in the trench coat replied that he'd been standing here before, he had to run home for money, he'd asked someone to save his place, but the ironworker shouted, "Forget it, no saving places here," if he needed something he could stand in line himself and wait like every decent person, and he shoved the man in the trench coat so hard that he fell right on his behind and got all muddy, and when the man in the trench coat stood back up the worker shouted at him to get going to the back of the line, but then the man in the trench coat said he wasn't about to stand in line again and that they could all go choke on those bananas and oranges as far as he was concerned, except they wouldn't be so lucky at all, they were wasting their time standing here, in no time the store would run out of everything, and anyway they could go drop dead, and he turned around and went away, but just which way I didn't see because by then I was standing at the end of the line.

The line wasn't really moving, no, around ten minutes passed and we'd gone only about one step ahead, so I tried asking one of the ladies standing in front of me how long she'd been standing there, but she didn't want to tell me, she only hissed for me to shut up, but then another lady did speak, she said they'd been there a pretty long time, a good two and a half hours already, and she added that I could see for myself how slowly the line was moving and that the people up front by the display windows said the line inside the store wound around the shelves maybe three times, and right as she was saying this, a commotion erupted up front by the door, as if someone wanted to come out of the store even though the door up there was supposed to be only an entrance, yes, someone was trying to get out but the people in line up front didn't want to let whoever it was do that because no one wanted to step back even a little. Instead everyone tried shoving the person in front of them back toward the door, which caused a whole lot of pushing and shoving up front, but then somehow the line edged backward after all, even the woman ahead of me was shoved back, she hit me dead-on and I too almost fell back, but by then the people way at the end of the line had begun jostling their way forward, yes, someone pushed right into me from behind and I fell forward, but by then the whole line was piled up just like when people try cramming onto a bus, and now someone elbowed me in the side and I tried kicking right back and then pressing forward even more. Sure, I was still being shoved pretty hard from behind, but then the line edged backward again, so suddenly this time I almost fell flat on my back, and I would have too, if not for all the people behind me, and then the ones all the way at the end of the line also had to take a step back because way up front by the store entrance some lady was jostling really hard to get out, you could hear her shouting, "Make room, comrades, back up already, don't you understand, step aside, can't you see my arms are full?" Right away I recognized her voice, and then as she shoved the people in line out of her way, I saw that it really was Miss Ani, she was holding a bunch of stacked wooden crates and using them to clear a path, and meanwhile she was shouting for everyone to keep quiet and back up. "Quiet already," she yelled, "this is uncivilized behavior, it's completely intolerable, you people must back up at once away from the door, it's outrageous what you comrades are doing," yes, that's just how she put it, adding that she didn't understand what some people were thinking, where they thought they were, to be standing four-deep in line and yelling like animals instead of waiting in a civilized, courteous manner for their turn to come, so they'd better back up right this instant. While shouting on and on like that, she kept shoving people back with the crates, and finally she did manage to push everyone away from the entrance, and the line gave way and the people in it now gathered around Miss Ani or were pushed onto the street, and Miss Ani was standing by the entrance, and I could see that even on the inside the store really was full of people, they were at each other's heels by the shelves every bit as much as the people outside. Miss Ani then put the crates on the ground and took a big rusty lock from the pocket of her smock, slammed shut the front door, and in one nimble move slid on the bolt and clicked the lock, and then she leaned down and picked the crates back up and again started shoving people out of the way, snarling at them to let her through, to let her pass, she had work to do, and then all of a sudden the ironworker stepped right in front of Miss Ani, grabbed the crates with both hands, and asked her why she had locked the front door, couldn't she see how many people were waiting out here, and Miss Ani yelled at the worker, "Let go of the crates at once," couldn't he see for himself that the store was closed or, well, it wasn't really closed, but they weren't letting in any more customers, they were out of goods, they'd be lucky if there was enough for those comrades who were already inside, everyone should just go on home, there would be tropical fruit distribution tomorrow too, or if not tomorrow, then next week at the latest, it was worth coming early in the morning, she said, but everyone knew that anyway. Suddenly people started yelling left and right and the crowd surged forward, sweeping me along, and as I was shoved ahead I felt that big wheel nut drop out of my pocket, but by the time I reached out to catch it, it had already rolled somewhere among all those legs, and meanwhile the ironworker was yelling really loud that this wasn't fair, and he wrenched the crates right out of Miss Ani's hands and flung them on the ground so hard they broke into pieces, the boards flew all over the place and slipped every which way over the pavement. People were pressing toward the entrance and someone shoved me so hard I fell down and my palms got muddy, one of the boards from a crate happened to be right there in front of my eyes, and printed on it in big black letters was the word CUBA, but I saw that only for a moment before someone kicked the board away, and I crawled forward really fast, and when I tried standing up to keep from being trampled, suddenly my palm came down on the nut, but right then someone stepped on my calf, and as I jerked away my leg, the nut again went rolling out of my hand, but this time I didn't crawl after it, no, I was pretty scared. I remembered what Jancsi had told me about how a crowd trampled a person to death one time in the stadium, so first I struggled to my feet and only then did I try sidling in the direction the nut had rolled, toward the middle of the road away from the crowd, but then someone's knee hit my thigh so hard that I almost fell back down before I finally did squeeze out of the crowd somehow, and there in front of me was the nut, so I leaned down right away and picked it up and wiped it on my pants to get the mud off.

By then everyone was shouting and pushing and shoving like crazy, and they were scuffling too, so instead of going back in line I looked on from the middle of the road.

Although I couldn't see the ironworker or Miss Ani any-where, people were pressing toward the door with its two thick panes of glass, four or five of them were banging it so hard that the lock rattled really loud, and that's when I noticed that another worker had fought his way out of the crowd and started screaming, "That's not the way to go about it, I'll show you how!" and he leaned down and with both his hands he grabbed one of the drain grates from next to the sidewalk and picked it up, and above everyone's heads he slammed it into the biggest display window. Well, that huge pane of glass popped right out of its frame in one piece before splintering into a thousand pieces, sending the canned sardines in oil and sardines in tomato sauce that had been stacked in pyra-mids just behind the display window tumbling all over the place, and by now even the folks inside the store were at each other and shouting, I heard someone yell "Fire!" and then the other two display windows also got smashed in, and I saw two ironworkers lifting the front door off its hinges and rock-ing it back and forth before flinging it onto the road right in front of me, the glass showered out of its broad, blue-painted iron frames and sprinkled all over the pavement, but I saw that the rusty lock was still there on the door at the end of the ripped-off bolt.

I knew I shouldn't stick around any longer since I remem-bered Mother begging me not to get mixed up in anything, but all I did was step back a little as I stayed there looking on, everyone was jostling their way into the store, some people ran up to the window and leaped right in, and the shelves inside toppled over and folks started throwing canned foods and glass jars outside, someone was crying for help and somebody else, a woman, kept shouting that the store was on fire, and then suddenly this old lady next to me shrieked that people shouldn't be going in through the front but through the stockroom in the rear, because if they did that, they would find what the sales clerks were hiding back there, and by the time she finished, a bunch of people were already scrambling toward the stockroom door, but they hadn't even gotten there when the door was flung open and out stepped that first ironworker, he was yelling, "Look, just look and see what they're hiding back here, take a look for yourselves!" and he emerged with a big sack on his shoulder, he put the sack on the ground and shouted that it was full of genuine unroasted coffee beans, they could take his word for it, that stockroom had everything in it that they could imagine, it really did, chocolate and oranges and dried figs and dates and crates full of Greek lemon juice, everything, understand, everything, why, it was plenty itself.

In no time people were running out of the stockroom door one after another, lugging bags and bales and crates and oranges in red netting, while others were coming out the front, not only had all the display windows been smashed in, but their frames had been ripped right out of the wall, a tall thin woman was trying to clear a path for herself out of the store using a board from one of the shelves, and under her other arm she was squeezing a really big pickle jar full of green olives, and by now people were trying to yank things out of each other's hands, two old ladies next to me were clawing at a huge cluster of bananas packed tight in clear plastic, both of them were baring their teeth, and finally the plastic ripped and the cluster came apart, and as it did, a nice big banana fell right in front of me. I leaned down and picked it up, it was really cold as if someone had just taken it off a block of ice, but right away I stuck that banana under my T-shirt at the neck, and then I saw a man trying to put all these big bars of Swiss chocolate that had spilled on the ground back into a ripped-open cardboard box, and I began heading that way so I could get at least one bar for myself. Which is when someone started shouting, "Where are the clerks, where did they go hide, now they'll get what's coming to them!" and right then I noticed Miss Ani lying there on the ground by the front door. She must only have passed out though, because in no time she began coming to, and as she tried standing up, a thin redheaded woman noticed her and pointed at Miss Ani and shrieked, "There she is, there's that fat, shameless whore!" and then two people ran at Miss Ani and wrested her to her feet, and suddenly the first ironworker was standing next to her, holding this big steel fire-hose reel that's in every store next to the fire extinguisher, he'd already wound the hose halfway off, and in no time he tied a noose on the end and hung it around Miss Ani's neck, and Miss Ani started shouting hoarsely for them to let her go, she was innocent, she didn't do a thing, they should let her go, what did they want with her, and then all of a sudden sirens blared from the direction of Long Street, from beyond the bridge, I could hear them coming closer, and someone started yelling, "Let's run, the police will be here in no time along with state security and they'll take everything back," and then the crowd surged all at once, I was shoved so hard I almost fell, but someone caught my arm and yanked me up, and although by then everyone was running back toward Harvest Street, I could still hear Miss Ani screaming, "Help, leave me alone, don't, don't do that," but by then the sirens were so close I could hardly hear a thing, and not even I was about to look back anymore, so instead I started running home so fast that I could feel the blood throbbing in my eardrums and the banana sliding slowly downward under my T-shirt, but I caught the banana through the cloth and pressed it to my belly, and on I ran.

15

Cinema

.....

THREE OF THE FOUR SCREWS came out no problem, but the fourth wouldn't move no matter what, it did no good tightening the monkey wrench that Feri took from his dad. I sucked in a deep breath and then yanked that wrench again, but one more time the screw didn't even budge, all that happened was that the wrench slipped off the screw head, and then I heard Feri whisper, "What in your pop's prick are you shitting around for when the light might come back on anytime and then we're done for," and he said this as if I didn't also know that this vent we were in under the movie screen went into the wall no more than two feet deep, and lying there on our bellies, both of us were hanging out up to the waist, meaning that if the room lit up all of a sudden the whole school would see our asses sticking out of the vent, so I whispered over to Feri, "Leave my pop out of this, go give my ass a kiss," and even lying there like that I gave a kick his way, I think I caught him right in the side with my knee, I heard him swearing under his breath as

I gave the monkey wrench another hard turn, and with my other hand I even yanked the grating with all my might. But it didn't move, the screw seemed to give a creak but still held its ground, and meanwhile you could hear everyone behind us in the theater shouting like crazy and stomping their feet and whistling even as Comrade Principal screamed his lungs out, he was standing there somewhere in front of the rows of seats, we could hear him really close to us shouting for everyone to stay in their places because we were going to sing patriotic songs in the dark, that's how we'd pass the time waiting for the power cut to end, and no one should dare to throw anything unless they wanted big trouble, he'd have us know that the electricity would be back on within minutes and the film would then go on, and he'd see to it that anyone not in their seat when the lights came back on would be impaled and hung in the schoolyard, and he'd personally tear out their heart, he would, because the time had come for the lousy bunch of good-for-nothing slackers that we were to learn once and for all what discipline was, and I knew that even while shouting, Comrade Principal was walking back and forth and panning the theater with his super-duper eight-battery flashlight, so I tried hard not to think what would happen if by chance he passed that light under the screen toward the air vent or if he tripped on our outstretched legs, and again I gave the monkey wrench a yank, but again the screw only stayed right where it was, and then I whispered to Feri that our crawling in here was stupid, we should go back to our seats instead, this vent didn't lead anywhere, there was no secret screening room here, we should just forget it, damn it, but then Feri elbowed me in the side and said I should go back if I wanted, but he for one wasn't about to give up, he'd stay right here because he wanted to see those banned film reels, and I should cut the shitting around and give that wrench a good yank already because the lights really might

197

come back on any second. "So don't screw around," he said, and I wanted to say that I wasn't screwing around and that he could go to hell, but instead of saying it I decided to set the monkey wrench even tighter around the screw head, and after wedging my elbow against the wall of the shaft I yanked again at the wrench, and this time the screw head broke right off, all in one piece, so fast that the monkey wrench almost dropped out of my hand, and Feri whispered, "Okay, now we can take the grating off, but careful, there's hardly any room," and I whispered back that he should say something I didn't know already, and I kept pulling hard at the grating until it finally came off the iron frame around it, and Feri and I held it from both sides, but there was just no way of turning it, it was too big for that, and so we had to back out of the vent almost completely, that was the only way we could lay the grating flat, and meanwhile the voice teacher joined the principal, but luckily he stood a bit farther over, not right beside the vent, so he couldn't tell we'd crawled out, and then we set down the grating really carefully and slid it into the vent, and that's when I overheard the voice teacher say under his breath to Comrade Principal that if he really wanted there to be singing, then he should be so kind as to light him up so the children could see him conducting, but the principal didn't say anything back, he kept swearing away because someone had just hit him on the head with a piece of chalk, so anyway, we climbed back into the vent, slipped through where the grating had been, and began crawling through the narrow shaft toward the secret screening room.

Feri was up ahead, and although at first I could hear him gasping and sometimes hitting his knee or the tip of his shoe against the wall of the shaft, he must have crawled really far ahead because before long I couldn't hear him anymore, all I could hear was the drumming and shouting from out in the main theater.

Meanwhile the shaft got so narrow that I could feel its wall brushing against my shoulder on both sides, which made me worried I'd get stuck any second, like the time I crawled into that concrete drainpipe to get the Prodán brothers' leather ball, and as I now crept ahead on all fours my back started rubbing against the top of the shaft, and I knew that even if I wanted to, I couldn't turn around anymore, and so I thrust myself forward as hard as I could, and I wished like hell I hadn't won the bet that morning.

Feri and I had made our bet right after Comrade Principal came to our classroom and announced that the first three periods were canceled so the whole school could go to the cinema and watch the documentary *A Nation Being Built*, about the five-year plan, which is when Feri said to me, "Let's make a bet about whether or not they'll cut the power during the screening," and Feri said they wouldn't because that would be sabotage, cutting the electricity during a film like that is sabotage against the state, but I said it would be sabotage *not* to cut the power because managing the nation's electric power supply was a big responsibility, and industrial production was much more important than even patriotic films, so Feri then said, "Okay, let's bet on it," and we did bet, and I promised that if he won, I'd give him my rock-shooting slingshot, which I had made by using strips of genuine upholsterer's rubber I'd got my hands on, and he promised that if he lost he'd show me where the entrance was to that secret projectionist's room in the cinema, the room his grandfather told him about, where they stored the reels of banned movies that never got into cinemas, the room that had every movie we'd only heard about but could never see, all six parts of *Spider-Man* and all the Tarzan and Zorro films and a whole bunch of cowboy and Indian movies.

Feri and I asked Janika to seal our bet by chopping down his hand on our clasped hands as we shook on it, though we weren't about to tell Janika what we were betting on, and Feri then told me that if they really did cut the power, we could even try crawling right into the projectionist's room, it was pure luck that he happened to have one of his dad's monkey wrenches with him, he'd brought it to school for fighting, but it would be just right for this too, we could use it to take the screws off the grating. I asked him right away, "What grating?" but Feri didn't tell me, all he said was that I'd find out if they cut the lights, but I'd do better to say goodbye to my slingshot because he had a feeling that by afternoon it would be his slingshot.

The Flame of the Revolution Cinema was the biggest one in town, and I used to go there all the time a while back, but by the day we went there with our school I hadn't been in more than a year, seeing as how the people's economy was in trouble and the energy industry was in special trouble, and you never knew in advance when they'd cut the power, and when that happened you had to sit there in the dark because the generators weren't working in a single cinema anymore, no, at most places even the reserve diesel oil had been stolen long before, and during power cuts you had to wait a long time in the pitch-black theater either until they didn't turn the power back on or until the security people or firefighters didn't get there to let you out, and I didn't really like it when that happened, so instead I didn't go to the movies at all. True, since they took Father away I didn't exactly have money either, but I could have sneaked in without money, it wasn't hard slipping in, you just had to know how to kick and shove a bit and also where to stand in the crowd, yes, back then I sneaked in a bunch of times when I couldn't get tickets for *The Colossus of Rhodes, Spider-Man, The Sheriff and the Space Kid,* and *Hercules Conquers Atlantis,* but the movies they were playing these days weren't even worth stealing in for, they were nothing but rehashed war movies and cheap films about partisans, like

The Seventh Comrade, Shod in Iron, and *Long Winter in the City of Tears.*

Other times we used to sit more toward the back, in the last row or the second to last, but this time Feri said we should sit up front and by the aisle so we wouldn't have to go crawling around for long in the dark if by chance I was right and they did cut the lights, and so we sat in the fourth row, really low in our seats to keep from getting hit on the head from behind with chalk or spitballs.

Before the film began, Comrade Principal stepped out in front of the screen and waved an arm for everyone to stand up and sing the national anthem, but not even when it was over could we sit down, no, we had to wait for Comrade Principal to give his speech about what a great thing motion picture presentations were, how they were one of the biggest technological achievements of our progressive age, and then he called upon us to display disciplined and devoted attention, and he wished us all a good time.

At first the film was mainly about integrated industrial works and wheat fields, it showed tractors plowing and combines harvesting and then the great railroad being built, the one that would cut right across the mountains, and next the film showed the subway being built in the capital city, at first this four-eyed comrade showed the viewer a map of where all the stations would be, and then you saw the tunnel being built right there under the ground, with this huge revolving disc boring into the earth and workers already laying concrete in its wake, and then the camera zoomed in on the revolving disc, right up to its middle, and then all of a sudden the theater went dark and everyone began whistling and shouting, and from his seat next to mine Feri said, "You won, goddamn it, let's get going fast," and he told me to hold his ankle because in the dark I wouldn't see which way he was going, and I said, "Let's wait, maybe the film just ripped," but Feri replied that if that was so, at least the exit sign would be lit, it wouldn't be so dark, and I knew he was right, but by then we were already crawling, edging forward down the aisle and then up front right across the wood floor, which smelled of the petroleum they cleaned it with, and we crept right behind Comrade Principal to the middle of the screen, and then Feri went straight into the vent between the floor and the screen, and he hissed at me not to shit around but to climb in too, and once I was lying there beside him, he whispered that he'd get out his monkey wrench right away, that all we had to do was unscrew the rat-proof security grating, and we'd be in the shaft in no time.

By now the shaft was so tight around me that I couldn't even move, I wanted to shout to Feri to come back and help except that the pitch-black was squeezing my lungs, I couldn't get any air, but then I remembered what Mother had said after the firefighters took me out of the concrete pipe and then every night afterward I was afraid of suffocating under my blanket, she told me not to think about being smothered but instead imagine I was on top of a mountain and that fresh alpine air was streaming into my nose and mouth, so there in the shaft I tried imagining that, but it did no good shutting my eyes, even then I saw nothing but darkness, and it crossed my mind that if I stayed here stuck in this shaft, no one would ever find me, I'd die right here, yes, I'd stay here forever, and that scared me so much that somehow I managed to edge forward again. As I turned to my side the wall chafed my shoulders even through my school uniform, but what did I care, I just kept crawling on, it was slow going but I could tell I'd gotten a little bit ahead, and then all of a sudden I heard Feri say from somewhere in front of me to come on already because there was another grating up ahead to detach, and not to worry, the shaft was about to widen, and he was right, after slithering just a little more I was able to

get up on all fours, and I didn't even have to crawl much farther before I was right there next to Feri, and Feri said that
this was where the shaft ended and that the grating was right
above our heads, and he told me to reach up, I'd feel it right
away, he'd already tapped it all around and figured it wasn't
screwed on, and although it was pretty heavy, the two of us
could handle it, so we should try lifting it up nice and easy,
and then we grabbed it on both sides and pushed it up at the
same time, and while at first the grating didn't budge, then it
did lift up after all, and I told Feri we shouldn't knock it down
because it would make a loud bang, instead we should slide it
to the side nice and easy, and Feri said okay, and he said that
we didn't even have to move it all the way, but just enough so
we could squeeze out.

I was the first to climb out, it was dark, all I could see was
this really faint red light, and as I headed in its direction I
accidentally kicked the grating, and from the echo it was obvious we were in a pretty big room. By now Feri had also
climbed out, I could hear him approaching, and when he got
up next to me he whispered that he really didn't think we'd
get this far, he hadn't even believed that this secret screening
room existed, he'd figured it was just a legend like that tunnel
that supposedly leads from the old fortress completely under
the city all the way to the forest and the clay pit, and I then
told him to shut up, or if he wanted to say something, then
to whisper and not shout, and Feri whispered that he wasn't
even shouting, and meanwhile we reached the red light, it
was a rectangular red button lit up in the middle of this big
control panel that had buttons all over it, and on the middle of
the red button it said, in black letters, EMERGENCY GENER-
ATOR TO BE USED ONLY IN JUSTIFIED CIRCUMSTANCES,
and Feri said that as he saw it, this was a justified circum-
stance, and before I could grab his hand, he'd reached up and
pressed the button.

The red light went out right away, it was all dark and I got so frightened I couldn't even breathe, and Feri must have been scared shitless too because he didn't even swear, he just stood there next to me in the dark. After about a minute we suddenly heard this loud rumble from somewhere beyond the walls, at first it was a really deep, bubbling sound, even the floor shook, and then it kept getting higher pitched and softer, and finally it was almost like a whistle, and then came a bang, and all at once the lights went on.

I looked over at Feri and saw that he was blinking just like I was, but then we sighed at the same time and I told him he was plain nuts, and he just shrugged and turned and went to look around, and I also began exploring the place, and then Feri gave a whistle, and what I saw almost made me let out a whistle too.

There we were standing in a proper big movie theater, except that instead of being full of regular seats, it had these huge leather armchairs, two of them next to each other in the middle of the theater and another ten or so in a semicircle on two sides behind us, and a colossal red curtain covered the wall across from the armchairs. A projector stood on a little cabinet behind the two main armchairs, and Feri went right over and told me to come over too, "Get a load of this," he said, "this is incredible," and he was right, the projector even had a film reel on it, and by the time I got there Feri had opened the door of the little cabinet, which was full of flat round metal boxes, and right away Feri said we sure hit gold, all those secret banned movies really were right here, and that I should be careful because these film reels were extra heavy, we should pick them up together and I shouldn't try removing even one on my own, and I told him not to worry, I wasn't about to touch those reels, and he said good, but I could give him a hand, we should start by taking out the one on top, nice and easy, but I said I wasn't about to help, I didn't want to take those reels out at all, and I wasn't curious about the movies either. We should climb back in the shaft instead because if someone caught us in here we'd be done for, secret places like this all count as military establishments, and sneaking into one of them was treason for sure, but Feri just gave a big laugh and said there wouldn't be any trouble, why was I being such a chickenshit, if we'd already gotten this far it would be crazy not even to take a peek at these movies, imagine how cool it would be to tell the others what happens in the sequel to *Zorro,* but even then I just said I didn't care, we should climb back in, I didn't want to get in trouble, and then Feri asked if I was really such a chickenshit that I wasn't even curious about what movies were here, and he said, "At least let's look at the titles, so we'll have something to tell the others," but I told him to cut the crap, it wasn't like we could tell anyone about this anyway unless we wanted them to report us, but by then Feri had already pulled a reel halfway out, and he told me to help him already because he was about to drop it on his foot, and I told him not to shit around, it couldn't be that heavy, but then I took hold of the reel all the same, and together we set it down on one of the armchairs and turned the reel all around because, according to Feri, the bottom or the side would say what movie it was and what number reel, because most movies had more than one reel, but there was nothing written on this one, and so we took out the next, but there wasn't anything on that one either, and we looked at around three more, and on one of them we could at least see a mark where the label had been, but the label was almost completely torn off, only the very end remained, and all it said was *84,* but Feri said that couldn't be, because not a single movie could be eighty-four reels long, and then I said again that I didn't care, we should go back because if they turned the lights back on we'd stay here forever, and then Feri said, "All right, we'll be going in a minute, but first we should at least see what's on the projector," and he began turning the lower reel by hand, and the film rolled slowly from the upper reel onto the lower one, and as Feri was busy turning the reel I leaned closer and saw the images begin moving, I could see the film like normal, except that I couldn't read the title and the director and all the other words because they were all backward, in a mirror image, plus they were also moving, but then I saw an empty room, its door slowly opened and in came this lady, she walked around and sat down on a bed and got up again, and then she went over to an armchair and sat down, but then she got right back up from there too and went over to the window and opened it, and she picked up a newspaper from a little table and fanned herself with it like she was really hot. And then Feri asked what was happening on the film, and I said, "Nothing, it's really boring, some lady is traipsing about this big room," and then Feri asked if she was alone, and I said, "Yeah," and now Feri also leaned closer to the film and went on turning the lower reel, and then the lady on the film took off her costume jacket and then her skirt, and there she stood in a blouse and a half-slip and high-heeled shoes, but I could tell she was still hot because she kept fanning herself with the newspaper, and in no time she also took off her blouse, but she was still really hot, and Feri asked why I'd said this was boring when it was actually really interesting because this must be one of those movies with totally naked women and men, he'd heard of movies like this, and if we kept reeling the film, we'd see in no time that this lady would take her clothes off all the way, even her bra and her panties, and so we leaned even closer, and Feri kept reeling, and then the lady really did remove something else, her half-slip, so there was nothing on her anymore except panty-hose, a bra, and panties, but the pantyhose weren't real panty-hose, from what I could tell they reached only as far as the middle of her thighs, and from there they were held up with ribbons of some sort, and those ribbons were tied to a belt around her waist, like Indians' leather leggings, and then Feri tried reeling the film even faster, which made the lady's movements speed up but in a jerky sort of way, but she didn't want to hear about taking off her pantyhose or whatever it was, no, she just kept traipsing around that room, she dropped her paper and leaned down to pick it up and lit up a cigarette, and she puffed on that cigarette a long time. I could see her face really close up, her lips were smeared with lipstick, but right then the lights in the room flickered, and I told Feri we'd better watch out because the generator was jamming, and sure enough, I looked at the control panel and saw that the big switch in the middle was flickering red, so I told Feri we should stop this right now and climb back in the shaft because there would be trouble, the generator was about to stop or else they'd turn the lights back on, and Feri said all right, but he hadn't paid any attention to what I said, he just kept reeling, and then the red light started flickering really fast, so I told him again that we'd better get going already, but Feri told me to shut up and get a load of the film because the lady was now unfastening her bra. "Bet you've never seen anything like this," he said, but I said I didn't care, even though I really did care a whole lot, but with my eyes on that flickering red light all I could think of was what would happen if they caught us in here, no doubt we'd end up in reform school, so this time I flat out begged Feri to get going, but by then he was pulling the film itself by hand, and he said he didn't care, he wanted to know what was under the lady's panties, and I saw him reach into his pocket and take out a razor, and I asked him if he'd gone nuts, what was he thinking to do, and Feri said that the lady was about to take off all her clothes, and he didn't give a shit, he was going to cut out for himself that couple of yards of film, and I told him not to touch it, that it wasn't allowed, plus it would be evidence that we'd been here, but by then Feri had already flicked open his razor and he'd just about sliced into the film when I grabbed his arm and asked him what the hell was the matter with him, was he bored with life, did he really want to end up in reform school that bad? All he said was to leave him alone, and he gave me a shove, but not even then did I let go of his arm, no, I shoved him right back and told him I didn't care, I was climbing back in because I didn't want them catching me, and then Feri pushed me again, but so hard this time that I fell against one of the armchairs, the one with switches built into its arm, and my hand came down right on one of the switches and I could feel it click under my palm, and then a motor began droning and the big red curtain on the wall in front of us began opening up slowly, and meanwhile Feri shouted was I nuts, what had I done, and I said he was the one who was nuts, he was the one who'd done it, and as I tried standing up, I accidentally pressed another switch, and then all the lights went out in the room, but the projector light turned on and the reels began spinning on their own, and I could see the picture on the screen. Although it was out of focus, I could make out the lady leaning forward and taking off her bra, but I saw that only while running because by then I was hurrying back to the shaft and Feri was running right behind me, and then the lady flung away her bra, and I could see both of her boobs and her nipples too, and the camera zoomed in so close that her two boobs filled the whole screen, and the lady then sat down in the armchair and leaned back and held her outstretched legs up high and began slipping off her panties even though the pantyhose were still on her, and then Feri and I just stood there by the shaft, and I knew we should climb in, but I didn't climb in and Feri didn't either, we just stood there and watched the lady slowly, slowly pull the panties off her rear end and her thighs, and then the camera zoomed in completely on her hand and showed her scrunched-up black panties and began gliding down all along her thighs, and it went right up between her legs, and all of a sudden that lady in the armchair spread her legs wide open, and at that instant the generator turned off and everything went dark, and all I could hear was one of the reels still turning on the projector, and then Feri and I made our move exactly at the same time, yes, both of us lunged for the hole at once, it was just like we were wrestling, we both wanted to get in there first so we could crawl to the main part of the shaft. Feri was holding my arm and pulling me back really hard and telling me to let him go, but I didn't, instead I raised my knee and kicked him with it right in the belly, so then he let me go, and in no time I was in the main part of the shaft, and I began crawling forward, and I could hear Feri creeping right behind me, and the shaft narrowed exactly like before, but this time instead of getting scared I turned onto my side and kept moving as fast as I could, the wall of the shaft chafed the skin off my palms, but what did I care, and while crawling ahead I suddenly heard the whole school singing really loud out in the theater, singing about heroic coal miners thrusting their pickaxes deeper and deeper, and I slowed down because I knew they hadn't turned the lights back on yet, and I knew that if we did it right, we'd get back to our seats before the end of the song, and then we too could sing along with everyone else, just as if we'd never sneaked away at all.

16

Pact

. . . . .

B Y THE END of the main recess I already knew there
would be trouble because by the time the bell rang, I'd
won almost all the money off Lupu and his gang, at
first I didn't even want to play the coin-toss game with them,
I'd heard they were into cheating, that it was hammered
money they threw at the hole so whatever fell in never did
bounce out, and that's just how it was, but it didn't do them
any good because when it came to calling heads or tails, that
white ivory king I got at the ambassador's and had with me
in the pocket of my school jacket kept bringing me luck, I
won every time we tossed coins, so by the end I was getting
so scared that I tried calling out the opposite of what I was
thinking, heads instead of tails and vice versa, but I kept winning all the same. Not even letting little Zoli toss instead of
me helped any, I just kept winning and winning, and finally
Lupu made the sign of the cross and spit on his coins and
threw them so high that before they came back down he had
time to turn on his heels three whole times and call out the

name of Tudor Vládimireszku, protector of the poor, but it did him no good, I won even then, and by the end of the main recess, from the way Lupu and the others were looking at me I didn't want to put away the money at all, but I didn't dare give it back either because that would have been admitting I'd ripped them off, when it wasn't me who'd cheated at all, but them. All that change really weighted down the pocket of my school jacket, I'd won so much, and although I didn't dare count it, there must have been more than two tens there, and as I went up the stairs to the classroom I knew I wouldn't get out of this in one piece, on my way home they'd get me for sure.

So on purpose I took a detour, toward the waterspout and then along the hill and on the footpath behind the apartment blocks. By the old soccer field I went off the path because I didn't want to go near that long ditch that had been left half finished, the ditch where the new sewage line would have gone, no way did I want to meet up with that worker called Pickax because one time when some construction workers had us do some volunteer work they played a joke on me by lying that Pickax was my father and that the only reason I couldn't recognize him right away was because smallpox had done a job on his face, and I almost believed it too because I was really waiting for my father to come home from that labor camp down on the Danube Canal. Since then, Pickax had tried passing along messages to me a few times to go pay him a visit. He'd built himself some sort of house at the end of the empty ditch and that's where he guarded the pipes and waited for the other workers to return and the project to pick up where it left off, but it did him no good leaving those messages for me because I didn't want to see him ever again, even though I couldn't help thinking a lot about his face, which really was all eaten up by smallpox, besides, for a moment I had in fact believed he was my father. So I walked along the bottom of the hill between the bushes, it was almost twice as far going that way, but at least I didn't meet up with anyone, I was just about home already, all I had to do was get back on the path a bit and then cross the yard behind the apartment block across from ours, and I was already thinking I was home free when, all of a sudden, someone whistled really loud.

When I looked over, who did I see but little Zoli sitting there on top of the Big Tree, and that's when they came out from behind the bushes, they were all there, Lupu and the gang, and they surrounded me without a word, even little Zoli climbed off the tree, and then Lupu stepped up and said they caught me, and now I'd find out what happens to cheating rats, and I said I hadn't cheated and they should leave me alone, but Lupu and the rest only laughed. Máriusz spoke next, he said there would be no mercy, that they were going to kill me, they were going to knock my skull to smithereens, and that's when I saw that he had a plastic bag with him, a bag with a brick in it, but he wasn't the only one who had one, everyone did, Lupu even spun his around his head, and the bag swished so loud I got really scared because I knew that if one of those brick war clubs hit me only once, my skull would crack just like that, and Máriusz said I must think I'm pretty smart, huh, for taking this detour, but I should get it through my skull that by doing so I'd signed my own death warrant because if they'd met me on the street, then at most they would have beaten the shit out of me and taken their money back, but out here there was no one around, so they could do with me whatever they wanted, so I should prepare myself for the worst. While he was busy talking I slipped a hand into the pocket of my school jacket nice and easy and then yanked my hand out and flung a whole bunch of coins at their faces, but it didn't turn out too good, the change went all over the place and didn't smack any of them square in the face. I was hoping they'd at least start snapping up the coins so I could somehow fight my way out of the circle around me and try running home, but not only did not a single one of them bend down to pick up the money, Lupu was already swinging his bag toward me, I was barely able to lean out of the way, the brick buzzed right by my head, and I knew that this was it, I was done for, they weren't kidding around, they really did want to beat me to smithereens. I cried out for help as loud as I could, "Help, help!" I shouted, and meanwhile I reached in my pocket again, but this time not to fling the money all over the place but because I knew that if my fist was full of coins I'd be able to punch harder, and then I socked Máriusz right in the belly before someone kicked me from behind, which made me fall forward, but it was lucky I did because by then two of them were swinging their plastic bags toward me at the same time, but only one of the bags hit me, and it only grazed my side. As soon as I fell over I turned and pulled up my knees because I knew they'd be giving me boot kicks in the belly in no time, and I brought my arms in front of my face just the way Zsolt had taught me to do, but without shutting my eyes, and then Lupu swung his bag, and I knew he'd hit me in a second, and from between my arms I could see him baring his teeth, but then all of a sudden I heard this loud shouting and I saw, as if in slow motion, a brown bottle of beer smack Lupu on the side of the head just above the right ear. Lupu staggered and the bag fell out of his hand, and maybe he would have fallen down if Máriusz hadn't grabbed his arm, the skin on Lupu's temple was torn open and he was bleeding a lot, but the bottle wasn't broken, and as it fell to the ground I could tell it was still at least a third full, the beer was all foamy as it trickled out onto the path, and meanwhile I heard someone yelling, "What are you all doing? For God's sake, leave him alone or else I'll beat the brains out of every last one of you!" The voice was one I'd heard just once before, then it was a laugh, but now I recognized it all the same, it was Pickax. I looked up and saw him running toward us on the path, he had a long crowbar in one hand and a sledgehammer in the other, and while running he knocked the two of them together so hard that the whole hillside echoed, and he was shouting, "Victory, victory!" There was a miner's helmet on his head, and from where I was lying on the ground I could see its lamp sparkling in the sunshine just as if it was really lit. He ran right up to me, and Lupu and the others all pulled back, you could tell they were scared, I didn't want to look at the man's face, but I couldn't turn away, his face was really ugly, true, but not as awful as I remembered, and then Pickax stopped above me and shouted at all of them to get themselves home while they could, because in a second he'd show them what beating brains out really means, what was this, what were they thinking, nine of them ganging up on one, and with bricks no less, like gypsies? He'd show them what honor's all about, and while he was at it, what the wrath of God really means. On account of all the pockmarks, his face looked like boiling hot, bubbling yellow wax while he was shouting, but it was more strange than scary, so anyway, Pickax then thrust the crowbar into the ground like it was a spear and told them to come get him if they wanted, but he'd have them know he wasn't just anyone, no, he'd learned to fight among the Lipovans across the country down in the Danube Delta, but by then Lupu and the gang were running already, Máriusz, Zolika, Pustyu, every single one of them was racing as fast as his legs would take him, and then Pickax threw the sledgehammer on the ground by the crowbar and looked down at me and said he just couldn't understand what the world was coming to, back in his day kids still knew what a fair fight was all about, "One on one, with bare hands, just like decency demands, but these days they come in hordes, with weapons worthy of thugs, like rats, terrible," he said, "just terrible," and then he asked me how I was, how much of a beating I'd got, and if I was able to stand up.

Slowly I staggered to my feet and said, "Luckily nothing really bad happened, all in all I got only one kick and I banged my knee and one of the bricks got me in the ribs just a little, it was nothing, I've survived worse." But, I added, an arm of my school jacket got torn half off and my pants got scuffed up, and when Mother saw that, she'd know I'd been fighting again even though I'd promised her I would never ever fight again. Pickax replied that in today's world you shouldn't go making such promises, and he told me to take off my jacket. Only then did I notice that the laborer's jacket he had on was all covered with bird feathers, feathers sewed on next to each other and on top of each other in thick rows, so much so that the jacket was more like a strange sort of scaly armor, the plumes were mainly grayish, from sparrows and pigeons and crows, but there were also colorful songbird feathers here and there, and this surprised me so much that my hand froze as I was pulling it out of my torn school jacket, but for a moment only, before the jacket finally came off. As Pickax now took it from me without a word, the remaining change jingled in its pocket. After inspecting the tear by pulling on the sleeve and putting his hand inside and turning it half inside out and tapping the lining, Pickax pronounced that it wasn't such a big deal, it would take just five minutes to fix it up, plus of course two able hands, a little needle, and some thread. Then he gave me back the jacket and waved a hand toward the beer bottle and told me to go get it for him, because as far as he could tell, there was a little left on the bottom, which was really lucky, it would be a shame to just leave it there. Not wanting to smear my hand with Lupu's blood, I picked up the bottle carefully, by the neck. Pickax drank down the remaining beer in one gulp and flung away the bottle before wiping his hand on his pants and saying, "Let's go." I thanked him for the help but said I had to go home because I had a geography exam the next day. Pickax then grabbed my shoulders, turned me toward him, looked me in the eye, and asked if I was scared of him, and I said, "No," and meanwhile I was looking at his eyes, they were really blue, almost as blue as water. "No," I said again, "I'm not scared," and then Pickax let go of my shoulders and said he was glad to hear that because lots of folks were scared of him on account of his face, though there really wasn't any reason to be frightened because he was a very good person, and more important, he was honest through and through. Then he told me to walk back with him to his hut because he'd been wanting to show me something for a while now, and anyway, it would be best if I brushed myself off a bit before going home. He picked up the crowbar and the sledgehammer and he gave a kick at Lupu's plastic bag, which was on the ground with the brick still in it, and the bag whirled rustling through the air maybe twenty feet before plopping in the mud between clumps of grass, and then Pickax pointed the crowbar toward the old soccer field and said, "Let's go."

Pickax had built his hut in the upper end of the sewage ditch, where it went up beyond the soccer field and into the wheat field. He widened out the end of the ditch and then closed it off with cardboard and tin and plywood, and covered the top with planks, plastic bags, and tarpaper, and he must have gotten his hands on an iron stove somewhere because as we walked along I could see the stove's chimney from far away, sticking up out of the hut's roof and giving off plumes of whitish smoke. Pickax didn't say a word the whole way, he just whistled to himself and kicked at clumps of grass, and when I asked him what it was he wanted to show me, all he said was that if I waited I'd find out, and he went right back to whistling, and then I thought of all those stories the guys told about how he ate cats and dogs, injected shots of plum spirits into himself with a needle, and climbed up the balconies of the apartment blocks at night and peeped in windows to see what folks were up to, and although I hardly believed any of this, I thought I shouldn't go with him, that it would be best to run home instead, but curiosity got the better of me, I'd never heard anything about Pickax inviting anyone over, and so I kept following along behind him all the same.

As soon as we reached the ditch Pickax jumped right in without a word, even though it was around ten feet deep, and he must have noticed that I was thinking of jumping in after him because he called up to say I should climb down the steps instead, I was such a little wimp I'd break my bones, and then I looked down into the ditch and saw a bunch of rusty car fenders sticking out along the wall that you could walk on all the way down, so that's what I did. After tossing his crowbar and sledgehammer on a pile of rusty tools, Pickax picked up a tin watering can, went over to the oil barrel, lifted off the wooden board that covered it, and dipped in the can, and as he put back the cover I heard him say, "The poor things need some water, they do, they must be really thirsty by now," and then he went over to the door and opened it, and all at once I heard the singing of birds louder than I'd ever heard it before, and when I stepped in after Pickax, in no time my head was throbbing from the sudden heat and the earsplitting birdsong and the burnt smell of scalded bird feathers. Pickax told me to shut the door fast because the warm air would escape and the poor things would get cold, and that's when I saw that the walls were full of hollowed-out little nooks, some of them closed off with woven willow twigs or metal screens, and others with nothing but pantyhose or a scrap of gauzy curtain stretched over a frame. But there was something moving inside each nook, and when I stepped closer I saw that they were birds, an awful lot of them, including many I didn't recognize at all, but there were also blackbirds, buntings, and larks, and every single one was hopping about, excited and fidgety, and some flew straight at their screens over and over again when they saw me. There must have been more than three hundred birds in all, maybe even five hundred, because the walls were completely covered with screens and nets. Pickax waved a hand all around and explained, "These little ones are my wee feathered kids, but they're ungrateful, they are, they're such harebrains that despite all the love I give them, they'd still rather fly away, yes, I keep them caged so they won't go freeze in this late autumn cold, why, they'd all croak if I didn't take care of them. Just look at them," he said, "even now they're making a racket instead of singing pretty songs, but no problem, in a second they'll quiet down, just watch how quiet it'll get," and as he said this he took off his miner's helmet, which is when I noticed what light, whitish blond hair he had, and after putting the helmet on the kitchen table, which had three good legs and a fourth one of stacked bricks, he stepped to the middle of the room, raised his arms above his head, and stretched his head so far back that his Adam's apple jutted out on top, and then after shutting his eyes he let out this screech maybe six times in a row, and everything really did get quiet on account of that, the birds all hushed up at once and didn't even move, no, they just stood there behind their screens and nets as Pickax opened his eyes and gave a wink and said, "They got scared, this is the call of the golden eagle, and every bird is scared of that, even those that never heard it before, the fear is in their guts, but if we now give them something to drink, pretty soon they'll be singing beautifully for us." Picking up the watering can, he poured some water into a broken-necked glass bottle in a straw case, which he then handed to me, telling me to be careful not to give even one bird more than a little sip, too much water weighs them down so much they won't want to sing, and then he stepped over to the wall of the ditch, and with flittering movements he began pouring water for the birds. On stepping over to the wall myself, I noticed that every nook had a crooked little trough leading into it that was made of a folded tin can. Lifting the bottle, I started pouring a little water into each trough as best I could, even though the bottle was hard to hold, the straw around it was so slippery, but somehow I managed to splash only a little water the wrong way. The birds must have been scared of me because they all drew back and kept an eye on me with slightly slanted heads, motionless, from deep inside their grottoes. Pickax was going about it a lot faster, and the sound of the water as he splashed it again and again into the cans was always a little different, and that's what I was listening to when, all of a sudden, Pickax asked if I remembered the time I once called him Father.

Hearing that made me turn all red and I was just about to spill the water, but then I said, "Yes, I remember really well." Pickax said he was sorry about it, it was a nasty prank, folks shouldn't go joking about life and death. He asked how long it had been since I'd seen my father. I said it would be more than a year and a half pretty soon and that we hadn't gotten any news about him in a really long time and that I was worried that my mother was starting to believe he died, but I knew he was alive, I could feel it in my bones, and I knew I'd feel it right away if anything happened to him. Pickax meanwhile came over to my side of the hut and went on pouring the water. He said he hoped I was right, but I should bear in mind that feelings don't always show the truth, no, lots of times they show only what someone wants to feel, but I didn't say anything to that as I stood there with that broken-necked bottle still in my hand, staring at a finch in a nook closed off by pantyhose stretched out over the head of a badminton racket, the birdie was scratching its spiny little feet against a twig stuck in the wall, and its leg was all green and really, really thin. Pickax took the glass jar out of my hand and said now that they'd gotten their water we should go sit down because as long as we were standing so close to their nooks, they sure wouldn't drink, and if there was no drinking there wouldn't be any singing either, and he would really like for me to hear what a concert they could give, so it would be best if we went and sat down there at the table. Nodding his head toward the three-legged kitchen table, he went over, pulled a stool out from under it for me to sit on, and waited until I took my place before sitting down across from me.

After rummaging about a little in the table's drawer, Pickax took out a spool of thread, pulled a long sewing needle from his jacket collar, and told me to give him my jacket, so we could do something useful in the meantime. He broke off a length of thread with his teeth, passed it through the eye of the needle, and began sewing up my jacket with nimble little stitches. From the way the skin on his face stretched tight, it was obvious he was concentrating really hard, the pockmarks looked deeper, and his thick, milk-blond eyebrows twitched as he leaned really close to the jacket, his hand working rapidly, and it was so quiet that I could hear the swishing of the thread between his fingers, as if the birds, which I couldn't hear at all, weren't even there. When I then asked Pickax where he'd learned to sew this well, all he said was that a long time ago he'd been training to become a taxidermist. "But better to forget about that, yes," he sighed, "that was a different life," and Pickax looked up at me, bit his lips, and asked me to tell him about my dad. My belly knotted up and I knew I should say, "No, I won't say a thing, it's none of your business," but then somehow this old memory hit me from when I was in nursery school, and I started telling Pickax about how back then my father hardly ever came to get me after school, he was so busy that I usually saw him only at night, but one winter afternoon for some reason he did come get me, he wanted to help me tie my shoes even though I'd been tying them by myself for years. I was big already, just six months away from starting school, so I didn't even want to hold his hand, but the fog was thicker than I'd ever seen, cottony thick and white as snow, my father said it was like sour cream, you could see hardly two feet ahead, even the yellow headlights of cars got lost in that fog, which sucked up light like a sponge, I remembered looking down and barely seeing even my own legs. Anyway, then my father took my hand just so we wouldn't lose each other, and he began telling me about Roald Amundsen, the famous Norwegian polar explorer, about how Amundsen once crossed all of Greenland on skis, except that by the end he got so lost in the fog that he didn't find his destination, his friend's hut, and figuring that his compass was shot, he turned around and with superhuman strength he struggled his way back to where he began, and a couple of months later he got a letter from his friend, and in it, his friend told him he found ski tracks on that day two yards from his hut, yes, that's how deceptive and dangerous fog can be. Back then my father's voice was all raspy from night work and cigarettes, but the fog really softened it up, it hardly seemed to be my father's voice at all, and I held his hand as we walked along, and I was thinking we were lost for sure, just like Amundsen, that we'd long passed by our apartment block and were on the far side of town by now, only that my father didn't dare admit it, he didn't want to be ashamed in front of me, but I felt as if we'd been going for a long time already, and my father was still telling me about Amundsen, about how he found the Northwest Passage, but by then it was obvious from his voice that he was nervous, and then, right when I was sure that we were lost forever, suddenly I tripped on something, and I looked down and saw that it was the step leading up to the entrance to our building, and I was so relieved and happy that I cried out, "Wow, we got home, we really got home!" and it was like my father didn't even notice how happy and relieved I was, no, he just went on telling me about how Amundsen's boat, the *Gjoa,* met up with a San Francisco whaling ship in the Bering Strait after three years, and how happy they were to have found the Northwest Passage, to succeed in accomplishing a mission that so many before them had undertaken in vain, that so many courageous polar explorers had paid for with their lives, and even though the Northwest Passage didn't fulfill the hopes people had for it from a commercial point of view, its discovery was really important all the same. And as we went up the stairs I realized that my father knew full well I'd been thinking we were lost, but because he didn't want me to feel ashamed about it afterward, he didn't want to be obvious about having noticed it. When I realized this, I got so ashamed that by the time we reached the fifth floor I was almost crying, that's how sorry I was about doubting my father even for a moment. That story hadn't popped into my mind since then, even though I once had to answer quiz questions out loud in class about Amundsen, but not even then did I remember the story, no, it was like I didn't want to remember at all that I might ever have doubted my father. Anyway, after telling Pickax about this I fell silent and shook my head and looked at him, and I said that I didn't even know why I'd thought of this story just now, and I especially didn't understand why I was telling a complete stranger, but Pickax told me not to be sorry, it was a really nice story, and then he gave back my jacket and told me to just try finding even a trace of a rip on it. After putting the thread back in the drawer he raised a finger and whispered, "Listen up, now, quietly, quietly," and he himself began listening so attentively that he didn't even take a single breath, so I also held back my breathing, and it got completely quiet around us, and then all of a sudden a titmouse started twittering, and from the opposite wall another one answered, and then a third bird called out, I couldn't tell what kind it was, but by then a fourth was singing, and a fifth, and then all of them, but not at the same time, and not helter-skelter either, like when we came in, but according to some really complicated order, as if one great big song had formed from all those little ones, it was like a real concert only a lot louder, and there we sat, Pickax and I, right in the middle of it. It lasted for a few minutes, maybe even fifteen, and meanwhile Pickax shut his eyes and just sat there listening, smiling all the time and swaying back and forth in his chair, and my legs began moving and a couple of times I too rocked in my chair as the air around us became completely saturated with a strange, vibrating birdsong, as if we were sitting in steam or thick warm fog, and my head was on the verge of throbbing again. But then the birds must have gotten tired because their singing started slowly unraveling, and once more you could hear this bird or that bird apart from the crowd.

Pickax then gave a big sigh, wiped his eyes with the sleeve of his jacket, looked at me, waved a hand toward the birds, and whispered that they couldn't stand being so close to each other, that's why they were singing, and what we heard as such heartwarmingly beautiful music was really just shouting, swearing, and threatening, because songbirds actually hate one another's guts, a person couldn't even think how much. Golden orioles are the most savage, they're even feistier than the skylarks, lots of times they just die on account of being locked up, but until then at least we could enjoy their voices because to our ears this was singing, beautiful singing. Pickax said I couldn't even imagine how much work it took to make this concert, how much he had to experiment with where to put each bird, how one particular bird reacted to another one, no, this was the product of many years of work, and when he was transferred here he almost had to start from scratch, but it was worth it because you could hear singing like this only in heaven, and maybe not even there. "That's right," I said, "never in my life have I heard anything as beautiful," and then I got on my school jacket and thanked him for sewing it and for helping me, and I told him he was really a good person, and I thanked him very much but said I now really did have to go because my mother would be worried sick by now.

Pickax then said all right, I should go if I wanted, but that he'd like me to see what he invited me over for, because it was much more important than the birds even, it was something no one had seen in a really long time.

With that, he unbuttoned his jacket and took a yellowed envelope from the inside pocket and put it down in front of me on the table. I reached out for it at once, but Pickax told me to wait, first he wanted to ask me something, he wanted to know what I knew about what had happened to his face. So I told him what I heard from the other workers, that he'd caught smallpox down on the Danube Canal and he was lucky he didn't die, but that it had scarred his face forever. Pickax shook his head and said, "No, that's not true, but just what the truth is, it's best you don't know that." It went without saying that ugly things had happened to him, he explained, that was plain enough anyway, but when they took off his bandages and he looked in the mirror for the first time afterward, he fainted, and when he came to he couldn't remember his old face anymore. Pickax then pointed at the sealed envelope he'd taken from his pocket and said it contained his old ID holder, which was returned to him when he was let out of the military hospital. There, in that ID holder, was the only picture of him from back when his face was in one piece. Not that he was a coward, but he never had gotten up the courage to look at that old picture, no, instead he always lied that he lost it, and he'd had a new ID made with this new face of his. Pickax then got all quiet and looked down at the envelope and then up at me, and he said he wanted to ask me a big favor, I shouldn't say a thing, I should just take the ID holder out of the envelope, open it up, look at that old picture, and then slip it back in, put the ID holder back in the envelope, take it with me, and hang on to it. That's all he was asking me to do, he knew it was no little matter, but it would mean a lot to him, and if I did it, then he would ask that when I think of him from now on, I should try thinking of him with that old face of his, I should try imagining what he would look like now, after so many years, how he would have gotten older, where the wrinkles would be. Sure, he knew this would be hard, and he wouldn't even mind if it didn't work, but he was asking me all the same to give it a try because it would make his life a whole lot easier. Of course, if I thought I didn't have the strength or the courage to do it, then I didn't have to, I could feel free to go home.

I looked at Pickax, at his face with all those wounds and scars, and I said, "All right, I'll do it," so I opened the envelope, whose yellowed paper was so thin from being carried around in his pocket that some of it crumbled in my fingers, and I took the ID holder out, the national coat of arms and the words had completely worn away from the gray, greasy cover, and I opened it at once and looked at the picture, which was right there on the first page, it was a poor-quality black-and-white photo, Pickax couldn't have been any older than seventeen, his hair was parted neatly on the side, he was smiling, and he was in a white shirt unbuttoned at the collar. His Adam's apple really stuck out, and his name was typed underneath in Cyrillic letters, not that I could read it, but I didn't want to either, instead I looked at his mouth, his nose, his eyes, his smooth clear skin, and the overall contours of his face, and even though he was smiling, the way his mouth curled sharply upward at the edges gave him a look of unyielding severity, but anyway, I then tried imagining what he would look like now, just like he'd asked, but I couldn't really do it. While looking at that young man's face I somehow thought of my father, of the picture of him that I'd taken out of his old military ID holder, and I could feel a tear trickling out of each of my eyes, and then I closed Pickax's ID holder, slipped it back into what remained of the envelope, put it in the inside pocket of my school jacket next to my ivory white king, and I looked at Pickax and thanked him and said I'd take good care of it, and those two teardrops flowed all the way down my face, and after wiping them away with the back of my hand I said, "I'll be going home then."

Pickax stood up, came over beside me, put a hand on my shoulder, and said thanks, that I was a really brave boy, that my father would no doubt be awfully proud of me. I nodded and said sure, but I just wished I knew how he was because maybe Mother was right, maybe he would never come home again.

After taking his hand off my shoulder Pickax said that if I wanted, he could show me my father. An old Lipovan had once taught him to see faraway through a mirror, did I want him to give it a try? He didn't like doing this sort of thing, but if I asked him, he would. I knew I should have said I didn't believe in this stuff, but instead I said I wanted him to give it a try, and Pickax said all right, but I had to promise not to tell anyone, and so I promised. Pickax turned around and went to the wall, where he opened one of the cages and took out a little bird and told me not to watch, but by the time I turned my head it was too late, he'd already wrung its neck, which let out a soft crack. He then came over to the table, pulled out a pocketknife, and cut off the two wings of the bird, which was just a sparrow, and after throwing its body onto the ground he scooped up a handful of thick loamy mud, held it in front of me, and told me to spit on it, and so I did. Suddenly Pickax reached for my head and ripped out a strand of hair, which he then pressed onto the ball of mud. Then he pulled the big sewing needle from the spool of thread, put it in my hand,

and said that all we needed now was blood, that I should prick my thumb and let three drops fall onto the hair. The needle was so sharp that at first I could hardly feel it pierce my skin, only when I pulled it out and the blood started dribbling in big red drops did my thumb begin hurting. Holding the ball of mud under my fingers, Pickax waited until three drops of blood dripped onto the hair, and after telling me to suck out the wound so it wouldn't fill up with pus, he went about kneading the mud while chanting words I barely understood, and nice and slowly he shaped a human figure. It looked more like a rag doll than anything else, its arms and legs were just barely formed, and as a finishing touch he stuck the two sparrow wings in its back, making it look like some ugly angel. Next he went over to the back wall, took a flashlight and a little shaving mirror out of a toolbox, put an empty beer bottle on the table, leaned the mirror up against it, and put the doll in front of the mirror. Pickax told me to look into the mirror but to keep my eyes on the reflection of that little mud figure, and so I did. He then asked me what I saw, and I said that all I could see was the doll and nothing else, and Pickax said that was okay, that's all I needed to see just now. Then he picked up the flashlight, pointed it at the mirror, and explained that in a second he'd turn it on, and when he did, the light would shine right back into my eyes from the mirror and would be blinding, but that not even then should I shut my eyes or look the other way, and I shouldn't blink either, no, I had to keep looking straight into the light, I had to keep my eyes open nice and wide, and I had to be thinking of my dad. When Pickax then clicked on the flashlight, at first I saw only the light and the clay doll, but then all at once the doll began to move and started beating its wings, and just like that, it flew straight into the mirror and disappeared. A chill poured through me as the mirror now billowed like waves on water, and then all I could see was brown, muddy, wavy water, it seemed I was a bird flying above the water, but before long I arrived at a clay wall, and I started scampering up it, the grains of earth and layers of slate were clear as day. And then that image faded into the distance and suddenly I saw all sorts of ramps and roads scooped into that high clay wall and people working on them, so many people that they looked like ants, they were digging and swinging pickaxes and pushing wheelbarrows, and then the image turned, and there was my father, he was really thin and he was trudging up a ramp with a sack of cement on his shoulders, and I could tell he was out of breath, there were a whole lot of others in line in front of him and behind him, each was wearing the same sort of striped prisoner's outfit, and all at once I felt my heart up in my throat and knew I'd burst out crying in no time, but suddenly the mirror again started billowing like waves on water, and then the image faded away, and again all I could see was the light and the mirror, but the winged doll wasn't on the table anymore, and that is when Pickax clicked off the light and asked me if I'd seen my dad, and I said yes, I had. Pickax asked what I would give to bring him back from there, and without thinking I said, "Anything, I'd give anything at all," and right when I said that, the beer bottle tipped over and the shaving mirror fell off the table, turning once in the air before flopping face up on the mud floor, but it didn't break, no, it just cracked lengthwise. Pickax's face froze and he made the sign of the cross, and he said I didn't know what I was talking about. After picking up the mud-smeared mirror, he drew his finger all along the crack and said it was his fault, he shouldn't have asked me, but maybe it could still be undone, and he looked at me and asked if I would give even a life to have him back, and he shook his head as if to say no, and he told me to think it over carefully before answering, to think it over really well. The air around me felt cold, and with my eyes on that long crack on the mirror I said, "Yes, I would give a life, my life," and the mirror then split in two right there in Pickax's hands, and he said just above a whisper that it didn't matter anymore, it already happened, it couldn't be undone, he'd have me know I couldn't give my own life, only someone else's. I would lose a loved one, but my father would come home. He nodded and put a cup before me on the table, and then he filled the cup from the watering can before telling me to drink the water and go on home, and to take good care of his ID and never show it to anyone.

I raised the glass to my mouth, the water was ice-cold but I drank it anyway, and then I stood and left the hut. As I climbed back up the ditch wall on the fenders, the change rattled in my jacket and I heard the birds down below start singing once again. Then I thought of Mother, and I thought that somehow I really should tell her I'd seen Father and that he would return, but then I felt the pinprick on the tip of my thumb start bleeding, and I knew I wouldn't say anything to her after all. I wiped my hands on my pants, reached into my pocket, and held Pickax's ID, but instead of taking it out I just went on home without a word.

17

View

.....

WHEN I STEPPED OUT of the restaurant that used to be The Lion and was now The Hunter, with the two ice-cold bottles of Czechoslovak beer in my hands, I saw the gray van right away, parked on the other side of the street, so I knew I didn't have a choice, I had to run right by it, and I knew the van would follow me as I went running back to school with the two bottles of beer in my hands, but I also knew I couldn't do anything about it, that I'd have to keep running because Comrade Sándor, our gym teacher, said that at the end of the term he'd flunk anyone who didn't get back with the two bottles of beer by the time the class bell rang because this was more important than any timed run, he won those four cases of beer on Sunday while arm wrestling the head waiter at The Hunter, and he knew that he if didn't have them picked up quickly, the regulars would drink them all up. "So get going," he said, "run like hell, everyone, and as for those who get back fastest, I might just offer them a bit, a little glass of beer never hurt anyone, you sure will see how good it feels after a run, pure medicine."

By then the gray van had been tailing me for two days already, but I didn't dare tell anyone because I knew they wouldn't believe me anyway, and if they did believe me, that would be even worse, because no doubt they knew full well what usually happens to people whom state security tails in a car, so if I told them, no one would dare speak to me ever again. Luckily the van wasn't following me all the time, I usually saw it on my way to and from school, and a couple times when I went to the waterspout or the soccer field, but its license plate had only three numbers on it, so I knew it could only be state security, who else would have a gray van with mirror windows after all, but I couldn't imagine what they could want from me, maybe they somehow found out that I was there when the ironworkers set fire to the grocery store or that not so long ago during a power cut Feri and I climbed into the cinema's secret screening room, anyway, I didn't want to think about it, and I always pretended I didn't even notice them.

The two beer bottles were so cold that they practically froze to my hands, after a minute my fingers got so numb I could barely hold the bottles any longer, all I could feel was the icy cold, and that made me just stand there for a moment outside the tavern after noticing the van, besides, with my limp, I'd been the last one to reach the place, my ankle was still hurting because the day before I had tried a penalty kick with a punctured leather ball the guys had stuffed full of stones as a prank, so now I didn't head off right away from in front of The Hunter, there was no one else on the street except me, the others had headed back a while ago already, so I wondered what would happen if I went the other way instead of toward the van, but I knew that would mean going toward the main square, which would be at least a mile longer, and with my foot hurting like it was, there was no way I'd make it back that way before the class bell, and so I took a deep breath and started running toward the gray van after all, and meanwhile I thought that maybe it wasn't the same van at all, but just another one parked here by chance, that it wasn't here on account of me at all.

As I ran I could feel the beer swishing inside the bottles, and from far away I could see myself in the mirror window of the van's rear door, there I was, running in my white T-shirt and black shorts, but the mirror made me look distorted, sometimes I was really tall and sometimes really short, and when I got up beside the van I knew the engine would rev up right away and the van would start following me, but then nothing happened. I was so scared I could hardly even feel my feet hurting as I ran by it fast, the van still hadn't started up and I was already past it, five yards, ten yards, yes, I was halfway down the street at least twenty-five yards past the van, thinking I was home free, when it gave out a loud beep, and that startled me so much I almost stopped dead in my tracks and just about dropped the beer bottles, and then the engine roared and I could hear the van starting off, and before I knew it, it was right there beside me, and again it beeped loudly, but I didn't stop even then, no, I just ran on, but then the van headed me off and parked up ahead of me with its two right wheels up on the sidewalk, and I knew that this was it, they'd caught me at last, up until now they'd waited for some reason, but this was it, I was captured, they'd take me away. I looked back toward the restaurant and thought that if I ran back there, maybe they wouldn't come in after me, but I knew that was a dumb idea, they'd come in for sure, but I just had to turn around all the same, I couldn't give up, and I'd already done so when the van door began slowly opening up and I heard someone blurt out my name and tell me to stop moving this instant, it was my grandfather's voice, and once the door was wide open I looked and saw that indeed it was my grandfather, but I figured I was just imagining this on account of being so scared and that I'd better not look again, I'd better run, but then I did look, and I saw clear as day that it really was him, and he shouted at me not to even think of running because he swore he'd drive right through me, I should climb right in the car beside him, he just wanted to talk to me. All at once a sense of relief flowed through me, it was like being worn out after running except somehow hotter, but it lasted for a moment only before my belly knotted right back up because I couldn't imagine what my grandfather could want from me, we met only twice a year, and this was neither my name day nor my birthday, and so I took a step back and said, "I can't climb in, Comrade Secretary, I'm on a timed run and I don't want to fail, I don't want to give Mother another thing to be sad about," and my grandfather now told me not to bother myself about this run, he'd take me the distance and we'd get there before those other poor buggers, and he didn't want to repeat himself, I should get in at once, so I climbed in and sat down on the imitation leather seat and put the two bottles of beer down by my feet on the ribbed rubber floor mat, and I started rubbing my hands together to warm them up.

My grandfather slammed the door shut, pressed on the gas, turned off the sidewalk, and drove away. For a while he didn't say a word, but then all of a sudden he said he always did hate running, and he hoped I couldn't stand it either, and I said, "You bet I can't," and my grandfather nodded. "Very good," he said, it seemed that I was indeed his grandson, and I didn't say anything to that, I just looked at my grandfather, and I wanted to ask him where he'd got the van from, and if it was he who'd been tailing me for three days already, and if so, then why, and as I was thinking all this, I suddenly noticed that my grandfather's shirt was buttoned up unevenly and that he didn't even have a tie on, and that his shirt collar hung completely out of one side of his suit, and I was so shocked to see him looking like that that I didn't ask a thing, I just kept looking ahead and out the window, which was easy because the seat was a lot higher than in a regular car, and I could see farther too, no, I had never sat in a van like this before.

On reaching the corner, we didn't turn toward the school but in the other direction, onto what used to be Mud Street, and then at the end of that street we didn't turn left toward the main square, but right instead, toward the hill called Calvary Hill, and then I thought I'd better ask my grandfather where we were going after all, but before I could say a thing, he turned toward me, shook his head, and said I was a sad sight to behold, that's how terrified I looked, and he couldn't understand why I was so scared of him, and I wanted to say that I wasn't frightened at all, it was just that my leg still hurt from running and that I was cold in my gym clothes, and I hadn't even said a thing yet when my grandfather grumbled that I should stop worrying so much, he gave his word of honor that I'd get back in time for the class bell, but first he wanted to show me something, it was something he'd shown my father too, back then, so I should calm down and stop being so scared, he didn't have any bad intentions, and I didn't say anything to that either, I just stared in shock because my grandfather had never mentioned my father before, not even once, and he didn't let anyone else mention Father in front of him, no, he always acted as if he didn't have a son at all, that's how angry he was at Father for besmirching our name, for bringing shame on him and the whole family by signing that petition, everyone thought that he, my grandfather, was the one who'd signed it, since Father had exactly the same name as Grandfather, and so did I, every firstborn son in the family had always had the same name, it was an awful scandal, my grandfather had to resign immediately and go into retirement, and he could thank his lucky stars that nothing worse happened to him, so I really was pretty surprised now to hear him mention Father. Not that I replied at all, but as we kept going I thought to myself that I should say something already, I couldn't just sit there and not utter a single word, and I thought I could ask how my grandmother was, if she was any better, but if I didn't bring that up, I could at least ask him what it was he wanted to show me and why it was so important that he'd come for me specially with this van, and I was already wondering how I could ask him, but then all of a sudden my grandfather spoke, and even though he didn't look at me, I could tell from how the edges of his mouth crinkled that he was smiling, and he said he was really glad to see that I wasn't being nosy but was instead waiting patiently, like a grownup, because I had enough brains to understand that I didn't need to know everything ahead of time, yes, it was obvious that I was already a really big boy, and so I still didn't say anything, instead I only nodded and went back to looking out the window.

By then we were almost at the top of the hill, we'd already passed the military cemetery and we'd reached the hunting palace of the commander in chief of the armed forces, which the commander in chief used only once every five years, whenever he visited our town, and for a second I thought my grandfather wanted to take me in there, that that's what he wanted to show me, Feri's uncle had been there one time to do some electrical work, and he said that everything inside was pure gold, the faucets and the coat rack and everything else. Not that I was really excited about going in there, but I would have taken a look all the same, except that we drove right by its tall brick wall and black iron gate, yes, my grandfather didn't even slow down, no, we went on through a stretch of forest before reaching the big meadow way up below the observation tower where May Day cookouts were held after the parade. And then all of a sudden my grandfather drove right off the road and over the sidewalk, around the benches and by the helicopter landing pad, and the van was bouncing so much that the two bottles of beer kept rattling against each other down by my feet, and I had to grab the side of the seat as my grandfather drove the van straight to the big walnut tree at the right edge of the big meadow where the cliff began, and then he slowed down, stopped, shut off the engine, and said we had arrived and said to me, "Get out."

I was a little carsick, the drive had really shaken up my belly, so I took deep breaths, just the way Mother had taught me, and sure enough, in less than a minute the queasiness was gone, even though I could see in the reflection of the van window that my face was still pretty pale. Meanwhile my grandfather had gotten out and gone over to the big walnut tree, from where he called for me to come over and take a look, saying the whole city was here before our feet, the view was loveliest from here, from this tree, there used to be a bench here, but every last bit of it including its armrests had been plundered by now. "But that's all right," he said, "spring is in the air, the ground is pretty warm," and as he said that he'd already taken off his sport coat and laid it down on the clumps of grass under the big walnut tree, and then he sat down cross-legged on one side of his coat and tapped a palm on the place next to him and told me to sit down too, what was I waiting for, and I wanted to say that I wouldn't sit down, that the ground was chilly and I didn't want to catch a cold, but then I sat down all the same, and my grandfather patted me on the shoulder and said that when my father was little, he'd brought him here and shown him the city, his home-town, because way back when he was just a kid he'd been brought here too, by his own father, who was my great-grand-father, although I didn't know him, and at that instant I knew that my grandfather was about to make me promise I'd bring my own son here, but then he didn't say a thing, he only gave a sigh. Then he picked up the two beer bottles from the grass next to his sport coat, which surprised me, since I hadn't noticed him taking the bottles out of the van, and then I knew that my grandfather would now drink both bottles of beer, but I didn't say a thing because I knew it didn't matter anyway, and my grandfather looked at me and smiled and told me not to be scared, my gym teacher was an old comrade of his, and if he dared to say even a word to me I should tell him that my grandfather sends his regards, and I shouldn't worry because there wouldn't be any trouble, I should keep in mind that I wasn't just anyone's grandson, and my grandfather then got all quiet and he held the two bottles up against each other so one of them was upside-down, and he hooked their caps together, never had I seen such a thing, it looked like an hourglass, and somehow he made it seem like he planned to break the necks off both bottles, but in one fleeting move he opened both of them at the same time, flicking off the caps with his thumb, white foam spilled out onto his hand from the upside-down bottle and he shook off his hand over the grass, and then he told me to remember well that a gentleman never drinks in the morning, but for him it really didn't matter anymore, and he raised one of the bottles and drank down almost half the beer in one swig, and then he lowered the bottle and reached it out toward me and asked if I wanted some, and I said no, and my grandfather nodded and said, "Right you are, you can still become a gentleman," and I looked at my grandfather's hand clutching the bottle, his skin was nothing but wrinkles, I saw, the wide brown band of his watch was really tight around his wrist, causing the skin touching the watchband to crumple up, as if his skin was made of paper or he'd suddenly lost a lot of weight, and then my grandfather smiled and took another sip of beer, and he gave a nod toward town and told me to just take a look at that city down there, to take a good look, to do so as if I was seeing it now for the first time in my life, for the very first time or else the last time, and I really could see the city perfectly, all of downtown, the old fortress, the main square with its three churches, the theater, the museum, the old hospital, city hall and, a bit farther out, those big gray neighborhoods full of apartment blocks, the newer five-story buildings and the seven-story ones, which is not to mention the river on the other side of town, the big dam, and the ironworks, and my grandfather then put a hand around my shoulder and told me not to look at where every single different thing is, but instead to try looking at the whole thing, all of it as one, as if I was looking at a painting or a pretty girl, to try and see everything at the same time, it wasn't easy doing so, he said, but if I could do it, then afterward I'd see the world differently. My grandfather then got all quiet as he just kept staring down at the city and taking sips of beer now and again, and I was looking at the city too, but all I saw were all the different buildings and streets and squares, and then the wind started blowing a little, my arms and legs got goose bumps, and then my grandfather spoke again, he said he'd have me know that this was the loveliest town in the whole wide world, even in this dull gray weather it shimmers and it shines, but he'd advise me to leave it at once if I ever got the chance, to leave and not come back ever again, to leave not only the city but the country too, to leave my home behind. He fell silent, gulped down the last of the beer from the bottle, and then suddenly flung it straight toward town. A couple of seconds passed, but then I could hear the bottle smashing on the big rocks at the bottom of the cliff, and I was still looking at the city, but I couldn't make out either our apartment block or our soccer field, and I didn't know what to say to my grandfather, and so I only nodded, and my grandfather then asked if I'd heard what he said, and I said, "Yes, I'd heard," and then my grandfather asked if I'd understood, and I said yes, but my grandfather shook his head and said he didn't think I could have, no, I was still too young to understand, but I should keep it in mind, and when the time comes I should remember what he said, and I said, "All right, I'll keep it in mind," and my grandfather nodded and picked up the second bottle of beer and began sipping that one too, and he went on looking at the city down below.

By now the wind had really picked up, and I'd begun getting seriously cold, and I knew I'd start shivering soon, but I also knew that until my grandfather finished that second bottle of beer we wouldn't be going anywhere, and then I remembered what I'd read in a yoga book that Szabi lent me one time, that if you concentrate on your bellybutton then you won't be as cold, so I tried my best to concentrate on that part of me, but nothing happened, I was just as freezing as before, and I thought to myself that I should just stand up, I should get going, I wouldn't get back for the class bell anyway and maybe not even by the end of the main recess, I'd be in a heap of trouble for sure, they'd send me down to the principal and Mother would be called in, and I tried figuring out what excuse I could cook up, but nothing came to mind, and then I looked at my grandfather, figuring maybe I could see the time on his wristwatch, except that he was holding the bottle of beer in his left hand so I couldn't see his watch, but he must have noticed me looking because he turned toward me and said he'd heard that I always had my father's picture on me, and I nodded, and then my grandfather asked if it was with me now, and I said it wasn't, because I was in my gym clothes, which didn't have normal pockets, so I'd left it hidden in my school jacket, not in the pocket but on the side, in the lining, and my grandfather then gave a big sigh and said too bad, he would gladly have looked at it, because unfortunately he didn't have a single picture of my father, but no matter, if it wasn't here, well then, it wasn't, he still remembered my father's face pretty clearly, fortunately things like that were impossible to forget, and then he fell silent and took a sip of beer, the bottle was still almost half full, but my grandfather leaned up with one hand against the ground and said, "All right, let's go, we've been here long enough," and then he began struggling slowly to his feet, and I stood up quickly and grabbed his elbow and helped him up, and my grandfather leaned against me and stood, and he said thanks, and then he let me go, and with one hand he smoothed out the wrinkles on his pants, and he told me to hand him his sport coat, and I leaned down and picked up the coat by the collar and gave it to him, but my grandfather didn't put it on, no, he just lay it over his arm and picked up the bottle of beer, which was still a third full, and he said he wasn't going to finish it up, and all of a sudden he turned the bottle upside-down and poured the remaining beer out on the grass, and as the beer spilled out, he stretched out his arm and started lifting the bottle up high, the stream of beer thinned and the wind caught the drops and the smell of beer hit my nose, and the beer foamed white on the grass, and my grandfather lowered the bottle, and I thought he was about to fling it away, but he just dropped it on the ground, and he said, "Let's go," and he swung his sport coat to his shoulder and stuck in one arm, and he headed back toward the van, with the other arm of his sport coat swinging about as he tried to stick in his other arm too.

The ground had completely soaked up the beer by now, so all I could see was the black earth among the clumps of grass where we'd been sitting and the flattened grass where my grandfather's sport coat had been, and on noticing the two gold-colored bottle caps I leaned down and picked them up and closed my fist around them, and then I too headed back toward the van, after my grandfather.

18

Funeral

■■■■■

NEVER HAD I SEEN so many cars at one time as on that day, on the road to the cemetery. Traffic was really down since gasoline rationing began, but cars and taxis kept going by us one after another as Mother and I went to the cemetery on foot, yes, there were even people riding bicycles in black suits, and by the time we reached the stations of the cross there were a whole lot more people walking, and everyone who went by us said to Mother, "I kiss your hand," and some even said, "My sincere sympathies," and whenever that happened Mother always nodded and gave the same reply, "Thank you, thank you very much." Sometimes people on bicycles turned their heads when passing by us, giving a wave of the hand or a tip of the hat, so anyway, it sure was something, I had no idea that so many people knew who we were, that so many folks in town knew Mother and knew me too.

The cemetery was much farther than I remembered, even though every winter my friends and I would walk up there pretty often to go sledding, but somehow the road now seemed a whole lot longer, my patent leather shoes chafed my feet like hell, and my black tie, which Mother cut from out of Father's tie, was so tight around my neck that once or twice it felt like I was hardly getting any air at all, and the only reason I didn't reach up a hand to loosen the knot was that I didn't want Mother getting mad, because before we left home she had spent at least ten minutes fixing that tie around my neck so it would be just right, exactly like Father would have tied it, so now I really wished we would get to the cemetery at last.

At one point along the way a white taxi stopped beside us, the driver opened his door, thumped his peaked leather cap, and said to Mother, "My sincere sympathies, ma'am, would you allow me to take you a bit?" But Mother only gave a wave of her hand and said that was out of the question, we'd already managed to walk up this far, so this last couple hundred yards really didn't count, and then the man in the leather cap said that was too bad because he really would have been glad to take us, and then he leaned down a bit and asked in a whisper if there was any news about my father, and Mother shook her head and said there was none, at which the cabbie knit his brows and said, "Well, well," he thought they'd let him come home for the funeral at least, to which Mother said, "Oh come now, don't go talking nonsense," and then, as the cabbie shut his door, she said, to herself this time, "Stinking rotten informer."

The day before, Mother washed and ironed my school uniform for the occasion so I'd at least look somewhat presentable, but I told her that doing so wouldn't turn my uniform black, no, it would stay dark blue, and besides, the dark blue had already faded a lot from all the washing it got anyway, so we should dye it instead somehow because I heard you were supposed to wear black at funerals, but Mother said she didn't think my grandfather would mind I wasn't in black, yes, seeing as how he'd shot his head to smithereens, everything was all the same to him, to which I said that in school I heard that my grandfather didn't really shoot his head to smithereens, that the words "sudden tragic passing" in the obituary didn't mean at all that he'd killed himself, only that he'd had a stroke, but while standing there in my room the day before, Mother just laughed and said that was just the version that idiot grandmother of mine was spreading all about town simply because she didn't want to live in shame, but everyone knew the truth, which was that somehow my grandfather got hold of a pistol and stuck it in his mouth, and he'd shot his head apart so good that there wasn't even much to pick up, I'd see for myself that the coffin would be closed, it was just disgusting what my grandmother was cooking up, somewhere or other she'd found herself a black-veiled hat she'd practically glued to her head and was parading about town in, playing the part of the grief-stricken widow, crying like crazy about what a heavy hand fate dealt her, what a tragedy this was, about what would become of her now that her poor darling was gone. But she sure never called him my poor darling while he was alive, no, she just nagged him all the time with her never-ending jealousy and a slew of imagined illnesses, no wonder my grandfather couldn't stand it any longer, no wonder he'd put the barrel of that pistol into his mouth, and when Mother said that she suddenly started crying, I'd hardly ever seen her sob so hysterically, she had to brace herself against my desk, her shoulders were shaking so much, and then she sat down on the edge of my bed and she tried wiping her face with the corner of my blanket, but she was crying so hard I knew it wasn't about Grandpa, no, she couldn't have been weeping like that on account of him but only because of Father, who'd been at the Danube Canal for almost two years already, we hadn't heard a thing about him in a long time, and then I almost started crying too, except it wasn't my father I thought of but my grandfather, and not even his face but only his hand, the way he'd moved his hand when opening the door of his Renault to let me in, the way he'd nudged the window with his fingers so the door would open all the way, yes, at such times I always saw him through the glass, how the pads of his fingertips flattened and turned all white, and now I saw this so clearly that it was like he was right there in front of me, for a moment I even shut my eyes, thinking that maybe then the image would go away, but even then I saw my grandfather's hand, except that this time I saw his fingers curling tight around the neck of a beer bottle until turning all white. I shook my head and let out a sigh, and I stroked Mother's shoulder and told her what Iron Fist, my geography teacher, had told me in school when he took me into the science supply room during the main recess to fill me in on the bad news about my grandfather and tell me I didn't have to stay for the rest of the classes that day but could go home, and so I told Mother not to cry, to calm down, life goes on.

When we turned onto the narrow street the cemetery was on, I noticed that both sidewalks were filled with parked cars way up on the curb and that each side of the black wrought-iron double gate was open, and that inside the cemetery a whole bunch of folks were gathered around the flower stand and also at the chapel, where everyone was carrying bouquets or big wreaths with ribbons in the national colors or in red or black, and I asked Mother why we hadn't brought flowers, to which she said that as I could see for myself, there would be plenty of flowers here, and my grandmother had called us dirty Jews so many times anyway that we might as well put a rock on the grave instead if need be, and besides, it was all the same to my grandfather, she didn't think the old man would be bothered much to see one more or one less bouquet, especially not like this, with his funeral being made into such a public spectacle.

Up until then I'd seen so many people in one place only when we were preparing for the visit of the commander of the armed forces, though there were a lot more police there, here I saw only around fifteen or sixteen of them, standing in uniforms by the cemetery entrance, and right then a short man in a hat went by us and I heard him say to another man next to him, "It seems the police are worried that something is brewing here, which is why so many of them turned out," but the other man just shook his head and said, "Oh come on, what can happen at a funeral, they'll bury the old man and then everyone will go on home just like they should, and that will be that," but the man in the hat replied that he didn't buy that, because he'd heard that . . . But right then Mother and I got up beside them, and as soon as they saw us they got all quiet, the man tipped his hat and both of them told us to accept their sympathies and that they were really sorry about my poor grandfather, and once again I didn't know what I was supposed to reply, but Mother said right away that she thanked them for their kindness and also for having come, so I also said thank you, and they nodded and went on toward the mortuary, the crowd was already really pretty big over by that building, and parked along the edge of the cemetery's broad main promenade were all these old-fashioned black cars sparkling with wax, cars with Party license plate numbers, I think I even saw a couple of old Soviet specials like Pobedas and Chaikas and Moskoviches, and of course Renaults and Citroëns, the ambassador we went to one time to ask for help finding out what happened to Father was also there, he was smoking a cigarette while leaning up against one of those black cars, I recognized him even though I saw him only from behind, but luckily Mother didn't notice, no, I don't think she would have been too happy about meeting up with him.

Even though the main promenade was pretty long, from

far away I could see big black flags fluttering on top of the cemetery's new mortuary at the end of that path, and as we went along, Mother tripped all of a sudden. "It's okay," she said, explaining that the clasp had loosened up on her shoe, that was all, I should wait a minute while she adjusted it, and she squatted. Meanwhile I took out of my pocket the medal I got from my grandfather for my birthday, and with one hand I undid its safety pin and pinned the medal over my heart, right where my grandfather had pinned it back when he wore it, and I pricked myself a bit while trying to fasten the medal to myself, but what did I care.

Mother noticed that medal the moment she stood up, and I knew she was about to tell me to take it off, but before she could have said a thing, this lady stopped right beside us, she came over so fast that I could even hear the swishing of her skirt, and she had on a hat that was bigger and had a wider brim than any hat I'd ever seen before, and this black veil was hanging from that hat all around so you couldn't make out the lady's face at all, and for a moment I thought that maybe it was my grandmother, but then I saw that it wasn't, this lady was much taller and much thinner, and when she then folded the veil back over the top of her hat I saw that she was much older too, not that I knew who the lady was, but she must have recognized us, for she said to Mother right away, "Hey there, dear," and she leaned close to Mother's face and gave her a peck on each cheek, and then she stepped back and all of a sudden she began crying really loud, and she raised an arm and pressed a big white handkerchief to her eyes and just stood there like that for around two seconds, and as she pressed that handkerchief to her eyes I noticed that she had on white threaded gloves, but she'd slipped a big ring with a seal on it onto her ring finger over the glove, and now that the handkerchief was covering this old lady's face completely, Mother gave a little hiss in my direction, motioning with her head that we should go, but then all of a sudden the lady lowered the handkerchief, her eyes were glistening with tears, and she said what a sad day this was, seeing as how this dear man had left us like this, and then she leaned close to Mother and asked, in a whisper, "Is it true what people are saying, did he really kill himself?"

Mother shook her head and said she didn't know, and she gave me a little wink to signal that we should get going already, and she said, "Don't be angry, dear Miss Yvonne, but we must be going," and as she stepped away the old lady grabbed Mother's arm and yanked her back, pulling mother right up to her and whispering with such a hiss that I could hear it clearly too, that she would have my mother know that my grandfather had killed himself because he'd always loved her, his dear sweet Yvonne, yes, he'd shot himself in the heart because he could no longer bear having lived his life without her and that she would also have my mother know that my grandmother hid his farewell letter because that would reveal the truth. "But it's all right, it's all right," she said, "fate will do him justice, anyway, you'll see, you will, yes indeed," and she nodded so hard while saying this that the veil fell back over her face. Then she began sobbing again, and she pressed the handkerchief to her eyes through the veil this time, and that's when Mother took my arm and pulled me with her toward the mortuary, saying we should go because we really wouldn't get there for the start of the service, and I looked back because I was scared the old lady would come after us, but she didn't move an inch, no, she just stood there on the sidewalk along the cemetery's broad main promenade adjusting her hat, so then I asked Mother what this was all about, and she said it was nothing, just Miss Yvonne, a crazy old woman who used to be my grandmother's best friend a long time ago and who was obsessed by the thought that Grandfather should have married her instead, for years she kept on his heels and stirred up awful scenes all the time, but this didn't matter now, we shouldn't talk about it, I should just forget the whole thing because we were just about there anyway.

The funeral march sounded a bit distorted and scratchy as it blared away from big black speakers set up on stands, and the closer we got, the more of a crowd there was, but all we had to say was "Sorry, please let us by," and everyone stepped dutifully to the side, looking at us like we were famous people or something, lots of folks said hello and almost everyone said my grandfather was a fine man and how sorry they were, and they asked us to accept their sincere sympathies, and Mother just kept nodding left and right, and I also nodded a lot, and that's how we went on ahead toward the main steps all the way up to the huge, black, gold-inlaid double door, which I'd never seen open before, not that I'd been at too many funerals, especially not one like this, and by now people were standing all over the steps, but when they saw Mother they stepped right aside, and then we went up the steps between all those men in dark suits and women in black outfits, and we went in the door.

I figured it would be dark in there, or at least low-lit like churches mostly are, but instead the light was so blinding I almost got dizzy, three whole circles of light bulbs hung one on top of the other from a steel chandelier that branched off in all directions, there must have been at least two hundred bulbs, so anyway, Mother took my hand and that's how we went forward, the room was really big, and even though there were red drapes all over the walls the picture of the general secretary of the armed forces wasn't on show, there were only all sorts of displays with long quotes from his speeches. And then, all at once, I saw the coffin.

The rear third of the mortuary floor was raised by about a foot, a little like a stage, and the coffin was laid on a red-draped table in the middle of a platform, it was big and black, and it really was closed, and its varnish glistened so darkly that it looked almost fluid, and three tall, black oil-burning torches stood on each side of the coffin, but they weren't lit.

As soon as we stopped, a young man came over holding a maroon leather folder, he greeted us and introduced himself but he was talking so fast I didn't understand his name, and he gave us his sincere sympathies and a warm welcome, he said he was Comrade Bherekméri's secretary, the city's Party committee had entrusted him with organizing this event, and would we be so kind as to step onto the platform, immediate family members have to stand up there, so would we please go on over, there beside the comrade, and he pointed toward the coffin, and that's when I realized that he was pointing toward my grandmother, who was standing to the right of the coffin, all alone, staring right at the coffin as if she hadn't even seen us arrive.

Mother didn't move, she just kept standing there before the platform, but then the secretary waved his folder toward the coffin and told us to hurry because Comrade Bherekméri would arrive soon to give his farewell speech in person, and as the secretary said this he pointed to the side, to a microphone-equipped pulpit by the red-draped wall in front of the platform, so we then started off, first Mother stepped onto the platform and then so did I, and the secretary came with us too.

Up on the platform the lighting was even stronger, what with a row of white neon lights above the rear wall of the mortuary, which was covered with a big ornamental tapestry depicting a machine-gun-toting partisan in the middle of a wheat field, symbolically forging a wedge from several swords broken in two, and in the background of this brightly lit tapestry, behind approaching tractors, were mountains plus our homeland's treasures, its pine forests and its oil wells, so anyway, Mother and I then went over next to my grandmother, but to the left of the coffin, and I said as usual, "I kiss your hand," but as if my grandmother hadn't even heard me, she just looked at Mother and said under her breath that she should be ashamed of herself, what was she thinking, how dare she show her face here, and my grandmother added that she'd like nothing more than to spit in Mother's face, yes, she said, she'd chase her out of here but good.

Mother smiled at my grandmother and said how very glad she was to see that she was feeling better, and that if she wanted, she should feel free to make a big scene right here in front of the whole city, no doubt my grandfather would be happier with a proper fight than with this awful circus, and I could see that this was turning Grandmother even paler under her mascara, she licked her lips and then took a big breath, and I knew she was about to say something really nasty to Mother, but then all at once a double door opened in the tapestried wall, the only reason I hadn't noticed that door until now was that it too was covered with tapestry, and in came this man in worker's clothes, he came straight over to my grandmother and said, "Ma'am, we'll begin bringing in the wreaths now because the chief comrade will be here shortly," and then he asked my grandmother if they could light the torches, at which my grandmother took a handkerchief from her purse, pressed it to her eyes for a moment, and then said that as long as the time had come, then they should go right ahead, at which the man in worker's clothes said, "Yes, ma'am," and no sooner had he left than he was back, but this time with one great big wreath in each hand, and five more workers entered after him, each of them carrying wreaths and flowers that they packed high up by the coffin in no time, and then they left and brought even more wreaths and flowers, and as they walked back and forth in front of me the smell of sweat was strong, and I thought that these must not be any old workers, no, these were the gravediggers, and they must have gotten so sweaty digging my grandfather's grave, and on looking down I noticed that the pant leg of one of them was all muddy at the knee, and I knew I was right, so I took a step back because I didn't want them accidentally brushing up against me. Meanwhile the gravediggers went about skillfully arranging the ribbons of the wreaths so the messages and the names of the people who bought each wreath could be seen clearly, and I read a couple of the names but not one was familiar, and meanwhile the first gravedigger brought in a little three-rung ladder and a decanter, and he took the ladder from one torch to another, climbing up fast and pouring a bit of oil into each one's black spherical top, and then he lit the torches with a long match.

After flickering wildly at first, the tall orange-red flames soon formed nice sharp tips, and as the funeral march got louder my nose was filled with the piney fragrance of the wreaths and the smell of petroleum, and I thought of Christmas, when they cut the power, and Mother and I had to celebrate by an oil lamp, and I looked at the coffin's glistening varnish and knew that if I went close enough to the black-painted wood I'd be able to see my own face in the reflection, and thinking that gave me such a lump in the throat that I could feel myself about to cry, so I reached into the pocket of my school jacket to remove the freshly ironed handkerchief Mother had put in there. It was one of Father's formal handkerchiefs, and while holding it I remembered what the cabbie had said to Mother, that Father would be brought home for the funeral, and I swallowed, figuring that this was reason enough to hold back my crying, just like a real man.

All at once, right in the middle of a measure, the funeral march stopped, the speakers buzzed for a couple more seconds, but then everything got all quiet, and again that double door in the tapestry opened up, and in hurried a tall bald man in a black suit who didn't say hello to anyone but went straight to the pulpit, and the secretary stepped away from us and raced over to the pulpit and put down that red leather folder, so I knew that this had to be Comrade Bherekméri. Stopping right behind the pulpit, Comrade Bherekméri tapped the microphone with an index finger and extended a warm welcome to all the comrades mourning here today, and asked that he be allowed to say a few words about my grandfather, Comrade Secretary, whom the city regarded as its own departed and whose distinctions were indisputable. Comrade Bherekméri turned suddenly quiet, cast his eyes about meaningfully, and reached into the upper pocket of his suit for his glasses, which he then put on before opening the red leather folder, removing a bunch of paper-clipped sheets, clearing his throat, and beginning to read his speech.

After giving those gathered here today another warm welcome, he said he'd begin by telling us how he got to know my grandfather, who was still a university student back then and who earned enough to cover his tuition by making his way each and every evening from one bar or restaurant to another peddling perfumes, colognes, facial washes, hair ointments, antiwrinkle creams, rejuvenating lotions, and scented soaps, yes, my grandfather lugged the samples with him in two big suitcases, and although those suitcases were terribly, terribly heavy, my grandfather carried this burden without a word of complaint, not whining even once, and he even put up with tipsy guests teasing him, and one time in The Elephant Restaurant, whose reputation was not so very good, the owner gave my grandfather a wager, saying that if he spread hair ointment all over . . . but right as Comrade Bherekméri said these words the crowd murmured and stirred, and I could hear someone shouting in a high voice, "Let me through, stand aside, let me go forward!" so Comrade Bherekméri fell silent midsentence, lowered his sheets of paper, and looked over to the source of the commotion, and when I also glanced in that direction I saw that old lady, Miss Yvonne, brandishing a big bouquet of red roses to cut herself a path through the crowd, shouting the whole time that she would not allow her poor darling to be buried without a proper farewell and that she would indeed go right up to the coffin because she was the one who should be standing there by my poor grandfather's desecrated body, because she, not my grandmother, had been his true love all the time, no, not that evil old hag. As Miss Yvonne kept jostling her way through the crowd ever closer to the front, I heard my grandmother flare up and say, "Take her out of here at once, this is intolerable, this is outrageous, why, I'll go and kill her, I'll go scratch her eyes out," but by the time my grandmother said this, Miss Yvonne was standing right there in front of the platform only two steps from the wreaths, but then all of a sudden someone grabbed her from behind and pulled her back, and I recognized who did it, it was the cabbie we'd met, yes, he picked that old lady right up with a wrestling hold while hauling her away, one of Miss Yvonne's shoes fell off and she dropped her bouquet of roses and she screamed, but the cabbie was already taking her out of there, with Miss Yvonne meanwhile shrieking at the top of her lungs that everyone should know the truth, that my grandfather had killed himself and that my grandmother had destroyed his farewell letter because that would have revealed the truth, which was that all his life my grandfather had loved her and only her, and the only reason my grandmother insisted on a closed coffin was so the truth wouldn't emerge, but by then the cabbie had carried Miss Yvonne out of the mortuary and it was impossible to tell exactly what she was shouting, and then all of a sudden she got all quiet, and then the tapestried door opened up and in came one of the gravediggers, he went really fast over to the front of the podium, where he picked up that one black shoe and bent down again and picked up the bouquet of roses too and put it among the other flowers, and with the shoe in his hand he went back out.

That's when my grandmother began crying out really loud, and she staggered and almost fell, so Comrade Bherekméri's secretary had to grab hold of her, and through her tears my grandmother told him something, all I understood was "coffin," and then the secretary took a blue handkerchief from his pocket and handed it to my grandmother, and he went over to the pulpit and whispered something into Comrade Bherekméri's ear, at which Comrade Bherekméri knit his brow and shook his head hard and cleared his throat, and meanwhile he gathered the pages of his speech, which had slipped all over, rolled them cylindrically lengthwise, and tapped the bottom edge against the pulpit until the pages formed a nice neat stack, and then he began reading again, but he picked up not where he'd left off, with that hair ointment and the wager, no, instead he began this really long sentence about how when he and my grandfather had begun their struggle, they knew full well that they themselves would not be able to enjoy its fruits, that they would not live to see their dream fulfilled, but they'd struggled bravely all the same because the future was much, much more important than their own happiness, it was much more important than . . . but I never did hear what was more important to my grandfather than his own happiness because that's right when my grandmother shook herself free of Comrade Bherekméri's secretary's hand and took a step toward the podium, and she shouted right at Comrade Bherekméri, "Aren't you ashamed of yourself, Pista, for lying in my face, what do you mean the coffin can't be opened, you know full well it can be opened, why are you doing this?" And then she stepped over to the coffin and slammed her fist down on it, and she shouted that they should open it up at once because after all this she wanted to see my grandfather one more time, one last time, it was her right to say farewell to him, and besides, she'd heard that all sorts of gossip was being spread about my grandfather having shot his head to smithereens, which was supposedly why the coffin was closed, so she wanted to put an end to every shred of such malicious hearsay once and for all, every last doubt about him having died by his own hand had to be done away with, every shadow of a doubt, she was sure my grandfather would also want this, yes, he too would insist on it by all means. "So open it up," she shrieked, because if they didn't, why then she would do it herself, it was her right, did they understand, her right.

Comrade Bherekméri's face was almost as red as his leather folder as he now slammed his sheets of paper down on the pulpit, I could tell it was all he could do to keep hold of himself, but then he let out a big puff of air and said, "Naturally, no problem," but the edges of his mouth were twitching as he nodded to his secretary, who then went over to the tapestried door, opened it, and went out, and Comrade Bherekméri said that for his part he'd go on with the speech, with paying our respects to our dear departed, and for a while he went back to putting his sheets of paper in order, and then he began reading his speech once again, but I wasn't paying attention anymore because I noticed the little door open again and two of the gravediggers come in, one of them had a monkey wrench and the other had a crowbar, so anyway, they went over to the coffin and got down to removing the screws from the black-painted varnished wood one after another, they worked really fast, not even thirty seconds had gone by and they'd already removed all three screws from the left side of the coffin, and then they went over to the other side, where the last screw took them some doing, but then that screw came out too, and they put their tools on the floor next to the coffin, and one of them stepped over to one end of the coffin and the other to the other end, and they grabbed the top of the coffin and in one swift move they lifted it right off, except that I couldn't see the inside of the coffin because they'd turned the top lengthwise and put it up against our end of the coffin, blocking the inside from my view, so all I could see was the red velvet lining in swollen pleats on the bottom half, and although the lavender smell of my grandfather's face cream then hit my nose, I knew I was just imagining this because no doubt they'd spread some sort of embalming fluid over his face. Then I heard the crowd in the mortuary let out loud gasps, much louder than when Miss Yvonne had come in, at first I thought it was only because the coffin had opened up and they could see my grandfather, but then Mother grabbed my arm and turned toward the door, and the crowd by the door began to part, and everyone looked in that direction, and by then Mother was squeezing my arm really tight and I heard her say, "It's your father, they're bringing your father," and then everyone began saying all sorts of things really loud, I heard them say my father's name and that he'd supposedly been at the Danube Canal, but someone else said he'd heard that my father had been in a reeducation camp, and then I too looked in the direction everyone else was facing, and I could see five people coming in through the crowd and one of them really was Father, yes, I recognized him right away even though I couldn't see his face, he was taking little steps with his head bent down, and he was in the same gray suit he had on when they took him away, and he was surrounded by five men in black uniforms of a sort I'd never seen, and even though everyone in the crowd had stepped aside to let them by, they were coming in pretty slowly, the uniformed men were now up front and Father was staring at the floor the whole time, and even though lots of people were saying his name, Father didn't raise his head, no, he didn't look at anyone at all, and I noticed that he was handcuffed in front and that a long chain was attached to the cuffs in the middle and that one of the guards was holding the other end of the chain, and even though Father's feet weren't shackled, he was taking such small steps that his ankles seemed to be chained together, and I knew I should run right over and give him a hug, and then Mother, who was still standing there beside me, said, "Holy Christ," and she had to lean up against me, and I felt the strength leaving my legs also, but I pulled myself together and told Mother not to be scared, Father was now here, now there wouldn't be any more trouble, but all Mother could say this time was "My God," and I heard her take gasping breaths, and meanwhile the guards had led Father slowly over to the platform, not to our side but across from us, to the other side of the coffin, and they stopped around six feet from the coffin. The guard holding the chain yanked at it and then Father gradually looked up, and that is when I saw his face and felt my belly bunch up, his face was gray with stubble and he'd lost a lot of weight, but that's not what scared me, no, it was his eyes, his completely blank stare, I knew he had to see us by now, he had to see Mother and Grandmother and me too, but his blank stare just wouldn't go away, as if he didn't know at all where he was, his eyes were glittering like glass and it occurred to me that it wasn't Father I was seeing, no, it was no longer him, he didn't remember me or Mother anymore, he didn't remember a thing, and he didn't even know himself anymore, and then I heard Mother give a sniffle, I was still looking at Father and hoping he'd say something, that he'd come to, that he'd notice me and say something, that he'd yank his hand out of that chain and come over to us and give us a hug, give me a hug and give Mother a hug, that he wouldn't just stand there, that he'd come to right away, and then I heard Mother give one more sniffle and gulp air, and I knew she was trying to keep from crying, to swallow her tears because she didn't want Father to see them, and I knew

I was about to give a shout, to call out to Father, and right then Father's nostrils flared, he took two wheezing sniffs of air, but the third time he inhaled he did so deeply, and then all at once he batted his eyelashes, winced, and looked down at the open coffin, and that's when I peered down there for the first time, the pleated red-velvet lining practically swallowed up my grandfather, yes, he looked a lot smaller and thinner lying there in the coffin, I looked at his face but couldn't see any injury, his skin glistened in the same oily way it had in life and his mouth was a bit open, almost all his medals were pinned to him, covering practically his whole chest, and then I thought I saw blood soaked completely through the gray fabric between the medals right above his heart, but I knew I was just imagining it, that all I really saw was the coffin's pleated red velvet reflecting off his burnished medals, and I was also imagining the smell of clotted blood, and then I thought to myself that this whole thing couldn't be true, I was just imagining that they'd brought Father back, that he was standing there on the other side of the coffin, but then I looked up and saw that Father was still there, he really was there, still standing as motionless as a statue, staring at the coffin, the coffin and my grandfather inside it.

The mortuary was dead silent, yes, Father hadn't stirred for at least a minute already, and I thought that maybe he didn't even really see the coffin either, just like he hadn't seen us, but all of a sudden his shoulders twitched and he stepped forward and put his two cuffed hands on the edge of the coffin, and then I knew that he was conscious of what was going on after all, that what he was seeing was sinking in, yes, for a moment I even thought he would take my grandfather's hand, but he grabbed only the edge of the coffin, and then he slowly turned his head and passed his eyes over the length of his father, and his stare fixed itself on the face, and then I looked at my grandfather's face along with him, at the contours of my grandfather's mouth, at how the stubble glistened bluish in one or two spots on the skin sunken under the cheekbones as if he'd just done a clumsy job of shaving, and I knew that Father would look up right away, that he would look again at us, at Mother and me, and I also knew that this time he would recognize us, yes, even if he wouldn't be able to smile he'd recognize us for sure, and he'd know that we were here for him, that we'd been waiting for him and that we would wait until one day they would let him come home forever, and then all of a sudden Father let go of the coffin and took a step back, and he really did look up, right at me, right into my eyes, and I could tell from the sparkle of his eyes that he recognized me, and then his lips parted, and it was obvious he wanted to say something, but he only winced, he couldn't get a word out, and then Mother said through her tears, "My God, what have they done to him? What have they done to the poor thing?" and she let go of my hand and stepped away from my grandmother and headed really fast toward Father, and she was already halfway around the coffin when one of the guards stepped in front of her and snarled, "Approaching a prisoner is not allowed," but then Mother cried out that she wouldn't have them giving her orders, she'd go over to my father, she sure as hell would, they could all go drop dead as far as she was concerned, and she shoved the guard so hard that he reeled back, but then the other guard gave Mother a backhanded slap, at which Father began crying out in a really loud wordless groan and stepped toward Mother before the guard with the chain yanked him back, and then Mother lunged at one of the guards, pounding his chest with her fists, and she shouted for people to help, to not let this happen, and that's when Comrade Bherekméri shouted into the microphone for everyone to stay in their places, to keep calm, and then my grandmother began wailing through her tears, "My son, my little boy, I want to go over to my little boy," and she too headed toward Father, but the guards had already begun wresting Father toward the tapestried door as he pulled with all his might against the chain, snarling and groaning while trying to free himself, but then one of the guards tripped his feet right out from under him, and they went on wrenching him toward the door, two of them were holding Mother by now, and my grandmother shrieked something loud while trying to pull one of the guards off Mother from behind, and then the tapestried door opened up and in stormed the police and the gravediggers, the police were armed with rubber truncheons and the gravediggers with the handles of their spades, and then I looked at all those folks in the mortuary just standing there and staring like they were at some kind of circus, and I shouted at them to do something already, to help, to keep these people from taking Father away, but no one moved, no, they just stood there looking on, and then Comrade Bherekméri's secretary told me to shut up and stop moving this instant, but I turned around and headed for the tapestried door, with Comrade Bherekméri's secretary shouting, "Didn't you hear what I said, stay right where you are!" and he shoved me from behind so hard I almost fell on the coffin, but what did I care, all I wanted was to see what was happening to Mother and Father, and although Comrade Bherekméri's secretary pushed me again, I just kept looking, I didn't see Mother anywhere but I did see Father, the guards were dragging him out the tapestried door, and after leaning down and snatching up the crowbar the gravediggers had left by the coffin, I took off after Father, except that by then the tapestried door had closed and the police were blocking it, so I knew I'd never get out that way even if I tried, and when Comrade Bherekméri's secretary now stepped in front of me I swung the crowbar at his thigh and he doubled up, swearing away, and then I turned around and jumped off the platform, and while swinging the crowbar high I cried out for everyone to make way, to stand aside, and I began clearing a path for myself toward the exit, like in school when we used to fight with the older students in the old air-raid shelter during the main recess. I didn't watch to see where the crowbar was going, no, I kept my eyes fixed only on the crowbar itself to be sure to swing it just right, jabbing and hitting as I went on ahead, with my eyes now also on the main door, and by then everyone was shouting like mad, but I didn't pay them any attention, not even when someone gave me a kick from behind, no, because by then I was already by the exit, in front of the closed double door, which opened just a crack when I gave it a kick, allowing me to slip out and kick the door shut behind me, and although I knew they'd open the door in no time and come after me, what did I care, I could hear everyone inside yelling and screaming away, and then I stepped forward and stopped on top of the steps, I turned completely around but couldn't see Father anywhere, not him and not the guards either, the whole cemetery was empty except for all those cars lined up one behind the other on both sides of the main promenade, and then for a moment I again thought that maybe I was just imagining the whole thing, that they hadn't brought Father home after all, but then a gray prison van turned out from behind the mortuary and began snaking its way down the main promenade, and I cried out for them to stop, to wait, and I started running after the van, and I knew it was about to speed up, but when I then glimpsed Father's bone-white face behind the bars of the rear window, I also knew that the prison van could go as fast as it wanted, I'd catch up anyway, and raising the crowbar above my head, I took off after the van, faster and faster, faster and faster and faster I ran.

A NOTE ON NAMES

Though set in a nameless land, *The White King* is inspired by Communist-era Romania—more specifically, by that almost mythical expanse of western Romania called Transylvania, which is home to various ethnic groups, Hungarians and Romanians most prominent among them. To Hungarian readers this variegated cultural-linguistic setting is apparent in the characters' names; all of them, regardless of origin, appear as per Hungarian orthography, since this novel was written in that language. The one exception, because the English spelling captures the essence of the original while also being fairly pronounceable, is the name of the narrator himself: Djata.

Readers wishing to imagine how the names sound in Hungarian may consult the list below.

Appears As	Pronounce As	Appears As	Pronounce As
Áronka	AH-rone-kuh	Laci	LUHT-see
Bherekméri	BEH-rek-mare-ee	Máriusz	MAH-ree-oos
Csabi	CHUH-bee	Miki	MEE-kee
Csidej	CHEE-day	Pista	PEESH-tuh
Feri	FEH-ree	Puju	POO-yoo
Gica	GEE-tsuh	Pustyu	POOST-yoo
Gyurka	DYOOR-kuh	Sándor	SHAHN-door
	(*dy* as a single consonant; *oo* as in *soon*)	Szabi	SUH-bee
		Szövérfi	SEA-vare-fee
Horáciú	HOR-ah-tsee-yoo		(*ea* as in *learn*, not *sea*)
Iza	EE-zuh	Traján	TRUH-yahn
Jancsi	YUHN-chee	Vászile	VAH-see-leh
Janika	YUH-nee-kuh	Zolika	ZOH-lee-kuh
Jánku Zsjánu	YAHN-koo DJAH-noo	Zsolt	zholt

ACKNOWLEDGMENTS

As small boy I was a great fan of James Fenimore Cooper's *The Last of the Mohicans.* I was convinced that this book, like all others, of course, had been written in Hungarian. Until the moment I picked it up in a different Hungarian translation, stunned and angered to find a different book rendered in different words. This experience shook me to the core, introduced me to the issue of translation, and made me understand that a translation of a novel is nothing short of a rebirth. So I'd like to thank all those who taught me about this and those who helped in publishing an English version of *The White King:* Nathaniel Rich, Radhika Jones, Philip Gourevitch, Anjali Singh, Jane Lawson, Janet Silver, Evan McGarvey, Géza Morcsányi, Katharina Raabe, Éva Schwartz, István Géher, Ádám Nádasdy, Peter Doherty, and Ferenc Takács. I'd also like to express my gratitude to my agent, Chris Parris-Lamb, for doing such an incredible job and being a true pathfinder. But above all, I have to thank another keen woodsman, the translator Paul Olchváry, for his unparalleled dedication and enthusiasm. *Nagyon köszönöm!*

—Gy. D.

■ ■ ■

Bringing *A fehér király* into English was immensely satisfying not only because it is as much a riveting story as it is a beautiful one, but also because I was blessed to be translating an author who himself has translated novels from English to Hungarian. Throughout, György Dragomán devoted painstaking attention to my queries, providing invaluable suggestions as he combed through revision after revision with keen insight, sensitivity, and kindness. For a translator this was a rare pleasure, and it was much appreciated.

—P. O.

About the Author

GYÖRGY DRAGOMÁN is thirty-four years old. A Samuel Beckett scholar and film critic, he has also translated works by James Joyce, Ian McEwan, Irvine Welsh, and Micky Donnelly into Hungarian. Awarded Hungary's prestigious Sándor Márai Prize, *The White King*, though strictly a work of fiction, is loosely based on Dragomán's own experiences growing up in the 1980s in Romania during the rule of Ceausescu. Part of it appeared in the *Paris Review*. The author lives in Budapest with his wife, a poet, and their two young sons.

About the Translator

PAUL OLCHVÁRY has translated many books from Hungarian, including Károly Pap's novel *Azarel* (Steerforth), and has received translation awards from the National Endowment for the Arts, PEN America, and Hungary's Milán Füst Foundation. His shorter translations have appeared in the *Hungarian Quarterly* and the *Paris Review*. A native of Amherst, New York, he lives both in Kismaros, Hungary, and various reaches of the American Northeast.